Murder on Deck

Deck

A Cruise Novel

Deb Graham

Murder on Deck
© 2017 Deb Graham

Other Books by Deb Graham

Peril In Paradise   a cruise novel

Tips From The Cruise Addict's Wife

More Tips From The Cruise Addict's Wife

Mediterranean Cruise With The Cruise Addict's Wife

How To Write Your Story

How To Complain...and get what you deserve

Hungry Kids Campfire Cookbook

Kid Food On A Stick

Quick and Clever Kids' Crafts

Awesome Science Experiments for Kids

Savory Mug Cooking

Uncommon Household Tips

Los Angeles, San Pedro Pier

What am I doing on another cruise? I could have talked them into a nice, safe camping trip instead. I should have taken up Nan's invitation to visit them on Kauai. I should have–

Fingering her new necklace, Jerria stood on the balcony of the *Ocean Journey,* watching the frenzied pace below. On the pier, forklifts shuttled pallets and crates of foodstuffs and other supplies to the waiting ship, while a stream of passengers made their way up the inclined gangway. The California sunshine warmed her face, but failed to touch the chill in her heart.

She mentally scolded herself, rubbing her arms. *Knock it off. The chances of another major crime on a cruise ship are as remote as Will ordering salad for lunch. Nothing's going to happen. I love Alaska, so what am I worried about?*

Will called from the stateroom. "What's taking so long?"

She squared her shoulders and stepped through the open doorway. *Nothing's going to happen; I'll enjoy this cruise like everybody else.* It wasn't her fault, after all, that trouble seemed to follow her.

Chapter One
Five Days Previous   Oman, Jordan

"Beautiful lady! Come, come see what I have for you today. Such a price you will find nowhere else."

"See the fine pewter I have for you. American, yes? Where are you from? Newark, have you heard of Newark? My wife's cousin's daughter's neighbor went to Newark. Is it near your home? Come, let me show you my lovely bowls...'"

Acrid spices filled the air. She quickened her steps, avoiding being snagged by yet another merchant hawking his wares.

"Gold bracelet for you, dear lady? Buy two, I give you another for nothing. No? Tell you what I do for you, only you. Buy two, I give you four more, my compliments. Please to step inside my humble shop."

The frenzied pace of the souk engulfed her, the labyrinth of colorful chaotic shops swirling across her vision. Carefully avoiding eye contact with yet another seller vying for her attentions, she paused to watch a tea boy making the midday rounds. Like a hummingbird, the little fellow skittered across the busy marketplace, carefully balancing a steaming glass teapot on a silver tray. The tray held a stack of tiny glass cups next to a bowl of sugar cubes. Hurrying into a shop, the child poured tea for the proprietor, accepted a few coins, then sped to the next stall on swift feet.

"Come see my beautiful pashmina, finest in all the souk, perhaps in all of the Middle East. No one else has such soft scarves. Only the best for such a lovely woman as yourself."

"Are you American? Where are you from?" A textile seller pulled urgently at her sleeve. "My brother-in-law's childhood friend is in America now. Chicago. Is that near your home? Come with me, see my beautiful robes. Hand-woven, silk."

Shaking her head, she stopped to finger a bolt of emerald green silk. *I wish I could wear these vivid colors at my wedding. Mom will insist on a white wedding gown, dress me up like a cake topper, and I know that's a battle I can't win. But, oh, this cobalt blue silk is gorgeous!*

"Ah, please, come into my shop; let me give you a good bargain on this perfume. Your husband will love you for it. Have you no husband? Let me introduce you to my nephew. A good boy, a little slow perhaps, but he will make you a good husband and you can get him the green card to go to America..."

She knew her boyfriend was waiting for the right opportunity to propose marriage; it was just a matter of time. Why, they would have already been engaged, she was sure of it, if not for the recent shake-ups in the Amsterdam Cruise Line. Staff members were transferred all around the fleet, and she'd been sent to work on the *Ocean Wanderer* for this contract. Four months away from her true love had been hard, but it was almost over. The ship was on its repositioning trip from Muscat, Oman to America. She'd almost worn out her new transfer orders sending her back to the *Ocean Spirit*. She'd looked at them daily, almost not believing her good fortune.

"Pee-*yew!* The camel market must be nearby. Oh, hey, there, good to see ya'll here. Are you safe, all on your own? We almost didn't recognize you without your uniform on. Ya'll have the day off work?"

Jolted out of her reverie by a distinctly southern twang, she straightened to greet the newlyweds from Louisiana. Nineteen days into the thirty-eight-day cruise, she recognized most of the passengers, at least the ones who participated in the activities onboard.

"Yes, a few hours. It's pretty pungent here, isn't it, between the camels and the incense? I think the big camel market is a few blocks from here. At least it's cooler in the souk. "

"Camels stink worse 'n the hog pit back home. Ya'll looking to buy some of that fancy cloth, Miss? I bought me a fine scarf a few shops back. Dunno where I'll ever wear it at home, but it was too purty to leave there. Kin I show you?"

The young woman's blonde hair fell over her face as she reached into her Amsterdam Cruise Line tote bag, the one the stewards left on every bed the first night of every cruise. Her diamond ring caught a ray of light, sparkling.

Won't be long for me. Wonder if Penn has bought my engagement ring yet?

"See, Miss, it looks like gol' durn church windowpanes, with the black velvet framin' the brighter bits."

"It's lovely! It'll remind you of your cruise every time you look at it. I'd better move along now; I want to buy a brass teapot. See you back onboard. Ship sails at five o'clock, remember."

"We'll be there," the man assured her. "No way I want my bride to be stuck here, so far from home, with the ship sailin' off into the sunset. Lessie here wants to buy one of them Turkish rugs before we go, if they'll ship it to Baton Rouge. 'Bye, ya'll." With a jaunty wave, the couple headed down a side corridor, hand in hand, the very picture of young love. Instantly, two sellers moved toward them.

"Rugs, you say? Buy my rugs, very good price for you. You are from America, yes? Do you know about Tulsa? My cousin's wife's brother lives in Tulsa. Let me show you these colors, hand made by women in the villages..."

"No, he will cheat you, rob you blind. Come see *my* rugs! Finest quality."

A muffled call to prayer from the minarets in the city drew her attention to her watch. A little more than three hours left until crew members had to be onboard; plenty of time to buy a teapot and stop for a snack. But, first, that blue silk caught her eye. She stepped into the textile shop, debating how many yards to buy. If she couldn't talk Mom into letting her have it made into a wedding dress, it'd make a gorgeous quilt. Oh, and valances for the bedroom she'd share with Penn before long. Eight or nine yards would be plenty.

Twenty minutes later, she signed her name to the shipping order. She hadn't planned on buying five full bolts of silk, but once she looked closer, she couldn't decide between the cobalt blue and the watery yellow silk shot through with gold threads. The vendor made such a good deal on the saffron and emerald green, she couldn't leave them behind. And he threw in the length of burgundy for free. She wouldn't need her bartering skills back in the States.

Her stomach rumbled–lunchtime had passed– and she moved toward a long narrow bakery across the hectic marketplace. Heaps of pastries filled the glass display window, making her mouth water. *Knafeh;* that's just what she wanted. She could munch the crispy shredded wheat pastry on her way back to the pier.

Or maybe she'd have some baklava. When would she get the chance again? Until this cruise contract to the Middle East, she'd never known how many varieties of baklava existed. From finger-sized tubes filled with chopped nuts or dates up to palm-sized triangles dripping with honey, they were a far cry from the mass-produced baklava Mom bought from Costco at Christmastime.

A female clerk greeted her warmly in English as she stepped into the bake shop. "Ah, here you are. Here, try a chocolate-dipped fig, very fresh. I have some warm anise pastries waiting, when you are ready. Take your time, look around; there is no rush for you."

Her filmy black-sequined *abayasare* swishing, the young woman greeted two customers in German, her voice impatient. Seeing their puzzled expressions, the clerk effortlessly switched to Spanish, then to Swedish. "Well, what *do* you speak? English? I can usually guess nationalities better. You will buy these lemon pastries. And here, take some jelly candy, rose flavored. I assure you, you will like it. Hurry along now, there isn't much time. No, that's all for you today; go to another bakery if you wish something else."

Almost pushing them out into the souk, the clerk removed her traditional veil, revealing almond eyes lined with elaborate blue and emerald green eye shadow. Red lips broke into a warm smile. "Now that they are gone, we will have our time. I will provide some hot sweet tea, for you look very tired. Come, sit here and rest." She led her to a tiny metal table in the back corner of the bakery, half hidden by a gauzy curtain.

Tea sounded wonderful; a headache was brewing, and she still had to walk back to the ship. Plenty of time. Buying the silk hadn't taken long. The teapot; she mustn't forget to stop at the brass seller on the way out.

"Tell me about yourself. You work on the big cruise ship, yes, a long way from home? Do you have a family?"

"I just bought some beautiful silk for my wedding. I'm from Indiana, in the middle of America. I may never get back to Muscat again, and I wanted to see the souk one last time. And hear it, and smell it, too, I guess. There's no place on earth like this."

"Yes, yes, when the wind is wrong, as it is today, the odor of the camel market is very strong. Soon the rains will come, and the dust will settle. Here, let me pour the tea for you. Sit back, relax, you have plenty of time, and you are so very tired."

"I didn't realize how much walking I've done today until I sat down. It's good of you to serve me tea. How do you know I'm from the ship?"

The younger woman placed a few delicate pastries on a china plate. "Taste these; I made them this very morning. Please, tell me why a pretty woman such as yourself is not a married lady. I have heard in America, it is common for a woman to work outside the home, but why did you go to sea, like a sailor?"

Sipping the sweet floral-scented tea, the American shifted in her chair. "I guess I thought working on a cruise ship would be an adventure. Good thing I did, because that's where I met my boyfriend, Penn. He's a sound technician onboard. He was just about to propose marriage, but then I was abruptly transferred to the *Ocean Wanderer.*"

She set the teacup down, smiling ruefully. "Sorry to ramble on. It's been hard, being away from him the past few months."

"No, no, please go on. I am most interested." The shopkeeper rose and placed a *Closed* sign on top of the bakery display case, the gold threads in her dress catching the light. "For this reason you came into my shop this day. You believe in destiny, don't you?"

Reaching for another braided pastry, the young woman nodded. "Oh, I surely do. I know Penn loves me. We're meant for each other. It's just that he gets distracted; you know how some men are. There's a woman on the *Ocean Spirit*, the ship where Penn and I worked, named Angela. She's pretty and all, but..."

Leaning forward, she confided, "She calls herself *Jelly,* for Pete's sake. I ask you, is that a suitable name for a grown woman? Even for a performer, it's unprofessional. She has these long looping curls, and those slinky sequined costumes-! She dazzled all the men onboard, including Penn, but I know he didn't mean anything by it. And then this transfer... well, it came at a bad time."

"Drink your tea. Please, go on. How will you win back the heart of this Penn, if you are so far apart?"

"That's the good news. The cruise line is having some changes, and the new owners are moving a lot of people around the fleet. I'll be on this ship just until it reaches Hong Kong, then I'll fly to Miami and transfer back to the *Ocean Spirit*. Once I'm back with Penn, I know I can make him forget all about Angela. Maybe *she'll* even be caught up in all the transfers." She stroked her temple. "I guess I'm more tired than I realized."

"Sip a little more tea. Tell me about your home? Indiana, was it?"

"Penn needs to remember he loves *me,* I'm his destiny." Her vision blurring, she strained to focus on the painted tiles swirling behind the clerk. "I don't feel well..."

Patting her hand across the table, the shopkeeper nodded knowingly. "Yes, yes, your destiny, of course. Another sip of tea, if you please. Do you feel able to walk?" She rang a little brass bell on the table.

The tea sloshed as she slurred, "Oh, I feel a little fuzzy-headed. I'd better go. Can you call me a taxi, please?"

The clerk soothed, "Destiny. What will be, must be. Go now, and do as you are told."

A small female form appeared from behind the gauzy curtain, clad head-to-toe in a black burqa. Only her birdlike hands showed, her eyes concealed behind a face screen. She pulled the young American to her feet, hissing urgently.

"I don't feel right...oh, my head is spinning. I need to get back to the ship. Please, call a taxi. Let go of me!"

The shrouded woman's claw-like grasp drew the young woman behind the curtain, out a back door. Half running, the black fabric swishing around her feet, the tiny woman pulled her insistently down a dirt path, into a bricked passageway, her fingers relentless.

Dizzy, she grabbed the gate's frame to steady herself, but the diminutive woman yanked her through it. She gasped, the odor of camel dung strong in the bright sunlight. Through blurred vision, she made out the words on a painted sign overhead.

Forbidden To Pass
Al Lawataya District

The sign triggered a distant alarm in her brain, half-buried in a confused haze. Blinking in the brilliant sunshine, her feet faltered on the uneven path as she was half-dragged through a flower-lined brick courtyard. Heat waves radiated through the soles of her shoes.

Al Lawataya, the Shiite district, where descendants of Hijazi Arabs live. It's strictly off limits to foreigners. I'll lose my job for sure; the cruise line won't tolerate a crew member being arrested. Arrested? I could be killed here, and no one would ever know. Will the newlyweds remember me? What was in that tea?

She felt dull, clouded, oddly unconcerned, as if listing facts that had nothing to do with her. The grasping hand jerked her forward, and she stumbled.

Even if I could get free, how could I ever find my way out of this narrow labyrinth? I don't know which way to go.

Eyes glinting through the burqa screen, the woman hissed at her, sharp, scolding her for not matching her pace. That, and her slippers scuffing the dusty path, were the only sounds, the world shut out behind the thick stone walls.

She sensed unseen eyes peering from behind lace-curtained windows. Bright flowers drooped in the relentless desert heat.

How can anyone that small be that strong? I can see over her head, easy. How can she move so fast in those preposterously small slippers? I'll never see Penn again. He'll probably marry Jelly after all. Their children will be born wearing silly sequined diapers. She slipped, caught her balance. *Serves him right.*

The black-clad woman clutched her hand, nails digging into her skin, rushing her down another maze-like path. At last, she stopped abruptly. The young woman bumped into her back. She leaned against a white stone wall, her breath coming in gasps. Exotic odors filled her nostrils: sweet flowers, cooking oil, pungent spices, and the ever-present camel dung.

From beneath the folds of her black burqa, scrawny fingers withdrew a slim bottle, holding it up to the sunlight, then pressed it into the other's hand. Staring at the tube, the American took it in: amber liquid, Arabic writing, skull and crossbones label.

A clipped British voice came from the depths of the burqa. "'Ere you go, take it. That'll set your love life to rights, Dearie, and you'll know when to use it. Not too much now, just enough to cause a scare. Take care not to spill a drop. You don't want to end up on CNN."

Light headed, the young woman strained to focus on her incongruous Cockney words, the pale liquid warm in her hand.

The other cackled, "'Urry back to your ship, luv, you're not safe here. Go past the pewter shop, take three right turns, cut through the camel market, and downhill 'til you see the harbor. Ta ta, Dearie."

A sharp shove propelled her through a rough wooden doorway. She slipped the vial into her khaki pants pocket. Ducking under a sheer curtain, she found herself in the souk, between two shops. Reeling, she leaned against a cool stone wall, overwhelmed by the market's cacophony and vibrant colors. She swiped at hot tears. To the left, she spotted a pottery shop, spilling its bright wares onto the walkway. Sellers called to passing tourists and local shoppers, beckoning them into their shops.

Her throat felt as dry as the dusty desert. Was there time for a cool drink? Lifting her arm to check her watch, she stared at a mesh bag containing a brass teapot dangling from her wrist. *How–?* She drew a shaky breath.

Only twenty-five minutes until crewmembers were required to be onboard. *If I'm late again, I'll be fired for sure. Hurry, I need to hurry.*

Shaking herself to clear her head, a green sign across the souk caught her eye: *Pewter*. She darted between vendors and shoppers, past the pewter shop, turning right into a dim, narrow passageway. At the first intersection, she brushed past a vendor carrying white boxes, and turned right. Another right brought her to a heavy wooden door. Shouldering it open, she stumbled out into the midday sun. She paused, letting her eyes adjust to the light. Coughing as a breeze kicked up a wave of dust, she straightened the black and gold-embroidered shawl around her shoulders. *Where had that come from?*

Men's voices flooded from behind the fence to her left. Pungent animal odors pummeled her senses, mixed with the distinctive spitting and braying of camels. Their huge padded feet, designed for hot desert sands, stomped and kicked. Men, seller and buyers alike, waved their arms and shouted to the auctioneer on the other side of the chain link fence, all wearing *dishdasha*, floor length robes, and embroidered pillbox hats. *How did the men keep them so dazzlingly white, surrounded by animals kicking up reddish dust?*

Men shot her curious glances as she rushed along the fence. Several shouted at her. Not comprehending, she rushed through the camel market, holding her breath, dodging green camel spit on the dusty floor. Her skin tingled, the heat oppressive.

Her thoughts bounced like balls in the ship's bingo tumbler. *There must have been something in* *that tea. Who was the small woman? I sure didn't expect a British accent. It's as though they expected me. Oh, my <u>head</u>!*

Darting across the busy street, she finally caught a glimpse of the harbor, its blue water glinting in the sun. She quickened her pace: only fourteen minutes to spare. Where had the afternoon gone?

What was in the vial? Skull and crossbones; the universal poison symbol, but how potent was it? Maybe she could use it to make Jelly sick once they were on the same ship; say, just enough to be transferred, or at least miss the next couple of sailings. That'd be long enough for Penn to get his head back in the game, to remember he loved *her,* not Jelly. *What had the clerk said about destiny?*

Hurrying around another corner, she recognized the main intersection; she'd been here this morning. The *Ocean Wanderer* should be in sight as soon as she rounded the tall hotel. Heat waves danced on the pavement, sapping her energy, but there wasn't time to rest. Blotting perspiration from her face, she pressed forward, every dry breath more painful than the last. Flipping her hair back over her shoulder, she turned onto the long pier, relieved to see the ocean liner towering against the horizon. *Home. And I'm not late.*

A few dozen passengers poured out of a tour bus parked by the curb. She circled them, mindful of the time; sailaway wasn't for another ninety minutes, but staff and crew were required to be onboard early. Festive music blared from speakers, almost drowning out the call to prayer from the city's minarets. She'd have time to take a quick shower before her scheduled assignment onboard. Cool water would sooth her headache.

At least the security line was short. She reached into her khaki pocket to retrieve her ship identification card, her hand brushing the vial. Someone called her name as she passed the security checkpoint.

"Over here!" A white-uniformed officer beckoned to her.

"No time to chat," she panted. "I need to check in. I can't afford another late return on my record."

"That's the least of your problems." The officer hurried to her, pressing a manila envelope in her hand. "Here are your new orders. You're being transferred again, right now, to the *Ocean Journey*. Jennifer Owen was fired for slapping a passenger. Jennifer's pretty laid back; it was probably well deserved. Somebody has to take her place, and you're up. Your flight to L A leaves in an hour."

"But– this can't be right! I'm transferring to the *Ocean Spirit* after this cruise. I don't want to go to the *Ocean Journey!* I'm scheduled to run the Cash Out Bingo at five o'clock–"

"Sorry, hon. I'm going to miss you, but you know how it is. I had your cabin-mate pack up your stuff. It's in that cab over there. Don't miss your plane."

The officer offered his hand, then caught her in a quick hug. "Good luck to you. You'll love Alaska."

The taxi honked its horn. Mechanically, she climbed into the back seat. As the cab pulled into heavy traffic along the pier, she pressed her face against the dirty window, watching the ship recede into the distance until a tall hotel blocked her view. *Alaska! I need to get back to Penn!*

She settled back into the seat next to her black roller bag, holding on as the driver whipped around a corner. No point in speaking; he couldn't hear her over the radio's noise. She set the bag with the teapot beside her. Her hand grazed the vial of poison in her pocket. The burqa-clad woman's voice replayed in her mind.

"That'll set your love life to rights, Dearie, and you'll know just when to use it."

Destiny. I'd better hang onto this. I know I can't get liquids through airport security, especially with a skull and crossbones label.

She slipped the poison vial into her suitcase, tucking it between the folds of her blue Amsterdam Cruise Line staff shirt. Sniffing, she glanced at a white paper bag on the seat next to her. Opening it, the sweet scent of fresh-baked shredded wheat pastry wafted to her nostrils.

Knafeh.

Chapter Two
Embarkation Day   Los Angeles

CLANG! CLANG!

Jerria jumped as the ship's gong sounded again.

"Hope they're not going to keep banging that thing the whole cruise. Making me crazy, and haven't even sailed yet." Will cast a malevolent glare over the railing at the five-foot brass gong. Two crew members in feathered warrior costumes stood stiffly at attention as the flurry of passengers boarding the ship brushed past them.

"We'd better get used to it." Jerria passed her husband a pile of folded clothes from the open suitcase. "You have to admit, the ship is gorgeous. I've never seen so much red and gold in a cruise ship cabin before. Hurry and unpack, so we'll be free when Nan and Charlie arrive."

Will reached for a wooden hanger in the closet. "Suite's bigger than expected. It's nowhere near as fancy as the ultra-suite in Hawaii, but it's nice. Didn't need three bedrooms and a butler on a cruise."

"Did you see the scrollwork on this desk? I think we'll enjoy having a balcony in Alaska, even without the VIP perks."

"Probably won't want to sleep out on it this time." Will hung up another shirt. "That was a great cruise, wasn't it? Overlooking the jewel thieves, and nearly getting killed a couple of times, had a wonderful trip."

"I sure hope this one's calmer. I'm so glad Nan and Charlie were able to come along. Charlie told me the timing couldn't have been better. He's working on some horticulture project, and wants to be home in time to transplant the grafted mangoes he's developing." Jerria placed a stack of clothing in a drawer. "The mangoes sound pretty. He said they have green and yellow striped flesh, like a candy cane beet."

The closet muffled Will's voice. "Sounds like Henrietta's bathroom wallpaper. Makes me think of citrus."

"Really, the wallpaper will look fine once it's up. You'll probably never even go in the new bathroom, and Great-Aunt Henrietta will like it. It's close to what I remember in her living room. She let me help hang it that summer I stayed with her."

"Can't fit the suitcases in the closet. Too narrow. Must have been a very patient woman to let a five-year-old hang wallpaper."

"I'm pretty sure my part was behind the big wood stove, where no one would see it. You were right; we could have converted the bedroom for Henrietta ourselves, but having a contractor fix it while we're away is better. A cruise to Alaska beats dealing with two weeks of endless hammering and sawing."

"Not to mention the power tools. Remember Jeff was so afraid of the chop saw noise when we built the upper deck? Screamed every night in his bed that summer. Amy finally admitted she'd told him that sound called in the dragons after dark, telling them where a tasty little boy lived. Wonder how our kids grew up, when their favorite activity was scaring the living daylights out of one another."

"Hard to believe they're all adults now, isn't it?" Jerria tucked a stray curl behind her ear. "It was fun choosing carpet and tile colors, then walking away. Oh, Will, you're going to love getting to really know Henrietta!"

"Still not sure about her moving in. Don't want her to be too much work for you."

"I'm looking forward to it. Can you fit the suitcases under the bed? We don't want to be tripping over them the whole cruise."

"Deal with the empty luggage later, okay? Hope she's as wonderful as you recall, Honey. At ninety-four, won't be as energetic as your childhood memories."

"Age is just a bunch of numbers. Her soul is still a twenty-five-year-old homesteader in South Dakota. She's always been my favorite of all of Dad's siblings."

"Must be mutual. What are you looking forward to most?"

"Oh, everything! Her stories, her advice, and I want her to teach me to make those Swedish cardamom pastries with poppy seeds. They look like little haystacks. She'd set them to rise overnight, and the aroma was enough to get me out of bed early, every time."

"So hungry, a haystack sounds good. Lunch? That sandwich on the plane didn't stay with me."

Jerria surveyed her husband, hands on hips. How did he stay so slim, when all he thought about was food? "Oh, you're always hungry. I thought we'd wait for Nan and Charlie." A knock came at the door. "Oh, there they are now."

A burly black man filled the doorway, ice bucket in hand, his voice booming. "Good day to you, Mr and Mrs Danson, my pleasure to meet you. My name is Griffin, and I be your cabin steward. Lucky you, havin' the good fortune to travel on the *Ocean Journey* to Alaska! Have you seen the Last Frontier?" Setting the ice bucket on the desk, he shook their hands in turn.

Jerria gulped as her slim hand disappeared in the Jamaican's ham-sized grasp. "Good to meet you, Griffin. Last Frontier sounds like *Star Trek*. Or was that final frontier? It's our fourth trip to Alaska, and we're happy to be going back. The suite seems nice."

"Yah, mon, it's an older ship, not like the new fancy mega-ships, but she's a beauty in her own way. You tell me if you need anything, yah?"

The steward's broad smile faded. "I heard your cruise in Hawaii wasn't so good—the story went across the whole fleet. You're some kind o' heroes. That kind o' crew member committin' crime makes us good 'uns all look bad. I aim to make this trip calm and smooth for you. Of course, the smooth part, that's up to the captain."

He brightened. "Did you sit on the bed yet? Give it a try. The fleet ordered new mattresses, hard as a table top. They always tryin' to improve things, never leave well enough alone. On the last cruise, the massage parlor onboard had a long line, I tell you. Captain McCann ordered new mattress pads, but they won't be in until the ship gets back to Seattle. I put a heap o' extra blankets under the sheets. If it's not to your likin', you let me know."

Jerria suppressed a grin, mesmerized by the man's accent. "Thanks, we'll be fine. That was pretty creative. Anything else we should know, right away?"

"Yes, Ma'am, the main t'ing is, you gotta know you have the best steward on the ship, at your service. With so much shakin' up across the fleet, you're in good hands. Mine."

Will ran a hand through his black hair. "What kind of shake up?"

The steward glanced around the cabin, as if checking for eavesdroppers. "I shouldn't say, you know, mon, but there be a lot o' new staff and crew this sailing." He ticked them off on his large fingers. "Lemme see. The First Officer transferred in, there's a new Hotel Manager, the Cruise director has two new assistants, and they tell me it took *two* new ones to replace the executive chef. That doesn't include the one-hundred-six new crew members, so if they seem as lost as you, have a little patience, as my mama always say."

Griffin whipped out a bright yellow handkerchief from his pocket, swiping at a nonexistent spot on the end table. "I always say, you can't make mud pie into chocolate, but they do keep on tryin'. But you're not to fret none, you hear me? This cruise will be a glorious one. Tell me, what can I do for you? Can I bring you anyt'ing? More hangers? Fruit bowl?"

Jerria asked, "I think we have everything. Do you know if our friends, the Callisters, have arrived? Their cabin is next door."

"The nice people with the Hawaii stickers on their suitcases? Yes, I met them, I t'ink they're unpackin'. Her bag was ripped. Those porters get aggressive, tossin' people's belongin's around like they be coconuts. I'll have it sewn up for her. Poor woman already shivering, and this is southern California. Gonna be so cold in Alaska. Me, I'm from the tropics, too, but I do just fine, I'm fat enough. I'll take your luggage and store it 'til the last night, so it be out o' your way."

A soft knock came at the door. Opening it, Griffin excused himself, taking their emerald green suitcases with him. Nan and Charlie stepped in.

"Oh, you made it!" Jerria hugged her friends. "I'm so happy to see you."

Charlie shook Will's hand warmly. "Wouldn't miss it."

"Glad we could make it." Nan pulled her lime green pareo close around her shoulders. "You'd think, being retired, we'd have more free time."

"Well, *we're* not retired yet, but the real estate business is slow enough to leave to the crew at the office for a while." Jerria tucked her novel into a nightstand drawer. "There, that's the last of the unpacking. Have you looked around the ship yet?"

"No, we came straight to our suite. It's not as glamorous as the *Ocean Haven*, but it'll be a fabulous cruise. But what's up with the beds? They're so puffy."

Jerria chuckled, taking Nan's arm. "Come on, let's go explore the ship, and find some lunch. We'll tell you what Griffin told us on the way."

Chapter Three
Embarkation Day

"Can't get used to the crew bowing all the time. Think they'll keep it up?" Will reached for ketchup as the waiter left the table. "Ship is more Asian-influenced than expected. At least some of the food is ordinary; couldn't face two weeks of stir-fried vegetables for lunch."

"You're missing out," Jerria wound a noodle around her enamel chopsticks. "You could eat a burger anywhere."

"Just wait until we reach Alaska," Charlie chimed in. "I haven't been back since college, but there was an awful lot of fresh salmon there. I know you're not a fan of seafood."

"Putting it mildly! First man to eat slimy sea creatures had to be pretty brave, or really hungry. How long did you live in Alaska, anyway?" Will stabbed a french fry, raising his voice over the din in the dining room.

"Just for one summer. The smaller towns don't have enough people to man the souvenir shops when the cruise ships come in. They hire college students from the Lower Forty-eight to run the little stores. I liked the contrast. The pace was hectic when passengers swarmed through town, but once the ships left at the end of the day, a tangible silence settled in. Pass the butter, will you?"

"Look, the butter's shaped like whales." Nan handed the silver butter plate to her husband. "Crime scenes aside, we had more fun with you that time than on any other cruise." Nan sipped her water. "I've never been to Alaska. That's the trouble with living in Hawaii; the rest of the country is so far away. I've never even seen a real totem pole."

"They're like tiki, only bigger, and not as spooky," Jerria teased, knowing her friend's superstitions. "Totem poles are like storyboards. I spent a month in Dutch Harbor my second year of college. I joined a research trip, thinking I'd go into Marine Biology. Sorting and counting the different species of fish in the nets on a stinky boat for days on end cured me of that. I think I still smelled of fish weeks later! I do remember that silence, Charlie. You're right; it was so thick, I could feel it."

"Good thing you changed majors, or wouldn't have met you." Will took Jerria's hand. "Love you. Looking forward to two weeks with no construction commotion."

Jerria smiled; after all these years, she still found his staccato speech charming. "I'm already a fan of the chef; here, try a bite."

Their waiter gathered the empty plates a few minutes later. "Would you like a dessert menu, or shall I bring samples?"

"I'm so full; I'd better skip dessert this time." Jerria set her napkin on the table. "I'd like to go up on deck. I enjoy watching the supplies being loaded onboard. Anyone coming with me?"

"I'll come," Nan volunteered. "We need to catch up, Jerria. Warming up in the sunshine sounds great to me."

Will stood, smoothing his cambric shirt over his frame. "Come on, Charlie, let's see if there are any basketball tourneys scheduled on the sports deck. With so many sea days, might enjoy a game or two."

Charlie kissed Nan. "Meet you at muster drill, okay?"

"See you later."

A few minutes later, Jerria sipped her root beer float, leaning against the teak railing. "So much for skipping dessert," she shook her head, her curls bouncing in the sunshine. "I can't lose that last ten pounds anyway, so why be deprived? Starting to think this is just the size I'm meant to be. I'm a grandmother, after all."

Nan chuckled. "The photos you sent of little Rowland were darling. I told you you'd love having a grandchild."

"It's even better than I expected. Getting old isn't as bad as advertised, at least in some ways."

Nan ate the maraschino cherry off her float, setting the red stem down on the table. "Speaking of age, I want to hear all about your great aunt. When is she moving in with you?"

"Under a month, I think; I'll drive her back from Utah after the cruise. I can't wait to have her under our roof. She's not an invalid, after all; just weak from that bout of pneumonia. The family nearly came to blows, convincing her to sell the ranch."

She brushed her wayward curls back from her face. "I know she hated being in the hospital. She wasn't happy about staying with her son while we're away, either, but I wanted her to have a finished place to move into. It works out great; she'll stay with Jim, and we get a cruise to Alaska, all at once."

"What is she like?"

"You'd love her, Nan—she's fiercely independent, like you. The upper plains are so flat; there's nothing to stop the harsh weather. Henrietta said a twister in '47 came and stripped the place clean, but she found the family Bible and the strength to go on." Her eyes followed a noisy group of passengers crossing the deck. "Oh, and the antique cookie cutters; they found them after the storm, too, intact in their old wooden box. It's Henrietta's pride and joy. I remember playing with them on her hand-woven carpet as a child. They must be worth a fortune now."

"Sounds like she loved you, to let you play with her treasure." Nan set down her empty glass. "You didn't grow up near her, though. How did you become so close?"

"Henrietta insisted they send me to stay with her on the ranch when my mother was on bed rest, until the baby came. I was only five. Long way from home, but the best option, I guess. From my perspective, it was heaven. I ran and played like a wild thing." Jerria sat forward. "She taught me to read that summer. I can still hear her saying 'a body needs to know how to read. The world can't put anything over on a reader.' She had such an impact on me."

"Sounds mutual! Is Jim her only child?"

"No, Jim is one of eight; those homesteaders had big families. The doctors wanted her to move to a care center, one of those old folks' homes, but she threw a fit. Henrietta insisted the only place she'd go is with Will and me. I'm honored."

"I think you're smart, to have one last vacation before she moves in with you. Why didn't she want to live with her children?"

Jerria grinned. "She flatly said she'd die of boredom in their city houses, and changing Henrietta's mind is like trying to move a fire hydrant. Her work ethic is incredible. I remember her always trotting off to help one neighbor or another, as her 'bounden duty.' I guess I see having her live with us as *my* bounden duty. I think we'll have fun together, even though she's ninety-four years old."

"I finally warmed up. If I'm chilled in Los Angeles, I don't know how I'll do in Alaska." Nan pulled her pareo off her shoulders. "Tell me about your remodeling project."

"We're having contractors convert our bonus room into an apartment of sorts while we're away. The French doors open onto the side deck, and the picture windows overlook my garden and the little stream."

"It sounds lovely! After the wide open spaces of North Dakota ranch, Oregon's scenery might be a culture shock for her."

"I hope the Northwest rain doesn't bother her as much as it does me. This past winter was one of the gloomiest ever. She's used to seeing open prairie and cattle."

"–and blizzards," Nan added.

"Well, yes, there's that. The Oregon coast rarely gets snow. Hat's Mill is a pretty small town, but I think it'll still seem civilized to her, after decades of running the cattle ranch."

"Did you know Charlie's father lived with us for while after his mother went to the Great Beach in the Sky? We had him for about two years, until Charlie's siblings saw how much fun we were having together." Nan leaned closer to Jerria. "Is your eye bothering you? You keep blinking. Let me see it."

"It's nothing, I'm sure. I've been working with some raw llama wool in my weaving class, and it's irritated my eyes. The itching is annoying." Jerria rubbed her eye. "You flew into LA yesterday, right? Did you have time to take that city tour you mentioned? Was it as touristy as you expected?"

Nan giggled. "Oh, was it ever! Talk about culture shock. I enjoyed the movie studios and all, but I had no idea how some *kaulana a* live, the celebrities, I mean! We drove past some of their homes, and I felt sorry for them. Imagine, not even being able to walk in their front yards for fear of a tour bus driving up. And the traffic-! Give me Kauai any day."

I could recite the muster drill safety speech; I've heard it so many times. As the canned voice came over the loudspeaker, Jerria idly scanned the Mandalay Lounge. The gold and enameled artwork would not have been her first choice for her house, but cruise ship décor tended to be over the top. The *Ocean Journey* was an older ship, smaller than most of the others they'd been on previously. She smiled to herself, remembering the *Vega*, a ship so small it didn't even have a theater. At an evening show, Will narrowly missed getting kicked in the head by a feather-costumed showgirl.

On cue, the uniformed crew member in front of the group slipped on her life vest, demonstrating how to buckle it with exaggerated motions. *At least we didn't have to bring our life vests to this drill. Somebody always trips on the long straps, and I hate to think of how many people have tried out the germy whistles.* Other than Nan and Charlie, she hadn't met anyone else yet. *Fifteen days ahead of me; they'll be like neighbors before it's over.*

Across the room, a lanky man tipped his cowboy hat to her, and Jerria realized she'd been staring. Embarrassed, she nodded at him, averted her eyes, casting a sideways glance back at him. *Starched western shirt with pearl buttons, wide-brimmed Stetson, red snakeskin boots and hand-tooled belt....he looks like he stepped out of a spaghetti western! Did he iron that sharp crease in his jeans?* Jerria wasn't a fan of ironing anything she didn't absolutely have to press. Her mother actually enjoyed ironing; she called it "meditative," but that gene had skipped Jerria.

"Fire is the most serious danger at sea," the disembodied voice droned on. "To avoid fire on the beautiful *Ocean Journey*, please note the following rules regarding..."

Jerria shifted on her feet. She found it difficult to stay in one place for long. An older couple holding hands by the bronze-flecked mirror caught her eye. They wore matching cornflower blue shirts, but it was the man's hair that drew Jerria's attention. He'd apparently tried to slick it down, a vain attempt to control his snow-white curls. *A person could surf on those waves.* Deep laugh lines framed the woman's eyes, and a smile played on the man's handlebar mustache. *If this drill ever ends, I want to meet them.*

"This concludes the muster drill. Please join us on the pool deck for the sailaway party in fifteen minutes, and don't miss the Glacial Ice, our drink of the day." Passengers cheered, drowning out the disembodied voice.

"Finally!" Jerria hissed. "They seem to take longer every time. Come with me. I want to snag this couple before they get away from us." Taking his hand, she pulled Will through the throng of passengers making their way through the wide double doors. He didn't protest.

"Jerria!" Nan called. "Are you two going to the sailaway party?"

"Yes, we'll be right there. Give us a minute, please."

The older couple hadn't moved, waiting for the crowd to dissipate. Stopping in front of them, Jerria realized she hadn't thought what to say. "Hello," she began. "Is this your first cruise?"

Will squeezed her hand. "Noticed your cap, Sir. WWII vet, is it? Where did you serve?"

The man drew himself to his full height, a head shorter than Will's six feet. "I served in the US Navy, long ago."

"And is that a USS Magpie pin on your cap? Served in Korea, too?"

"I did at that. Minesweeper out of Guam. Hit a bit of bad luck off the coast of Korea in September 1950. Not a good month, September."

"Hit a mine, as I recall," Will exclaimed, "with few survivors. Saw a movie about that raid."

"Twelve of us made it to shore, taken prisoner for a while there. Twenty-one lost that day, including the captain, a good man if one ever lived. You know your history, young man."

"Want to shake your hand, Sir. Thanks for your service."

Smiling indulgently, his wife took his arm. "Now, dear, no one wants to hear old war stories."

Will winked at her. "I do. It's a long cruise. Can we find time to talk, Sir? Would enjoy hearing your experiences sometime."

"I'd be honored." The man's blue eyes sparkled. "But first, you have to stop calling me sir. Makes me feel old, and I'm not even ninety-one yet. I'm Elias Wilcox, and this lovely lady is my bride, Penny."

"Good to meet you. Will and Jerria, from Hat's Mill, Oregon."

Charlie and Nan made their way across the lounge. Charlie shook hands with Elias and Penny. "Now that the crowd is gone, we can catch up." He introduced himself and Nan. "We're from Hawaii, good friends of Jerria and Will. Where are you from?"

Penny's brown eyes sparkled. "Hawaii? Oh, my, we love the islands! Such a change from our home in Kansas. We're celebrating our seventieth anniversary this cruise. I'm looking forward to seeing a real glacier. I've taught about them—Elias and I were both high school teachers—but to see one with my own eyes...I can't wait."

Charlie grinned at Nan. "You know who makes the best teammates for Trivia games, don't you? High school teachers. We'd be unstoppable. Penny, if you and Elias join us, we'll have a full team."

"Why, we'd love that! We don't know a soul on the ship."

"Great." Jerria grimaced. "Two teachers, two professors, and two lowly real estate brokers from

Oregon. Sounds like Will and I will be along for the ride."

Laughter broke out. Charlie retorted, "Not so; you two were amazing on our last cruise. Elias, I've been eyeing your cap. Are you a Navy veteran? I thank you for your service, and I'd enjoy hearing a story sometime."

Will good-naturedly elbowed his friend. "Did that part already. Come on, don't want to miss a party."

Twenty minutes later, passengers lined the railings, cheering as the *Ocean Journey* pulled away from its moorings. Southern California's sun glinted on the harbor like confetti on the blue water. Jerria held her sunhat on with one hand, raising her glass with the others in a toast.

Across the pool deck, the big brass gong sounded, nearly drowning out Charlie's words.

"North to Alaska!"

Chapter Four
Day One   At Sea

Eight minutes to Trivia. Checking her watch, Jerria opted to take the atrium's stairs to deck seven rather than wait for the poky glass elevator. Besides, she wanted to see the artwork in the stairwell. By the second flight of stairs, a stitch began under her ribs. *I should have skipped that chocolate French toast, at least the third slice.* But a whole day, chocolate-themed, wasn't to be taken lightly.

"Sorry!" she gasped, sliding into a plush chair in the Warrior Lounge. Other players straggled in, forming teams for Trivia. Across the lounge, Jerria noticed the lanky cowboy from the muster drill, his Stetson on his knee. "Where's Will?"

"Catch your breath," Nan advised. "Elias and Penny aren't here yet either. I don't even see the staff member who's running the game. Will and Charlie went to order some hot cocoa for all of us. What did the doctor say?"

"He agreed my eyes are just irritated from that new llama wool I was weaving at home. He gave me some antibiotic drops. Interesting guy. Dr Marsh is a weaver, too. We talked about Turkish hand looms while he examined my eyes."

Will and Charlie crossed the room to the circle of six chairs, each juggling three white paper cups with red dragons embossed on them. Will said, "Extra cream for you, Jerria. How are your eyes?"

"I'll be okay, thanks. I liked the doctor, not that I want to spend any more time with him this cruise. He has a sweet deal, works only four hours a day, and he's on call the rest of the time. He said he brings his wife and five-year-old twins with him every summer. Not a bad gig, spending all summer on a cruise ship."

"The kids must love that. I wonder how he can leave his patients, though. I read in the brochure that he's in private practice." Charlie stood to let Penny slip by him, into the circle of chairs. "Good morning."

"Oh, are you talking about the ship's doctor?" Elias pulled back a chair. "Good morning, everyone, sorry we're late. Had a nice stroll on the promenade deck, and lost track of time. We met Dr Marsh in the snack shop last night while his little boys ate a bedtime snack. Good man. He's an obstetrician at home. He said he plans which patients he accepts, passing ones who are expecting babies during the Alaska cruise season to his partners."

"Pretty smart! Here you go, Penny." Nan passed the elderly woman a cup of hot cocoa. "Enjoying the cruise so far?"

Penny rested her hand on her husband's knee. "It's been lovely, except our bed is as hard as my kitchen table. We tossed and turned all night."

Jerria suggested they talk to the cabin steward. "They can pull strings we don't even know exist." She nodded her head toward a crew member walking at a fast clip into the lounge. "Oh, she must be running the Trivia game today."

The young woman dropped her Amsterdam Crew tote bag on the piano lid, smiling as she scanned the room. "Hi, everybody! I'm Liza, part of the Cruise director's Activities staff. Sorry I'm late. Why on earth the other Activities staff decided to store the game prizes in the closet with the spare uniforms baffles me. But hey, I scored a new shirt or two while I was picking out these amazing prizes for you all."

She laid out score sheets and a box of golf pencils on the piano. "Okay, let's get started, shall we? Super. Teams of no more than six. Send somebody up here for a score sheet and pencil. Which team is most excited to be on the *Ocean Journey?* Let me hear you!"

Jerria stood and, along with eight other passengers, made her way to the piano as whoops filled the room. Liza high-fived each person, dancing like a cheerleader, her blonde ponytail bouncing with a life of its own.

"Okay, who's ready?" Liza's enthusiasm was contagious. "Let's start with an easy question. You all had breakfast, right? Super. How many sides do most bananas have?"

The room fell silent. Players' heads bowed, conferring with their teammates.

Will whispered, "Come on, Jerria, you like bananas. How many sides?"

"I just eat them, I don't count them. Charlie, you taught horticulture. How many sides?"

"Five, I'm pretty sure."

Penny wrote on the paper, her schoolteacher handwriting round and precise.

"Ready? Super. Where is the cheapest petroleum fuel in the world sold?" Liza giggled. "I was there on my previous ship, and let me tell you, the harbor was full of ships, waiting to fuel up. Worse than Costco on a Saturday morning!"

Will murmured, "Gibraltar. Saw those same ships last year." Jerria nodded.

"Next question: What US state consumes the most ice cream per capita?"

Soft guesses buzzed around the lounge. Jerria overheard "Florida," Mississippi," and "Texas". She leaned in, her voice muted. "It's Alaska, I'm sure of it. I bet few people will think of that; a warm-weather state makes more sense."

"Number three: what color is a giraffe's tongue?" Liza grinned. "Who wrote these questions? I'll make up some better ones for tomorrow's game, promise. Meanwhile, think back to the last time you visited the zoo."

"Navy blue," Elias contributed, "and don't ask why I know that. The mind is a remarkable thing, full of all sorts of useless knowledge."

"Navy, it is." Penny filled in number three.

"Next question: What island is the boot of Italy kicking?" Collective groans wafted across the lounge. Teams murmured, heads bowed over answer sheets.

"Honestly, the next one's worse. What is a baby skunk called?" Liza teased, "What's with all the blank faces? I chose some light-up necklaces for prizes, just the thing to wear to the Northern Lights dance party tonight. Super. Next question: what was Mark Twain's given name?"

In the end, Jerria's team tied with a younger team, with a perfect score of twenty.

"Super. Tie-breaker question!" Liza announced, "Send up a smarty-pants team member. First one to answer wins, and no help from the peanut gallery, got it?" Will urged Elias to go.

A smug twenty-something smirked at Elias as he carefully picked his way to the piano. Jerria suppressed a smile. The other players probably thought the wobbly old man stood no chance.

Liza challenged, "Two-part question. What is my name, and why was I late this morning?"

Without missing a beat, Elias blurted, "You are Liza, part of the Cruise director's Activities staff. Why on earth the other Activities staff decided to store the game prizes in the closet with the spare uniforms baffles you. But, hey, you scored a new shirt or two while you were picking out these amazing prizes for us."

Stunned, the lounge fell silent, then applause rang out. His opponent shook Elias' hand, apologizing for underestimating him. Liza congratulated Elias and gave him a handful of light-up necklaces. Elias clasped his hands over his head over his head like a prizefighter, his back military-straight, and returned to the group.

"Don't let it go to your head, dear; you know what pride goeth before." Penny smiled indulgently at her husband. "It helps to have an audiographic memory like yours."

"What's that?" Will asked. "A ringer on our team?"

"It means he remembers everything he hears," Penny explained, "like photographic, only with hearing."

"And it was a real burden, let me tell you, teaching high school," Elias cheerfully complained. "There are things I'd rather un-hear."

"Oh, his memory has been a benefit a few times," Penny said proudly. "He won five hundred dollars at the county fair last year by reciting the names of every state capital, alphabetically. Had his name in the local paper, too."

"Heard them on a local late night radio station." Elias's mustache twitched. "The things they do to avoid dead air space in the middle of the night. Here, take your prizes. Nan?"

Nan's attention was drawn to the floor-to-ceiling windows lining the lounge. "What are those spindly structures on the horizon? They look like oil derricks, but we're still within sight of the coastline."

The three couples stood to get a better look. "Yes, they're derricks," Will agreed. "California's on a shelf. Not far offshore, it drops off deep and sudden. Easier to snap California off when the Big One hits. Remember Sierra losing sleep over that when she was in fourth grade, Honey?"

Jerria bent to pick up her cup. "Why the schools assigned that awful earthquake book to those little kids, I never did understand. She was prone to nightmares as it was. Penny, do you and Elias have children?"

"No, we were not blessed in that way." Penny took Elias' hand. "Neither of us have any siblings, either, so we're the end of the line. We've had a good life, though. And now we're living another dream, going to Alaska!"

"Are you two going to the Captain's Reception this morning?"

"Oh, yes." Penny's plump cheeks crinkled in a warm smile. "We wouldn't pass up a chance to meet a real ship's captain, and a woman one at that. Captain Bay McCann. It's all so exciting!"

Charlie pulled a ship's schedule from his back pocket. "It starts in twenty minutes, and I'm not sure where it is. Oh, it says here it's in the atrium, deck three, midships."

Nan pulled her wrap around her shoulders. "This air conditioning is freezing. Let's go together, shall we?"

The three couples stopped to gaze over the railing on deck six, down onto the atrium floor. Penny's blue eyes sparkled. "Oh, did you ever see the like? I feel like I fell into an elegant movie set."

Two decks below, crew members scrambled, setting out drinks and trays of finger foods on mirrored stands. A man in a tall white toque directed traffic, barking orders, his voice drowned out by the violinists warming up on the raised platform.

"Is that the head chef, do you think?" Penny pointed. "My, that hat!"

"Must be." Jerria nodded to the left. "And here come the officers."

A parade of senior staff in crisp dress whites took their places in front of the musicians. Immediately, a crush of excited passengers rushed across the atrium, eager to meet the officers. Liza urged them into a ragged line.

"By the time we catch an elevator, the throng will subside. Come on, I could go for a snack." Will held out his hand to Jerria. "Haven't eaten in over an hour."

A few minutes later, they took their place in the receiving line. When Nan and Charlie reached the assembled group, the First Officer shook their hands warmly, clasping both of his over theirs. They knew John Hansson from previous cruises in Hawaii.

"Nan, Charlie, it's so good to see you! I just transferred here, and I was delighted to see your names on the passenger manifest. And Will and Jerria, too! Captain, may I introduce Mr and Mrs Callister? And Mr and Mrs Danson; they're the ones I told you about. This is Captain Bay McCann."

The slim African-American woman extended both hands, the gold stripes on her sleeves catching the light. "Delighted to meet you. You're legendary across the fleet, after that episode in Hawaii. I'm honored to have you aboard my ship. This cruise will be a quieter one, I assure you. One thing Alaska has is tranquility. Have you met our Cruise director?

Gretchen, may I introduce the Callisters and Dansons?" Captain McCann turned to the next passengers in the receiving line.

The tall Cruise director extended a limp, icy hand. "I've heard about you. The things some people will do to get a free cruise."

Jerria recoiled. Was she joking? The tall woman smiled, the effect never reaching her eyes. "Move along now, you're not the only passengers on the ship."

Jerria heard Captain McCann behind her warmly welcoming the Wilcoxes. Her heart sunk. *Their first cruise ever, and the CD is as cold a frozen trout. Sad.* Moving down the line, she greeted Dr Marsh, who introduced her to Joel, the naturalist onboard. The doctor's warmth didn't hide Joel's unease.

Joel pumped Jerria's hand. "Pleased to meet you. Do you like the Northern Lights? There's a ship-wide party tonight with that theme, and I'm required to attend, although I told them I have two left feet when it comes to dancing. But the real Northern Lights will be visible once we reach the higher latitudes. I hope you'll come watch them with me one night." His face red, Joel dropped Jerria's hand and sputtered, "Not just *you,* you understand. The whole ship can see the sky."

"Ignore him," Dr Marsh teased. "He's at loose ends without binoculars in his hand. Mrs Danson, your eyes still look irritated. Come see me again tomorrow in the Med Center, please. I have some eye drops that might help."

Jerria nodded, assuring Joel she'd love to see the Northern Lights, then moved across the atrium. A uniformed waiter approached, offering skewered prawns on a silver tray.

Elias and Penny soon joined them. Penny's cheeks were flushed. "Oh, my! Wait until I tell the girls in the garden club I shook hands with a genuine ship's captain! And she seems so nice, too, so professional."

"Unlike the Cruise director. Have you ever seen such a disdainful woman in your life? I'm surprised Captain McCann tolerates her." Charlie shrugged.

"Maybe her bun is pulled too tight," Will joked.

"It's a French twist, and I don't think hair styles cause rudeness." Jerria sipped her soda. "Maybe she's just having a bad day."

Nan stepped aside so a woman could pass. "Now, her assistant, on the other hand...Liza has a way of drawing people to her, doesn't she? She even made waiting in the receiving line fun."

A passing man jostled Jerria, nearly spilling her drink. "Looks like the whole ship showed up at once. Let's move outside, where there's some breathing room."

Carrying small plates of hors d'oeuvres, the three couples pushed through the double glass doors out onto the promenade deck. They headed for deck chairs under the shaded overhang.

"Fancy cheese toasts and shrimp at eleven o'clock in the morning, sitting on a beautiful ship with new friends, on my way to Alaska...this is a dream!" Penny relaxed into her seat.

"Don't wake me if it is; I'm content." Jerria pulled her sunglasses out of her pocket. "This sunshine is so bright! There are some interesting folks on board. Have you noticed the young family with the double stroller? And that man with the big cowboy hat looks like he stepped out of Central Casting."

"I saw him; I think his cabin is down the hall from ours." Nan popped the last cheese cube in her mouth. "I was pleased to see John Hansson onboard. A familiar face among the staff is a good thing."

"Interesting people right here, too." Elias set his plate down. "This being our first cruise, you're making us feel comfortable, like old hands. Nan, I'm curious, and I hope you don't mind me asking, but how did you get that red scar on your jaw? Looks recent."

Penny stiffened. "Elias, my *word!* You can't ask a lady such a thing!"

Nan chuckled, "I don't mind. At first, I kept it covered with makeup, but that wasn't practical. We live on Kauai, and you never know when rain might pelt or Charlie might want to take a break to go kayaking." She brushed her long hair over her shoulder. "Anyway, short answer, a horse kicked me."

"A horse kicked your jaw? You're lucky to be alive to tell the tale!" Elias' respect was tangible.

"No, it wasn't a big deal," Nan bit a toast point. "I was feeding the mare while a friend was out of town, and she didn't trust me. It wasn't the horse's fault."

Charlie cut in. "There was a little more to it than that. After the horse kicked her, Nan stood up and walked home, over a mile. Scared me out of a year's growth, seeing her walk across the garden, covered in blood. I wasn't sure if she'd murdered somebody or what."

Penny patted Nan's hand. "You poor dear! How very brave."

Nan brushed aside the sympathy. "You'd have to kick a lot harder than that to crack this coconut."

Charlie took Nan's hand. "She's full-blooded Hawaiian, and let me tell you, those are some tough people. Last year, Nan's auntie—"

Clang-! Clang-!

A nearby passenger spilled her drink. Will growled, "Charlie, want to help me throw a gong overboard sometime?"

Over the loudspeaker, a voice intoned, "Good morning, *Ocean Journey.* We're currently sailing at twenty-one knots, and will reach the port of San Francisco at five o'clock tomorrow morning. Seas are calm, with an air temperature of eighty-six degrees. The drink of the day is a California Capture. Don't miss the country line dance class at one o'clock. Please be sure to check your daily schedule for today's other activities and—"

"Anybody interested in the dance class after lunch?" Elias smiled. "For an old guy, I admit I can move my feet."

Nan said, "I don't know how, but I'm willing to learn."

Jerria stood, stretching. "I've seen your hula, and if you can do that, this will be easy. We'll be there, right, Will? We don't find many chances to dance. For now, I'm going to go fix my hair. I slept later than I planned, and I just ran my fingers through it. See you all later."

Jerria walked away, hearing Penny say, "Jerria's hair is naturally curly? What I wouldn't give to..."

Chapter Five
At Sea

Even before they reached the ship's gymnasium, Jerria heard raised voices. She exchanged glances with Will.

Gretchen bit off each word. "All I've got to tell you is, consider yourself on probation. The last thing I need on my staff is a chirpy cheerleader. Staff changes or not, I don't want you here."

Jerria slowed her pace. Another woman spoke, but she couldn't make out the words.

"Now get out there and make nice, and I mean it, do your job and stay out of my sight, hear me? And quit acting so perky, you look five kinds of stupid." Gretchen stalked around the corner, her eyes flaming. "Oh, passengers. Just what I need." The Cruise director stormed out onto the open deck.

"Whew, I felt a cold breeze! Wonder who she lit into?" Nan shuddered.

"She really sounded mad! Did you see her eyes? Such an unusual copper color." Jerria resumed walking.

"Yeah, like a witch's," Charlie grimaced. "Glad I don't have to work with her. A ship's a confined space, after all. Oh, not too many people here for the class yet."

A couple dozen passengers stood around the gym, as awkward as teens at a school dance. A technician in the back fiddled with a soundboard. In the center of the big room, Elias spun Penny in a slow twirl to music only they could hear, their faces wreathed in pleasure.

Jerria spotted the man she thought of as The Cowboy across the room. Dressed in a plaid western shirt and jeans, with red snakeskin boots and a ten-gallon hat complete with a peacock feather, he was hard to miss. Most of the other passengers wore shorts and tank tops in the California heat. That was the third Stetson she'd seen him wearing; how did he pack them for a cruise? Jerria suppressed a smile, imagining the cowboy carrying a heap of flowered hat boxes.

Several more people straggled in, waiting for the class to commence. An older man beside a woman in a pink jogging suit shifted on his feet. She probably dragged him here.

Her face flushed, Liza rushed to the center of the gym, dropping her Staff tote bag by the wall. Her eyes were red above her broad smile. "Sorry I'm late. Great turnout! Make three lines, facing me. Super. Let's start out slow, okay? Don't worry about a partner; it's not that kind of class."

Jerria and Will stood behind Elias and Penny. Nan set her wrap down on a chair, moving into place next to Charlie.

"No wallflowers. Come on, this will be fun! We'll start with some basic steps. You need to know how to pivot, or you'll end up in a tangle on the floor, and this is *not* a first aid class, okay?" Slipping her hair into a ponytail, Liza waved a few latecomers into place.

"Eyes on me, please. Step forward, lean your weight on your front foot and rock into a quarter turn right. One and two and three and –*whoops*, not that right, the *other* right, facing the windows. Let's try that again! To the right, four times. You folks catch on quick! Super!" Liza clapped, beaming. "Moving on. Cupid Shuffle. Like this."

Liza demonstrated, counting. "Eight to the right, tap your toes, eight to the left, eight heel steps right where you stand, eight heel steps forward, *pivot* to the right." Her easy laughter was contagious. "Super, you look great! Now, again."

The man with the pink-suited partner edged his way toward the open door. His wife, intent on her feet, didn't look up. Jerria smiled at Will and he winked. They didn't get much chance in their small hometown, beyond the Christmas Dance at the club.

"Next step, ready?" The group shifted to get a clear view of Liza. "This is the kick-ball-change, and it's important because you can make a lot of noise, and that's always fun. Super! It looks a lot harder than it is. Okay, weight on your left foot, kick your right foot in front with your heel leading, push your right foot in back and really *stomp* with your left foot. Two times, ready?"

The group followed Liza's lead. She faced them, hands on hips, giggles bubbling through her grin. "Look, people, I know you're trying, but that stomp was *pitiful*. Flip-flops and sneakers just don't have the same authority as cowboy boots. You, sir, with the fine hat on, come to the front, please, show 'em how it's done."

The lanky man wiped his hands down his jeans and strode across the gym, his snakeskin boots loud on the wooden floor. Liza extended her hand. "I've had my eye on you. I can tell you've done this before. Super! Tell us your name, and where you're from."

He tipped his hat, revealing short red hair. "Folks call me Cowboy Bob, and I hail from Split Fork, Texas, Ma'am, by way of the US Marines. And, yes, Ma'am, I can dance a lick."

Jerria suppressed a giggle. Hat's Mill, Oregon suddenly sounded like a metropolis, compared to any place named Split Fork. And his drawl was so thick, you could spread it on toast.

Liza grinned, "I bet you can. Show us a proper kick-ball-change, will you?"

Cowboy Bob nodded. Kick, push, *stomp,* kick, push, *stomp.*

"That's how it's done! Give Cowboy Bob a hand." The group applauded. "Try it one more time, then we'll take a quick break, and we'll get some boot-scootin' tunes playing. Super! "

Jerria wiped her face. "Whew, it's warm in here!"

"I know, right? Dancing is a real workout." Nan ran her fingers through her luxurious hair. "I want a drink. Did you notice the crew wheeled in some snacks?"

"Not worth the bother," Will grumbled. "Just vegetables on fancy skewers. Where's a cookie when you need one?"

Jerria reached for a cucumber-tomato kabab and a bottle of water. "Honestly, there's more to life than cookies." She'd tried for years to cure Will of his aversion to vegetables, but she admitted failure. At least he hadn't noticed her sneaking them into her cooking...or hadn't commented yet.

Penny and Elias piled veggie kababs on little plates and dolloped dip on top. Penny said, "This is so much fun! Look at me, dancing on real cruise ship."

Elias blotted his forehead. "And it's just started. Isn't Penny pretty when she's happy? We've been dancing as long as we've known each other."

"Yes, indeed," Penny nodded. "We danced up a storm in the USO club in Topeka."

Jerria smiled, taking in the other woman's flushed cheeks and warm smile. *I hope we're as happy as they are when we've been married seventy years.*

Cowboy Bob stood a few feet away, sipping bottled water, his back ramrod straight. Nan walked to him. "Hi, I'm Nan. I'm having trouble with the Cupid Shuffle. Would you mind showing me how again?"

"Yes, Ma'am, I'd be right pleased. Follow my eight count."

Jerria watched, amused. Side by side, hands on hips, Cowboy Bob and Nan moved through the steps. His wide shoulders dwarfed her slim frame.

Nan's grace made the steps look more Hawaiian than country.

"Ma'am, you're making the right moves all right, but ya'll gotta step a little harder. Country line dancing isn't nearly as dainty as all that."

"Sorry, I'm used to Polynesian dancing. It's not quite the same." Nan's bare feet mimicked Bob's leather boots through four turns. "Oh, I think I get it now. Thanks!"

Elias asked, "Bob, did I hear you say you're a Marine? Where did you serve?"

"Yes, Sir. My country sent me to Iraq and Afghanistan. This cruise takes up a good bit of my leave before I meet my unit in Europe next month. My wife's at some fancy art auction."

"Thanks for your service," Jerria put in. "Wow, Alaska is about as far from that climate as you can get. What did you do there?"

Bob studied the floor. "Well, Ma'am, I can't rightly say. Mostly, I tried to blend in with the locals, much as a red-headed Texas boy could do."

Liza clapped her hands. "One more step I want to teach you," she called, "then we'll tackle the Watermelon Crawl. Cowboy Bob, come on up front."

The passengers moved into ragged lines, facing Liza. "Let's try a grapevine next, to the right. Step out, cross over, step, cross, tip back, now step-ball-change and...*turn!* And again!" She kept a sharp eye, encouraging those who lagged. "You *got* it. Super! I think we're ready for some music."

"Louisiana Hayrack" blared through the gym. Concentrating, passengers turned, dipped, stomped and turned to Liza's count. Now that they had the steps down, the group moved smoothly across the wooden floor, smiling. Jerria winked at Will, admiring his easy grace. *We should book a vacation to Nashville sometime, just for the music. Maybe a long weekend in Branson-*

The door flew open, smashing into the wall behind it. Heads swiveled, dancers collided. A woman tripped and fell to one knee, and two people next to her stumbled. A young man in a Staff shirt rushed across the floor, heedless of the confused passengers. "Liza! Gretchen's on a tear. She found a file on the staff laptop and she-"

"Gregg, can it wait? I'm in the middle of a class here-"

"Turn that infernal noise off this instant!" The Cruise director steamed into the gym, heels clacking as she made a beeline for Liza. The music shut off abruptly. "Liza, I warned you to stay out of my way! You're a poor excuse for an assistant. I-"

She glared at the staring dancers. "You mind your own business. This silly class is over, as of right now. Go lie in the sun or something. *Out!*"

Grabbing Liza by the arm, Gretchen dragged her to a corner, waving her finger in her face. Gregg's training kicked in. His smile never wavering, he ushered the passengers through the wide double door. "Thanks for coming, hope you had a good time, don't forget Bingo starts at three o'clock, thanks for coming, 'bye now..."

Nan stopped to pick up her wrap from the chair. Jerria's heart went out to Liza; no one likes getting yelled at, especially in front of others. She took Will's hand as the group filtered out.

Gretchen's words rang through the gym. "I can't believe you touched the staff laptop! What were you thinking, you silly girl? Who told you to change the Trivia questions?"

Liza stiffened. "Gretchen, I had a class here. You interrupted it, over a computer file!"

"And that's another thing, young lady," Gretchen's face was mere inches from her assistant's. "I don't know how you managed before you got here, but on this ship, classes go forty-five minutes, no longer. You're late by sixteen minutes."

"Oh, seriously. The passengers were having a good time. This is my free hour, so why do you care?"

Jerria heard Gretchen's last words before she moved into the hall. "Just don't get too comfortable here; I swear I'll have you put off in the next port if you cross me again."

Passengers milled uneasily in the corridor. Nan suggested they go onto the open deck. "Can you believe that woman? I've never seen a Cruise director that hostile. I feel sorry for Liza."

Jerria shook her head. "Sure seems like Gretchen made the wrong career choice. For a job working with the public, you think they'd choose somebody who likes people."

"Maybe Captain McCann doesn't see this side of her."

"That could be, or maybe she's just stressed out. Our steward said there'd been some staff changes recently," Jerria said. "Either way, let's not let it ruin our afternoon. Anybody for a swim?"

Penny said, "We'd enjoy that, if you don't mind me and Elias tagging along."

Will assured her, "Of course not. Meet you at the pool in a few minutes."

Chapter Six

Jerria scanned the dessert menu. "I can't decide. Would you laugh at me if I ordered both the crème brûlée and the tangerine tart?"

"Never get between a woman and her dessert," Will smiled at her. "Your sweet tooth goes into overdrive when you're upset. Not still thinking about Gretchen and Liza, are you, Honey?"

"Well, yes, I guess I am. Cruise staff are usually so professional. I can't imagine what made Gretchen holler at poor Liza in front of everybody."

Nan gingerly adjusted her green flowered shawl over her shoulders. "Hard for a Hawaiian to get sunburned, but I think I managed by the pool. They probably smoothed things over by now. The music is nice, don't you think?"

"Trying to distract me, are you?" Jerria relaxed in her chair. "You're right; it's not worth another thought. Did you read the notice about tonight's show?"

""Haywood Jacallme. Odd name, even for a comedian." Will set his menu aside. "Can't figure out what nationality Jacallme is."

Their waiter refilled Will's water glass. "Excuse me, Mr Danson. The comedian's real name is Tom Wagner. He goes by his stage name. Say it slowly, like this; 'Hey, would ja call me.' Personally, I think it's a little hokey, but no one asked my opinion."

He pulled a pen from his vest pocket. "Before I take your dessert orders, may I offer some advice about tomorrow's port? We'll be in San Francisco at six-thirty in the morning, but if you want to see us sail under the Golden Gate Bridge, you need to be on deck ten around five o'clock." The waiter took their orders (two desserts each) and walked away.

Penny and Elias approached, holding hands. "Hello! Pardon our interruption, folks, but we thought you'd get a kick out of our cabin steward. You'll never guess what she did."

"I love a story. Pull up a chair," Jerria invited.

Penny sat next to Will. "We told our steward the mattress is too hard, as you suggested, and asked if she could find a mattress pad of some sort. When we went back to change after swimming, the bed looked different."

"It looked like something out of the *Princess and the Pea* story," Elias interrupted, "about eight inches taller, and rounded on top."

"What on earth–?" Jerria's eyebrows rose.

"We looked closer, and you'll never guess. She'd arranged bed pillows under the bedsheet, end to end, like a checkerboard! It's a–"

"–*pillow* top mattress!" Penny and Elias finished together.

Charlie joined in the laughter. "They do anything to make passengers happy, but that takes the cake."

"This is the best anniversary trip we've ever had," Penny wiped tears of laughter. "And we've met such nice people already. There are three other couples at our dining table, just as sweet as could be."

Jerria sipped her water. "Do you have plans for San Francisco tomorrow? Have you been there before?"

"Oh, yes!" Penny sat forward. "Elias was stationed here years ago. I didn't teach during the summer months, so I packed up and came to California. We were poor as they come, but we made great memories those few weeks before Elias shipped out. We thought we'd like to visit some of the places we went to all those years ago."

"Sounds lovely," Nan said. "This is my first visit to San Francisco. Jerria has the day all planned out for us. We can compare notes tomorrow night. Will, did you say something?"

Will's ears reddened. "May have muttered something– just in passing– about the color-coded spreadsheet on our cabin wall."

Charlie patted Jerria's hand. "Your planning serves us well, friend. Will may laugh, but we appreciate all your research."

Elias winked at Jerria. "Don't let them tease you. I fully understand. If you're going to see a place, you may as well see every bit of it."

The waiter arrived, wheeling a loaded dessert trolley. Elias stood, extending a hand to Penny. "Are you all going to the show this evening?"

"We'll be there. The comedians on ships are usually pretty good. Would you like to sit with us?"

Some hours later, Jerria closed the cabin door and slumped into the teal chair. "I led Elias astray. I told him comedians are usually funny, and I lied. Have you ever heard such a bitter performance in your life?"

Will unbuttoned his grey striped shirt. "More rage than humor. Definitely had a chip on his shoulder, maybe both shoulders. Man needs a good psychiatrist. Sure hope his wife isn't onboard to hear that. Can't tolerate a man who disrespects his family."

Jerria knew Will was still upset about his old college roommate. They hadn't seen each other in years, until the man approached Will with a business proposition a few weeks ago. It would have brought in more money than Will earned in months selling real estate. Over lunch, Paul boasted about having a long-term affair. Will broke off the deal on the spot, telling Jerria that night, "If his own wife can't trust him, how could I? Man who can't keep his word to his family is no man at all, in my book."

"Besides that, Haywood wasn't even funny. I kept wondering if the Cruise director would yank him offstage, but we never saw her after she introduced the guy." Jerria kicked her shoes off. "It's a pretty night. Want to sit on the balcony with me?"

They sat in the dark, lost in their own thoughts. Eventually Jerria spoke. "The cabin steward said the production team was all new this cruise, too. I sure hope tomorrow's show is better. Oh! Did you see that shooting star?"

"Good omen. There's another one. Stars are sure pretty against the dark sky, away from city lights. Better get some sleep, Honey, if we want to be up in time to sail under the Golden Gate."

Jerria yawned. "The ship will sail under the bridge with or without me, and five o'clock is awfully early. We'll have to sail back out of the harbor in the afternoon; maybe I'll watch it then instead."

"Heard they'll serve coffee and pastries on the upper deck," Will teased. "That get you up and going?"

"Don't count on it!"

Chapter Seven
Day Two   San Francisco

Will dressed in the dark, attuned to Jerria's steady breathing. She'd been sleeping poorly at home, and he wanted her to rest and relax on this cruise. He knew when they returned to Oregon after this cruise, she'd be caught up getting Henrietta settled, and helping Amy plan her wedding. Jeff was coming up on final exams at Cornell, but promised to come home for two weeks between semesters. It never ended, and Jerria needed this vacation.

Identifying his jacket by feel in the closet, Will closed the cabin door behind him, holding it so it wouldn't slam. His watch read 4:35 AM. The ship's corridor was deserted at that early hour. Two other passengers waited for the glass elevator near the atrium, bundled against the morning chill.

"Are we nuts, getting up this early just to see a bridge?" A woman greeted Will, her voice muted.

"Most likely," Will replied cheerfully, "but when else can we see the Golden Gate from the bottom? Hope the fog lifts in time. Couldn't see past our balcony railing."

The elevator doors slid open. Three other passengers welcomed them. "Ah, kindred spirits!"

They joined a knot of hardy passengers on deck ten, clustered near the railing. Fog roiled like a living thing, and spirits were low.

"Crazy, I woke up early for this!"

"I can't see a thing! I figured it'd be daylight by now."

"The fog will lift, right?"

"Come on, fog, give it up!"

"I'm freezing. I thought California was supposed to be warm."

The *Ocean Journey* blew her foghorn every ninety seconds, the sound lowing across the harbor. After waiting a few minutes, several passengers gave up and retreated to the elevators. Will pulled his knit hat down over his ears, shifting his feet.

A man nudged him. "Hey, man, do you see lights ahead, or am I imagining it?"

Will strained to see through the dark and fog. "Think you're right. Maybe it'll clear up in time."

The foghorn blared again. Suddenly, the fog broke ahead of the ship, wispy tentacles floating on the pre-dawn breeze. The Golden Gate Bridge loomed a few hundred feet ahead of the ship, and the ship was closing in on it fast. Streetlights on the bridge decking cast puddles of muted light, blurring details above. The angles of the bridge glittered eerily in the headlights of passing vehicles. A ragged cheer rose as the *Ocean Journey* approached the bridge, its superstructure mere feet from the traffic passing overhead.

Two bicyclists paused on the sidewalk above, waving to the cheering passengers. At the edge of the streetlight's glow, a figure in a grey trench coat faced the sea, seeming to not notice the huge ship. Will looked away, then back again as the aft of the ship cleared the bridge. Out of the corner of his eye, he thought he saw the figure above swiftly pull a dark shape from under his coat and lob it toward the darkened ship. Will blinked, but the figure was gone, swallowed by the fog. Will's breath caught in his throat. Was he seeing things?

Did I imagine that crash? Thought something fell from the bridge. Did something hit the ship? Did the man throw something? Couldn't be...

San Francisco's lights nestled on the city's hills, Oakland's visible across the harbor. Straight ahead, the first glimmer of sunrise broke over the horizon. Passengers chatted, delighted to be among the few to witness the bridge from that angle. Now that the fog was behind them, the day promised to be crystal clear. Good; that wasn't often the case this time of year in San Francisco.

Will unbuttoned his jacket, eying his fellow passengers. No one seemed to have noticed anything unusual. Will watched the city slide past as the ship eased through the harbor to its pier. *What did that man have in his hands? Something out of the corner of my eye. But–*

"Join us for some hot cocoa? The buffet just opened." The man next to Will held the door open.

"Thanks, sounds good."

A dozen or so passengers poured down the stairs to deck nine and into the buffet. Considering the early hour, the brightly-lit restaurant bustled with activity. Only a handful of guests were up and about this time of day, but the crew stood ready for the inevitable flood. Port days were especially hectic.

Will filled a mug, selected a warm pastry from a basket, and settled at a large round table by the floor-to-ceiling windows. Others joined him.

"That was an amazing sight," a woman sighed. "I expected more clearance. Too bad my family thought sleeping another hour was more important!" The group chuckled. Most of them had left cabin mates asleep, too.

"Wife said she'd rather see it the bridge this afternoon, on the way back out of the harbor," Will remarked. "Was wondering, did any of you see–"

"Good morning, you early risers!" a cheerful voice interrupted. "What a terrific start to a beautiful day! May I join you?"

Will dragged a chair from the adjacent table.

Liza slid into it and reached for the cream pitcher. "Thanks. Just look at that glorious sunrise. Super! Sailing under the bridge was really something, wasn't it?"

"Oh, yes," a woman agreed. "I'm glad I got up early to see it. But I guess it's old hat for you crew members. You must get tired of it, seeing every couple of weeks."

"Not me." Liza set her steaming mug down. "I'm excited about seeing San Francisco, too. I'm off duty until one o'clock. Ghirardelli chocolate, here I come!"

Will opened his mouth again to ask if anyone else had seen anything fall, but a young man spoke first.

"Liza, can I ask a question? Did you see the show last night? Usually, comedians are funny, and he wasn't, at all." Agreeing murmurs passed over the table.

"I missed the show, but I sure heard about it! Haywood was the talk of the staff lounge last night. Very unprofessional to dump his personal problems on an audience like that. The way I heard it, his wife—"

"Do I see a staff member consorting with passengers?" Gretchen's shrill voice jarred the group. The Cruise director stormed across the restaurant, and jerked Liza's chair back. Liza's cup was halfway to her lips. Dark liquid sloshed down the front of her blue Staff shirt.

Liza flinched, holding her steaming shirt away from her skin.

Will passed her a wad of paper napkins. "Gretchen, what is wrong with you? Barely daylight and already yelling."

Her glare would have melted a meeker man. "Mind your own business. What I do with my assistant is none of your concern." Anger flashed from her eyes. "You, Liza, I expect you to act like a staff member at all times. You're not on vacation. I don't want you talking to passengers any more than you absolutely have to, much less gossiping. Now, get going. You have disembarkation duty on deck four in forty minutes."

"No, I don't." Tears rose in Liza's eyes. "I have the morning off."

"You have off when I say you have off. Get out of here before I write you up for being out of uniform." Gretchen turned on her heel, glaring at Liza's retreating back.

A moment later, the First Officer strode to the table. "Good morning, everybody. Is there a problem here?"

Gretchen's fury turned off like a switch. Honey-tongued, she replied, "Oh, absolutely not, Mr Hansson. These fine people are just enjoying the lovely morning. The captain certainly did a great job bringing us under the bridge, don't you think? Nice and smooth. If you'll excuse me, I'll see about the disembarkation announcement. It's going to be a beautiful day."

John Hansson raised an eyebrow as the Cruise director hurried away. "There's something to be said for efficiency, but that woman is tightly wound. Everywhere she goes, fireworks follow. Well, I'd better get my coffee."

"Telling me a senior officer has to get his own coffee?" Will teased. "Not still drinking it with maple syrup, are you?"

John gazed at the stripes on his sleeve, averting his eyes. "No one ever adds enough for my liking. Have a great day, all of you."

The ship settled into its berth with a gentle bump. "That's my cue." Will stood. "Off to see if my wife is awake yet. 'Bye, everyone."

Halfway to his suite, Will remembered. *Should have asked John if he saw anything. Those guys with binoculars on the bridge...not much gets by them.*

In the dining room forty minutes later, Jerria set down her muffin. "Oh, there you are," she greeted Nan.

"Aloha." She slid into a chair. "Running slow this morning. I think the bathroom in our suite is haunted. Seemed every time we fell asleep, wailing started from somewhere in the wall. Charlie thinks it's the plumbing. He stopped by Guest Services, but I don't know what they can do about it."

Charlie arrived a minute later. "Sorry I'm late. Good idea, to have a leisurely breakfast while the crowds dissipate." He reached for the pastry basket. "What's the plan for today?"

Nan interrupted. "I hope it includes a department store. I saw a forecast for Victoria, and I can tell you, I'm going to need a warmer coat."

"Of course. We'll stop at Ghirardelli Square. Also, we–"

Charlie patted Jerria's hand. "The old chocolate factory? That's my kind of place! Good planning."

Jerria laughed. "It's been converted into shops, but we'll find you some candy before the day is out. I booked a hop-on hop-off tour. I figured that'll give us an overview of the city. And a cable car ride out to

Union Square, of course. I'm sorry I couldn't get tickets to Alcatraz; they sell out months in advance."

"It's just as well. That'd take all day, and we'd rather see all we can." Charlie sipped his juice. "We have to have some sourdough bread."

"And crab on Fisherman's Wharf?" Nan asked hopefully. "Sorry, Will, I know you don't like seafood, but we can't visit San Francisco and not eat crab."

"Or cioppino. I think I heard it was invented here," Charlie put in. "The Italian fishermen would go around at the end of the day, asking the other boats to *chip in* some seafood for the communal stew."

Will shuddered. "Good story, but still not eating slimy sea creatures. Better load up on breakfast. Lunch sounds iffy."

"Great Aunt Henrietta would say 'eat now against the later hunger.'" Jerria stood, taking Will's hand. "I'd just as soon skip breakfast and enjoy a big lunch."

Will told Charlie, "Jerria's great aunt is used to cooking for hungry ranch hands. *There's* a woman who appreciates breakfast."

Jerria stuck her tongue out at him. Will's favorite meal was breakfast. Personally, she'd prefer to sleep the extra half hour than face food first thing in the morning. At the buffet, she placed melon, sliced bananas and a plum on her plate. Eying Will's tower of French toast, she added a croissant, then a raspberry turnover. No matter how hard she tried, those extra ten pounds clung stubbornly to her middle, and she dearly loved the crisp pastry.

Besides, she rationalized, *if some poor crew member worked in the middle of the night to bake these for me, the least I can do is enjoy them.*

By the time they finished eating and headed for the gangway on deck four, most of the passengers had disembarked for the day, leaving only a couple dozen in line ahead of them. Gretchen's voice filled the corridor.

"Move along! Honestly, how hard is it to get off the ship? Just flash your key card at the nice man, and get going! If it takes you this long to get *off*, you'd better plan on being back early. Ship sails at five o'clock, with or without you. Makes no difference to me."

"I'm sure the captain wouldn't tolerate her treating passengers like this if she knew about it." Jerria shifted her bag to her other shoulder. "I've half a mind to report her."

Will took her hand. "Let it go, Honey. Need both halves of your brain to be our tour guide today. Where to first?"

"First, we'll take the trolley to meet the hop on hop off bus and-"

Haywood Jacallme scrambled into line behind them, muttering into his cell phone. He snorted in disgust, then slipped it into his pocket.

A man standing nearby jeered, "For a comedian, you're not a very happy guy. Do you ever smile? And that bit last night about soaping yourself and spinning clean in the shower wasn't even original. Where'd you get it, out of *Reader's Digest*?"

Haywood sneered, "Mind your own business, joker." His nasal voice broke. "*You* try making a bunch of strangers laugh while your world is coming apart."

Jerria made eye contact with Haywood. "Are you all right?"

He rubbed his jaw. "Oh, yeah, right, like you care. My wife's mad. She found out I coulda brought her along on this cruise for free. I'd like to know who told her that. I oughta punch them right in the nose."

Charlie asked, "Why on earth did you leave her home?"

"She'd harsh my mellow. Lot of pretty ladies onboard. Hey, it's your turn."

Gretchen rounded the corner, hands on hips. "I tell you, it takes a special kind of stupid. You folks can't even keep a line moving. How will you ever get around a big city?"

Her tone lightened abruptly. She flashed a broad grin over the heads of passengers as Jerria slid her card into the security slot. "Oh, Captain McCann, a good morning to you. Lovely weather, isn't it? Off to see the sights, Ma'am?"

Captain McCann stepped off the last of the carpeted stars, greeting passengers warmly. Her voice lowered to a hiss as she reached the Cruise director. "Hardly! I'm meeting the state police about the broken window on deck six. The officer on duty reported something striking the ship as we passed under the Golden Gate. Might have been a large rock.

Keep everybody calm, will you? I don't want anyone panicking."

"Yes, Captain, you can count on me."

Captain McCann passed the line of passengers on the gangway.

Nan adjusted her shawl around her shoulders. "I hope it warms up later on."

"Don't count on it." Charlie put his arm around Nan's waist as they walked down the concrete pier. "Hey, Will, I know you were up early. Did you see anything unusual? When I went to the cabin to get my sweater, two maintenance men were in the elevator with a big pane of glass. They were grumbling about it being an inch too small and having to order another. They said one of the canted windows in the Year of the Dragon lounge shattered coming into the harbor. How could that happen?"

Jerria kept her voice low. "You didn't hear what Captain McCann said? Something about a rock? Who'd drop a rock on a cruise ship?"

Will stopped in his tracks. "Saw…thought I was wrong. Right when the ship sailed under the Golden Gate, something fell, just as the aft passed the bridge. Man in a trench coat…Hoped I imagined it."

Tears welled in Nan's eyes. "Oh, I feel terrible. That's a bad omen, an *ouli*. Someone threatening the ship is dangerous. Maybe we should…"

Charlie squeezed her shoulder. "Now, Nan, this isn't Hawaii. *Ouli* don't apply here. It's probably a silly prank, not an omen. Shake it off; we can't let it ruin the day, much less the cruise."

"Try not to think about it, Nan. The captain's in charge, not us." Jerria well knew her friend's Hawaiian superstitions, and was determined not to let Nan dwell on it. "Besides, you need a new coat, remember?"

"And some sourdough bread, don't forget." Will winked at Jerria. Trust Will to have food on his mind.

"Hi, everybody!" Dr Marsh called to them, holding a little boy's hand. "Beautiful morning, isn't it? Last trip was socked in, fog so thick, we could hardly see the bay at all."

"Good morning, Doc," Jerria greeted. "Is this your family?"

The pretty woman with him extended her hand, her blonde hair falling forward. "I'm Jill Marsh, and these rascals are Jed and Jeremy."

The group introduced themselves, and shook hands with the five-year-old twins. Jerria noticed one had a Band-Aid on his chin; they were otherwise identical. Remembering her own children at that age, she admired Jill's calm exterior. She couldn't imagine keeping two little boys safe and entertained on a cruise ship all summer.

"Let me look at your eye, Mrs Danson." Jerria tilted her head back so the doctor could see better. "All clear," he said. "Looks like you were right about it being the new wool at home. Picking up any new fibers today?"

"No, I'll wait until we reach Alaska. I'd love to find some musk ox yarn there."

"Good idea. Maybe I'll get some, too. I'd like to buy some llama wool today. There's a shop on Union Square that sells exotic fibers."

"Yes, I saw their web site. We weavers have to stick together. Dr Marsh, can I ask you about Gretchen? Is she always that angry? She's been in a rage since we boarded."

"I don't know what's up with her. Guess she packed up cat and cauldron to be here this contract." Jed –or was it Jeremy? – pulled at his father's hand. "Well, we're on our way. As you can see, the boys are eager to go see the Maritime Museum."

Jill smiled. "Have fun today."

They waved at the retreating family. Nan drew a deep breath. "Okay, I feel better now. If it was a body that fell on the ship, Dr Marsh would be involved in the investigation, right? It had to be a rock. Oh, there's a sign for the trolley."

Jerria led the way, glad her friend had calmed. She didn't mention her suspicion that the ship's doctor wouldn't be involved in a death unless it actually took place on the ship. She shook off a chill as they stepped onto the old trolley. Nothing was going to spoil this trip; she wouldn't allow it.

Chapter Eight

As they climbed aboard a cable car a few hours later, Liza called to them, smiling broadly. "There are seats over here. Are you loving San Francisco? It's a glorious day, isn't it? Super!"

Jerria perched on the narrow wooden bench, arranging her shopping bags at her feet. "It's a pretty city. I can't get over these hills, and the way the buildings cling to them. Didn't I hear something about earthquakes?"

Liza's giggle sounded like bubbles. "Oh, you know humans, always wanting to live as close to the water as they can. Let me show you these necklaces, okay? I bought them for my bridesmaids." She bent to retrieve her bag, just as the cable car hit a bump.

Jerria grabbed her arm, steadying her. "Oh, I didn't know you're getting married. Good for you!"

Nan leaned over to get a better view. "Oh, they're beautiful! So delicate. When's the wedding?"

"I'm so glad you like them; I needed another female opinion." Liza beamed, flipping her hair back. "He hasn't actually proposed yet. May I show you his picture? Isn't he yummy?"

Jerria smiled as Liza whipped out her cell phone. Young love was a bright spot in the world, and Liza was deep in it.

Liza's young man reminded Jerria of one of those fishes that never sees the light of day, but there was somebody for everyone. She passed the phone to Nan.

"Oh, this is my stop. Have fun, you guys!" Liza gathered her bags and stepped off the cable car with a cheery wave.

"So bouncy. Sure a contrast to her boss," Will shook his head. "Don't know she stands working with Gretchen. Where do we get off?"

They grabbed handles as the cable car jerked through an intersection, then down a narrow street. The grip man in the middle of the car strained to hold its speed steady on the steep downhill. Beads of sweat rolled down his bald head, his fingers white on the grip.

"I smell burning wood," Nan nervously clutched Charlie's hand. "Are we okay?"

A man next to Nan looked up from his newspaper. "It's just the wooden brakes under the street, scorching. Nothing to worry about."

Nan gasped. "The brakes are wooden, they're burning under the street, and you say not to worry?"

The cable car leveled out on a flat stretch of street. The passenger nodded, "See, nothing to it. Happens all the time, part of the experience. Here's my stop."

As the man stepped off, he offered one last piece of advice. "Just enjoy the ride. You never know what life will bring."

"People are nice everywhere we go." Jerria sat back as the cable car passed an oncoming delivery truck. "Reminds me of that time we were here with our kids years ago. The cable car was packed. I had Amy on the seat beside me, and Will had the other three kids in the back. The car began to slide backward down a steep hill. I was terrified, but I didn't want to scare Amy. I think she was about four. The gripper couldn't hold the cable car, and I was sure we were going to crash."

She reached for her bag. "We slid down about two blocks. People were screaming, car horns honking. And there was little Amy, with her hands in the air, grinning and squealing, 'Wheee!' Halfway, another grip man jumped on, and the two of them were able to get it to a stop. That poor gripper...I can still see him, sitting on the curb, shaking like a leaf in a windstorm."

Nan's eyes were wide. "Oh, my gosh. What did you do?"

"We decided it was a lovely day for a walk, and we got off as soon as it stopped. The kids were scared, all but Amy. She said, "We're going to Knott's Berry Farm tomorrow. I'm going to ride a roller coaster, and I was *practicing*!'"

Charlie and Nan laughed, along with other passengers listening in.

"Fisherman's Wharf, end of the line!" bawled the grip man. "Everybody off!"

They stepped off the cable car, and stopped to watch two workers turn the cable car.

Nan exclaimed, "I had no idea the turntable was still operated by hand."

"Come on, let's head to Boudin. It's not far. Sourdough is legendary, and that bakery is as authentic as it gets. We'll circle back to Ghirardelli

Square, so we won't have to carry any shopping bags." Jerria stepped aside to let a family pass.

Matching his pace to hers, Will grumbled, "When's lunch? I'm so hungry, could eat a crab." He wrinkled his nose. "Well, not *that* hungry."

"I didn't forget. The bakery has a shop where we can see how the bread is made, then we'll find lunch. We still have plenty of time before sailaway."

"Would you look at that?" Charlie pressed closer to the display window, marveling at a baker deftly shaping sourdough into bears and turtles.

"It smells so good, my mouth is watering," Jerria said. "Let's go in."

Twenty-five minutes later, they stood on the sidewalk, ripping chunks off a crusty loaf.

"I had no idea there was that much history in the bread," Charlie broke another hunk off the loaf.

"I thought the most interesting part was learning about Boudin's great grandfather saving a bucket of the mother starter after the great earthquake of 1906. If I was fleeing a burning city in ruins, grabbing a strain of wild yeast might not even cross my mind." Nan chewed slowly. "On the other hand, this is delicious."

Will wadded up the empty bread bag. "Come on, that was a fine appetizer, but I want lunch. Great day for a picnic, don't you think? Head down by the water. Saw picnic tables not far from the seafood vendors."

"Sounds good, "Jerria said, "but what about you? You sound awfully eager for crab cocktails."

"Not happening." Will took her hand. "Saw a kiosk across the park offering half-pound hot dogs and curly fries."

Jerria laughed and took his hand. Trust Will to find the best compromise.

After a lunch of crab sandwiches and cioppino—and a hot dog—Charlie stretched in the sunshine. "We lucked out, having such a clear day. How about you women go shop for a coat, and Will and I will scout out some chocolate. Let's meet back here in an hour." They agreed, and walked across the green to Ghirardelli Square.

Nan quickly found a warm blue pea coat with a fleece lining. "I can zip it out if I get too warm. Fat chance." She and Jerria poked around the little shops, keeping an eye on the time. Eventually, they made their way back to the picnic table. Will and Charlie were deep in conversation, not noticing the women until they sat beside them.

"What's up?" Jerria took in the concern on their faces.

"Wish you'd been here sooner." Will shook his head. "Would have known what to do. Liza ran by a few minutes ago, obviously upset. Crying hard."

"We stopped her, "Charlie continued. "We wanted to make sure she was okay. She could have had an accident, for all we knew. She wasn't able to talk clearly. She said she'd had a phone call from somebody on another ship. Will, did you think it was the one she transferred from?"

"Don't know. Bawling so hard, it was hard to understand her. Wailed about somebody not having the sense God gave lettuce. Then she sobbed about losing a pen, and said she had to be onboard an hour early or Gretchen would have her head. That last part, I understood. Ran off and jumped in a taxi. You two would have known what to do with her."

"Oh, no. That poor girl! She was so happy a few hours ago." Jerria's heart fell. Liza reminded her of one of her daughters, and she grieved right along with them when they hit disappointment. "Maybe we'll have a chance to check up on her later. We'd better head back to the ship ourselves. Getting a taxi with three ships in port might take some time."

They slowly walked across the green to the taxi stand, where a knot of people waited. They heard Haywood barking at a child as they walked up. He popped her yellow balloon with his fingernail. The little girl burst into tears, and her mother scolded the comedian.

"I said, keep that away from me. Kids and dogs, neither of 'em belong in public."

Will grabbed the comedian by the sleeve. "Pull yourself together before somebody calls the cops on you. What's your problem, anyway?"

"A lot you know, with your pretty little wife by your side." Haywood turned on Will, his face stony. "*My* old lady cleaned out our bank account and went to her mother's. Just because I didn't let her come on the cruise. I could kill her. I could just kill her. I'd have to find some way no one could trace. Something exotic, you know? I'm better off without her, but I ain't gonna spend no time in jail over her."

Haywood walked past the open door of a waiting taxi. "Forget the cab. Fresh air will do me good."

"He needs more than fresh air!" Jerria slid across the taxi's seat. "The ship looks like one of the buildings from this distance."

"I'm feeling uneasy," Nan admitted. "Broken window, upset crew members, who knows what's next?"

Charlie took her hand. "Shake it off, sweetheart. With so many people onboard, somebody's bound to have a bad day now and then. We're going to have a great cruise. Lazy sea days ahead, and we're going to love Alaska."

The taxi pulled over on the pier. "Have a good trip," the driver. "I've always dreamed of a cruise, and you lucky people are on your way. Twelve ninety-five."

After paying him, Will took Jerria's hand, walking toward the gangway. "He's right. Couldn't be any more blessed. Wonder if they put out the afternoon cookies yet."

Chapter Nine

Liza sprawled on her narrow bed, sniffling. She sat up, threw another soggy tissue toward the waste basket, and squared her slim shoulders. *If Mom were here, she'd tell me not to give away my power. I can't give that awful woman any more space in my head. I just need a plan, that's all.*

At the stand-up meeting this morning, the First Officer made it clear Captain McCann wanted a party atmosphere for sailaway today. Liza's role was to encourage the passengers to have fun, moving, dancing, happy on deck. Once again, Liza mentally thanked her college theatre instructor, who'd spent weeks going over how to slip into a different persona at will. She'd put on a happy face for the passengers' sake.

Gretchen slammed the desk drawer in her cabin. She'd just about had it, and the cruise still had more than a dozen days left. Honestly, every trip seemed to include passengers more annoying than the previous one. All they did was eat and laugh and chatter, having no respect for her feelings one way or the other. And the questions! How fast are we going, what time does the buffet open again, bring me a lime, clasp my necklace for me, do these stairs go up or down? Who did they think she was, their servant?

Dr Marsh's little boys were sure cute, though. A smiled played on her lips, remembering the way their freckled faces lit up when she handed them the stuffed peregrine falcons she'd purchased for them at the market today. Only two more cruise contracts, and she'd be able to stay home for good. Maybe start a family of her own. She'd take them camping. She'd never set foot on another cruise ship.

The radio on her hip squawked. John Hansson's voice came through the static. "Gretchen, can you track down the band right away? They should be on the pool deck by now. We sail in twelve minutes, and the captain wants the sailaway party started."

Gretchen scowled. Didn't the First Officer have better things to do than badger her, as if she didn't know her own job? The disembodied voice continued. "Also, the passenger headcount is off by five, and I need you down on deck four ASAP. You'll need to talk to the pier officer if they don't get here quickly; we can't delay sailaway. Oh, and you set up the art auction for eight o'clock, didn't you? I emailed you that change. Are you there?"

"Yes, Mr Hansson, I'm on my way." How he expected her to be in three places at once wasn't clear.

Kids were great. It was the adults she could do without.

Jerria kicked off her shoes. She swiftly tapped out a text message on her cell phone, then displayed it to Will.

Ship sailing soon from San Francisco. Take care of each other. Phone off. Will call in a few days. We love you.

"I'm sending it to all the kids at once." With a flourish, she pressed the Send button, then walked across the suite and keyed in the code on the safe. She shut the phone inside with a satisfied smile. "I tell you, the stress at home was sinking my ship, pardon the pun. It's a relief to be away from everything. My phone's tucked away, and I'm ready to vacation."

A tap sounded at the door. Will yawned and opened the door.

Charlie poked his head in. "Nan's changing her blouse. Are you two going to the sailaway party?"

"Wouldn't miss it. Saw them setting up a giant grill on the pool deck earlier." Will called to Jerria, "Come on, Honey."

Jerria pulled a cardigan out of the closet. "Did you grab the daily schedule sheet? I don't want to miss anything."

Charlie said, "I see there's a city names Trivia game before dinner. I'm not sure how long Nan will want to stay on the open deck. With the fog rolling back in, it's getting chilly."

"Good thing I packed this new wool wrap," Nan's voice came from the corridor. "I hope we can see the bridge before the fog closes in. I already heard some foghorns."

As they pushed open the heavy door to the pool deck, music met them. A Filipino singer did a credible imitation of Johnny Cash's "Walk The Line."

Passengers milled around the pool, talking, laughing, heaping plates with grilled chicken and salads. Over by the bar, a handful of guests joined in a line dance, led by Liza. Laughing, she and Gregg motioned others to dance with them, and the group grew.

Jerria and Will took places next to Charlie and Nan in the second row, in front of a woman in pink shorts. They quickly caught on to the steps Liza called out. Elias took Penny's hand over by the railing, and soon they joined the other dancers.

Cowboy Bob started near the front, but within a couple of moments, he moved back beside Nan. Over the music, he encouraged, "Kick back, touch, turn, double step—that's right!" Sipping a drink by the railing, his wife stared at him, her brow furrowed.

Jerria concentrated, careful not to look down as she danced. She remembered her Driver's Ed teacher's advice from decades past. "You already know where your feet are, so keep your eyes up." Her heart lightened, surrounded by passengers reveling in the party atmosphere.

The ship eased out of its berth at Pier 27, made a sharp turn, then eased into the channel toward the Golden Gate Bridge. The band broke into "California Dreaming." Jerria and Will moved to sit by the pool with their friends.

Jerria accepted a soda from a waiter. "I was too tired to get up before dawn, but I'm excited about seeing the Golden Gate from underneath now." She sat back. "Penny, did you and Elias enjoy the city?"

"Oh, my, yes! It brought back such memories. We rode a cable car, then had a picnic of crab cocktails and sourdough at the Golden Gate Overlook Park. Alcatraz looked like a gem in the bay. Today was perfect."

"And I realized I love Penny even more than when we came here as newlyweds." Elias' white head bent toward his wife. "She's even more beautiful now."

Penny beamed.

"I hope we can be this happy when we've been married as long as you." Nan stood, extending her hand to Charlie. "Let's go up one deck, okay? I want to see the bridge close up." The three couples trooped up the teak stairs to the sun deck.

The Golden Gate glistened in the gauzy sunlight, tendrils of fog wafting around its surface. Traffic streamed overhead, oblivious to the cruise ship in the harbor below. Flashing lights from a state trooper's car gleamed on the car deck above. Two troopers stood at the center point of the bridge, scanning the ship and the passing cars behind them. Jerria waved, and they waved back. The knot of passengers on the upper deck cheered as the ship glided mere feet under the bridge, heading out into the open sea.

"How nice, a send-off as we leave the harbor!" Penny exclaimed. "They even had their police lights on for us."

Will held his thoughts, knowing it wasn't typical for state troopers to watch a ship sail out of harbor.

Did it have something to do with the broken window in the Year of the Dragon lounge? What had he seen falling from the corner of his eye this morning? He glanced at Nan. She was leaning over the railing, her wrap pulled tightly around her shoulders, waving at small sailboats below. Good, she'd forgotten about the 'ouli, the omen. Hawaiians could be so superstitious, and Nan was full-blooded.

Onshore, fingers of fog wafted down the steep hills spilling onto the harbor. Sunshine gradually ceded its place. Music from the pool deck drew the friends back to the party. Will caught Jerria in an embrace as the band segued into "I Left My Heart In San Francisco." Older couples danced around the pool, enjoying music from a familiar era. Elias and Penny smiled into each other's eyes as they twirled across the teak deck like professionals. Passengers applauded softly as the last notes faded.

Liza grabbed the microphone from the band leader. "Come on, everybody! Let's kick up the pace, shall we? Everybody dance! I have a bunch of light-up necklaces I dug out of the crew closet. Super! Come on, let's have some fun. You're on a cruise!"

The band broke into "Boot Scootin' Boogie," and passengers quickly formed a line, hands on hips. Liza moved between the dancing passengers, handing out Mardi Gras beads, plastic leis, and blinking necklaces, never missing a step.

Gretchen, near the salad bar, kept a close eye on her staff. Liza knew how to keep a crowd happy, she'd grant her that, but her chipper attitude grated on her one remaining nerve. *If she's going to stay on my ship, she needs to tone it down. I can't stand a chirpy assistant.*

An hour before dinner, Liza propped her staff laptop on the piano, and retrieved the City Names Trivia file. She'd have time to change a few. Repeat passengers likely knew the answers to the tired old questions. Deleting several, she replaced them from memory. She could wing the rest during the game if she had to. After all, how many Trivia games had she led?

She rifled through an assortment of ship-logo prizes in her canvas staff tote bag, deciding on keyrings. A wave of pride washed over her; that simple canvas bag represented a dream fulfilled. Well, almost: she figured she'd be promoted to Cruise director within a year or two. *And it'll be a relief to be the one giving orders instead of taking them.* She wondered again what Gretchen had against her.

Realizing someone had spoken, she blinked. "Sorry! Something on my mind, I guess. What did you say?"

Jed—or was it Jeremy?— Marsh grinned at her. "Miss Liza, can I stay here with you while the big people play the game? Mommy said it's about cities, and I know a lot about Chicago. That's where my house is, you know."

"Sure, you can. It's about funny names people give cities, so you might not know all the answers, but you're welcome to stay. You can help me keep any eye on the teams." Liza smiled. "Now, tell me which one you are. I bet you get tired of people mixing you and your brother up, don't you?"

"It's easy!" The five-year-old grinned. "I have a loose tooth, and Jed doesn't, and he has a skinned knee, and I don't, and I have–"

Liza caught the small boy in a bear hug, laughing. "You are just the cutest little boy, and it's a good thing there are two of you to go around."

A sharp voice crackled the air. Gretchen jerked Liza's arm, pulling her off balance. "What is wrong with you? You left the staff closet unlocked!"

Jeremy, startled, ran out of the Year of the Dragon lounge past a cluster of passengers trickling in.

Liza blinked. "I never...I didn't–"

Gretchen forced a smile at the puzzled passengers streaming into the lounge. "Here for the Trivia game? I'm sure Liza here has a good one lined up. Go ahead and take your seats. Over *there*." She lowered her voice, biting off each word. "See that you mind yourself. I won't tolerate anything out of order on my ship." She turned on her heel, nearly bumping into the First Officer. "Good evening, Mr Hansson."

"Everything all right here?" John Hansson's eyes bored into Gretchen's.

"Never better." She averted her eyes. "I'm just checking on Liza here, making sure she's set up for the game. Our guests do love their Trivia. Well, I'm on my way."

He watched her stalk out of the lounge. "Liza, what's going on?"

She bit her lip. "I...I don't know. Just working out the newness, I guess. I'd better get my pencils and papers set out, if you don't mind."

Passengers were beginning to stare. "I'll see if I can talk to her."

"Hi, John," Nan greeted him as she took her seat. "Here to play Trivia with us? As much as you travel, I should think you'd know a lot of facts about cities."

"My head's chockful of data, much of it useless." He paused, smiling at his friends. His previous assignment had been in Hawaii, and Nan and Charlie Callister often cruised on that ship. They'd become fast friends, along with the captain, even inviting the officers to their home on Kauai a few times. "I'd better leave you to it. Good luck." With a jaunty wave, the officer headed down the corridor.

Clapping her hands, Liza called, "Welcome, everybody! Gather into teams of six or less. We're playing for some great prizes today, Amsterdam Line key rings, one size fits all. Get your paper and pencils up here on the piano, and we'll start in just a minute."

Charlie rose. "I'll get the scoresheet. Your turn to keep score, Jerria."

"Happy to. Did you notice that broken window is taped off? Anyone heard for sure what happened? Cruise ships' glass has to be pretty sturdy; it didn't break by itself."

"I heard rumors, that's all. Somebody in the elevator said a piece of the bridge fell off and hit the ship, and another woman said she'd heard somebody dropped a big rock. I guess it was too dark and foggy to be sure. Too bad Cinci isn't here; she'd tell us." Nan turned to Penny. "On our last cruise together, the Cruise director kept no secrets. She talked like speech was a marathon and she had to come in first, but she had a heart of solid gold."

Will leaned forward. "Thought I saw—"

"Quiet, everyone!" Liza clapped her hands. "First question: what is the Emerald City? No, not the *Wizard of Oz* one, the American one."

Low comments from other teams wafted through the room. Jerria penciled *Seattle.*

"Next: What is Pittsburg's nickname? That's a harder one, but you can get it, I'm sure." Liza's eyes scanned the room, giving them time to write an answer. "Ready? Super. Number three: what city is called the Crescent City?"

Penny murmured, "New Orleans, I'm certain. We had such a nice time there."

"Where is Charm City?" Liza's giggle filled the lounge. "I don't know about that one; I've been there, and I think that's a pretty optimistic nickname."

"Next question is worth three points: There are seven cities claiming the title of City of Roses in America. Name three of them." Liza grinned as players growled. "Hey, these glamourous keyrings are worth at least fifty cents. I have to make you work for them, don't I? Super."

Jerria looked to Elias. "Portland is one of them, but do you know any others?"

"Used to be an old ditty about that, decades ago. Little Rock, Pasadena, Chico, Norwich, Springfield, and Thomasville, Georgia. Bada,dada da bin."

Will's eyebrows rose. "That memory of yours comes in handy!"

"He can't follow a grocery list to save his life, though." Penny took his hand.

"Selective incompetence," Elias smiled guiltily. "I learned long ago, if I do something poorly, Penny'll take over, and she's a much better shopper than I'll ever be."

Will grinned. "Selective incompetence? Charlie, why didn't we think of that years ago?"

"Next question..."

At the end of the questions, Liza called, "Okay, let's see who gets these great keyrings. Clap good and loud if your team scored five right." Every team in the lounge clapped. "Now, ten correct? Super!" The cheering lessened as she counted. "Who has fifteen right? Sixteen?" Two teams remained in the competition, Jerria's and a family by the piano. "Seventeen? Eighteen? Wow, you guys are *good.* Nineteen?" Both teams continued clapping. The other teams watched intently.

"On my other cruise ship, if there was a tie, somebody had to do pushups for a tie breaker. Just sayin'," Liza joked.

Elias nudged Will. "That's a job for a younger man, you or Charlie, not me."

Liza called, "Did either team get *twenty* right?"

The team by the piano fell silent, leaving Charlie and Penny the only ones still clapping. Warm applause broke out.

"Good for you!" Liza congratulated them. "That was a tough quiz. Here are your prizes, and thanks for playing, everybody. Super. Don't miss the variety show tonight."

"Oh, my, thank you so much," Penny examined her keyring through its plastic sleeve. "I can't wait to show the girls at home. This is wonderful!"

Liza put her hand on Penny's shoulder. "*You* are the reason I love my job. So many passengers are jaded, forgetting they're on vacation to have fun. I'd better run; I want to be sure the sound system is set up for karaoke this evening. Last night, the bass was stuck on low, and everybody sounded like Minnie Mouse. See you around!"

Chapter Ten

At dinner, Will set down his fork. "Eating turducken is mighty efficient. Turkey, duck, and chicken in one dish, sausage stuffing, and not a vegetable in sight."

Nan waggled a finger at him. "Jerria's right; I don't know how you stay alive, avoiding vegetables and fruits like you do."

Charlie chimed in, "Aw, leave the guy alone. You know what would cure you, Will, is some fresh Hawaiian fruit. I tell you, the produce I grow on Kauai is nothing like this mass-produced stuff. I'll show you around when you two come stay with us in February."

A loud cry rang out across the dining room. Heads swiveled. A passenger pushed her plate away angrily. "What is this, a dirty gym sock? If this is a lobster tail, it's gone bad. Are you trying to kill me? I never—"

Two waiters and the maître'd hurried to her table. One quickly whisked her dinner away while the others tried to calm the woman. Nearby diners resumed their meal.

"Yet another reason to avoid seafood," Will mused cheerfully. "A spoiled lobster can ruin a cruise right quick. Pass the rolls, will you?"

Jerria slid the basket toward Will. "Still, there's no reason to make such a fuss. Nan, are you and Charlie planning to go to the show tonight?"

"The Herman Hermit's tribute band? Yes, it sounds good. I doubt it'll beat the ABBA review we saw in Hawaii, though. I don't know how they danced on those platform shoes. They had to be eight inches tall, at least."

"The shows on ships have been pretty good, at least the ones we've seen." Jerria blotted her lips with her napkin. "I don't know about the comedian on this one, though. He's performing in the piano bar later tonight. I hope he's in a better mood."

Will sat back as the assistant waiter removed his plate. "Has a bee in his bonnet, for sure."

Their waiter offered red-leather bound dessert menus. "May I recommend the chef's special dessert? He has prepared an origami swan on lemon custard."

How could a dessert be made of folded rice paper? Before long, a platter with four graceful puff pastry swans floating on a creamy lake appeared.

"So elegant!" Nan exclaimed. "If I was a few years younger, I'd whip out my camera and take a photo to post online."

"Thank goodness, we're a smarter generation. Dig in." Jerria wielded her fork. "Mmmm."

Jerria leaned over the railing on the promenade deck after the show. The moon cast a streak of gold across the sea. "Gorgeous! I think there are more stars here than we have at home. You'd think, living far from a big city, we'd be able to see a lot, but this time of year, the Oregon coast is cloudy more often than not."

"The sky is pretty." Nan pulled her sleeves over her hands, shivering. "But it's already getting colder, and we're still in California."

"The theatre was so warm, the fresh air feels good to me. They were sure talented! I wonder why Haywood Jacallme was the emcee tonight. Usually, Cruise directors introduce shows."

"It did seem odd. Haywood managed to insult half the audience, first the older people, then the parents of young kids and the singles. I hope Elias and Penny didn't have hurt feelings. At least he was brief. Once the boos quieted, the Herman's Hermits band was great!"

"I may have 'I'm Into Something Good' playing in my head all night," Jerria agreed. "Shall we go meet the guys? Will probably picked up that map from the purser's desk by now, and we said we'd meet them for dessert."

"*Second* dessert," Nan reached for the door handle into the atrium. "I certainly don't eat this much at home!"

"I know what you mean. Something about cruising makes me forget all my good intentions. I sure haven't been choosing low-cal foods. And with two more sea days, I can't even walk it off in port."

"Once we reach Alaska, I intend to eat salmon as often as I can. Hawaii has wonderful fish, but there's something special about wild salmon."

"It's still fish," Will said cheerfully, behind them. "Charlie went ahead to find a good table in the dining room. Overheard somebody say the dessert buffet was already crowded."

"I guess I was spoiled on the *Ocean Haven* in Hawaii, "Jerria lamented. "That VIP service was really nice. Remember that night when the staff set up a mini buffet, just for the VIP passengers?"

"This ship doesn't have that kind of exclusivity, but the chef makes a fine dessert. Worth a wait." Will pressed the elevator button.

The door slid open, revealing the comedian and three other passengers. A heavy silence hung in the air.

Jerria smiled, "Room for us, too?"

"Oh, who cares?" Haywood snapped. "All you people think about is yourselves. Does anybody have a kind word for a lonely man far from home? Nooo." He elbowed his way out of the elevator, bumping Charlie in the process.

"What just happened?" Nan stepped into the elevator.

A man in a grey striped shirt shrugged. "He was going on and on about his wife leaving him, and his career being in the tubes. I can't believe the ship hired such an angry man for a comedian."

"I agree, and you can bet I'll complain about it." A woman grasped the handrail as the elevator rose. "We're here to have fun, after all."

The elevator doors slid open on deck ten, and they joined the line moving toward the dessert buffet.

"At least the line is moving along nicely." Jerria ran her hands under the hand sanitizer dispenser. "If I was going to complain, I'd aim for the Cruise director." Jerria brushed her hair back. "I've hardly seen her around the ship, and the way she snaps at her poor assistant is unreasonable."

"True," Will moved forward. "Seems like Liza is between the dog and the tree, so to speak."

"Oh, a chocolate fountain! I hope they have pineapple. I'm craving it." Nan spotted Charlie, sitting at a table by the railing. "Good, he found Penny and Elias."

Penny already had a plate of petite desserts in front of her when they reached the table. "Oh, my! I've never seen such pretty little treats outside of a big-city bakery. Would you look at this berry tart? And the chocolate sculptures! I've only seen those in magazines." Her blue eyes twinkled behind her glasses.

Elias smiled fondly at her. "I love seeing you happy. I'm going to get another cream puff. Can I bring you anything?"

"No, thank you, Dear."

"We'll come with you," Jerria set her sweater on a chair. She and Will moved through the crowded dining room to the center buffet, followed by Nan and Charlie. "Would you look at that cream puff display? It must be three feet across!"

"Mmm, hmm, and this tower of petit fours looks like art. I almost feel bad, taking them. *Almost.*" Nan reached for a glass dessert plate, and scooped three tiny cakes onto it.

Will grinned, "You ladies can eat all the doll food you want; heading for the pies over there. Come on, Charlie, chocolate cake on the way."

Jerria watched Will thread his way around the long tables, and confided, "Just wait until we reach Victoria. I booked a high tea for the four of us at the Empress Hotel. I've always wanted to do that, and it won't hurt Will to have some civility in his life once in a while. Sometimes I think we get lazy, living in a small town."

"Thanks! It sounds very nice," Nan chose a pink macaroon. "But I'll be surprised if Charlie doesn't find a way to get out of it, and take Will with him. We're used to Hawaii, where elegance is a foreign concept."

"If they weasel out, perhaps we can take Penny and Elias with us in their place. Penny would love it, and Elias seems agreeable."

"Maybe it comes with being married as long as they have. I'm glad we met them; they're wonderful. I can't fit any more on my plate."

"Just let me snag one of these chocolate mint parfaits." Jerria balanced the slim glass on the edge of her plate. "But tomorrow, for sure, I'm going to eat only low-fat foods. I don't want my waistbands hurting by the end of the trip."

Nan hid a smile, knowing Jerria fought a sweet tooth. She'd trade a good-hearted friend for a skinny one any day of the week, and twice on Friday.

Chapter Eleven
Day Three   At Sea

"Ahoy, neighbor! Heard your door close."

Jerria poked her head past the white partition on the balcony. Charlie, grinning, dried his hair with a towel on his balcony.

"Pretty morning, isn't it? Nice, having cabins next door," Jerria waved.

"Nan said to tell you she'll be ready for that yoga class in a couple of minutes."

"Thanks, I just need to grab some shoes. Will's going to the photography class at nine-thirty. What are your plans for this morning?"

"I think I'll join him. He told me about that flammulated owl by your place. He's determined to get a picture of it."

"I'm not even sure what flammulated means. It's a cute little thing with flame-shaped markings, about handful sized, and *quick*. It hoots loud enough to wake us most mornings, but takes off when Will grabs the camera."

"The class is something I wouldn't do at home, and that's part of cruising, right? Oh, Nan says she's ready to go. Have fun, you two!"

Jerria stepped back into the cabin, pulling the sliding glass door closed behind her.

Will set down his socks and caught her in a hug. "Look like one of our daughters today."

"Sweet talking so early in the day? I love you, too. Meet you at ten-thirty, okay?"

"Okay. Interested in Captain McCann's question-and-answer session with the senior staff this morning. Female captain is rare. Looking forward to it."

"Great, I'll go with you, and then let's try the Ping-Pong tournament at noon. You and I used to be pretty good."

"Back in the day. Age creeps up faster, now that I'm a grandfather. Give it a try anyway." Will ran his fingers through his hair.

"You remind me of Jeff when you do that. You have a few more wrinkles, though," she teased, reaching for the doorknob. She cocked her head, thinking about their son at college. He and his father had the same straight black hair, and many of the same mannerisms, including Will's economy of speech. *If Jeff turns out to be as good a man as Will...*

She almost bumped into Nan in the corridor. "Whoops, sorry! Good morning. Ready for a nice, relaxing workout? I see Gregg is leading the yoga class. How hard can it be?"

Forty minutes later, Jerria sprawled on the lime green yoga mat in Corpse Pose, her chest heaving. She'd underestimated Gregg. Besides breaking her concentration by clapping between every yoga pose, he'd urged the class into positions her yoga instructor at home hadn't introduced. Even in a silent room, peer pressure to keep up was strong. Her thighs were still trembling.

Around her, passengers lay still on the gym floor, soaking in the soft music. Jerria opened one eye and glanced at her watch. If she hurried, she'd have time to take a shower before meeting Will.

Nan hissed, "Jerria, you're supposed to be relaxing!"

"I did that already. I–"

Gregg clapped his hands. "*Namaste,* everybody! The divine in me salutes the divine in each of you. Don't forget the mega bingo game at three o'clock." He stood by the door, thanking the passengers. Jerria thought he looked entirely too fresh, considering what he'd put the class through.

"Mrs Danson, is it? Thanks for coming. I'm sure you'll be able to reach a few of the poses next time. Meanwhile, I suggest you lay off the carbs."

Jerria snapped, "I'm on a *cruise,* and I have no intention of–"

Nan took her elbow, pulling her out of the doorway. "Don't let him get to you. You're not going to listen to a twenty-something *kan'e* with rubber bands in his joints, are you? Come on; let's find one of those apple-crumb muffins at the coffee shop before we meet the guys."

"Now you're talking," Jerria glanced at Nan as they walked. "I have to say, I'm impressed with your flexibility. That pose where he wanted us to pull our shoulder between our knees...You made it look easy."

"Wish I hadn't tried. I think I felt six vertebrae pop. I'm not ready for the Senior Strut classes at our rec center, but I sure felt outclassed in a room full of bouncy youngsters in their cute little shorts. Some of those people looked so young; I wouldn't trust them to babysit."

"Good morning, Nan, Jerria! Can you join me for a bit?" John Hansson called to them as they entered the coffee shop. "The muffins are still warm."

"Hi, John. Great minds think alike. We were just coming to have one." Jerria scooped two of the fragrant muffins onto a plate, streusel crumbs scattering.

Nan took two bottles of chilled water to the table. "Aloha. Are you taking a break?"

"I'm supposed to be walking the public areas. Captain McCann likes the senior staff to be visible, in case passengers want a word. She installed a Comments box by Guest Service, too. She's more laid back than Captain Storkmann, but I'm getting used to her."

Conversation turned to the *Ocean Haven,* where they'd met. He'd served as First Officer on that ship as well, and he'd been involved in solving the international jewel theft ring in Hawaii.

"I prefer uneventful cruises. With hundreds of people on a ship, something always comes up, but so far, this one has been quiet. No complaints at all, except some missing luggage the first day. Porters have universally lousy handwriting."

"It'll be my first time in Alaska," Nan said. "I'm surprised the ship can make it all the way to Seattle in only two days."

"We're making good speed, around twenty-two knots." John set his muffin paper aside. "Have you met any of the other passengers yet?"

"I chatted with a nice woman who's lived in Saudi Arabia the last decade or so," Jerria said. "She said she markets those expensive Turkish rugs around the world."

"We talked a lovely couple into joining our Trivia team. They're celebrating their seventieth anniversary onboard." Nan sipped her water. "That's a nice thing about a sea day; there's plenty of time to relax and play a little."

"I prefer cruises with plenty of port days," Jerria said. "Being at sea is nice, but I admit I like seeing new places better." She told them about the trans-Atlantic cruise she and Will had taken two years ago from Miami to Barcelona, only stopping in San Juan and Gibraltar. She found the trip monotonous, like "Groundhog Day."

"Seven sea days was too much! Not a plane, not a boat, not a fish or a bird for seven straight days. There was no internet service, and the TV couldn't pick up a satellite for three days. It was a relief when we finally passed Madeira, and I could see lights in the distance. On the other hand, I met people who loved it."

Nan nodded. "I know what you mean! When Charlie and I took a trans-Atlantic five years ago, I was amazed at how vast and empty the Atlantic is.

And *deep!* Our captain said it was over six miles for days on end. I could understand how early mariners imagined mermaids and sea monsters."

"I've stood watch many an hour. I've never seen a mermaid, though." John chuckled. "I agree, it's more interesting with port days mixed in. Plus, it gives the crew and staff a chance to get away from one another, even for a few hours. On sea days, time off is spent in the crew quarters. San Juan is one of my favorite ports. It's part of America, but it sure doesn't feel like it."

"Will and I took a tour there, and stopped at the capitol building. Across the street is the Walk of the Presidents. There are nine life-sized bronze statues of US presidents. Just nine." Jerria leaned forward. "I asked the tour guide where the others were, and he said they only made statues of the presidents who visited Puerto Rico during their term in office. The ones who didn't make the trip, didn't get a statue."

"There's something to be said for just showing up. Speaking of that, I'd better get ready for the Q & A with the captain." He stood. "A passenger in the hall asked me how many hot tubs there are onboard. I didn't know, and it was embarrassing. I couldn't tell him I'd boarded the ship the same day he did. I'm bringing my folder with the ship's specs in it. See you around."

"You'll do fine. We'd better get a move on, too." Jerria smiled as the tall officer walked away. "You're going to love Alaska, Nan. It has a feeling all its own, a barely-tamed wildness. And the people are wonderful."

"That's one of the things I like about America, the variety. Nebraska isn't anything like Maine or Texas or Hawaii. I'm looking forward to driving into the Yukon most of all."

"We lucked out there," Jerria agreed as she pressed the button for the glass elevator. "Skagway only had three rental vehicles. Nothing's going to spoil this trip!"

Chapter Twelve

"I thought John Hansson held his own, no reason for him to feel embarrassed," Jerria commented as the four of them left the theatre after the Captain's Q & A session. "He even handled that question about the engine capacity well."

"I'm impressed with Captain McCann, too," Charlie sidestepped a little girl. "She's *sharp.* I have the feeling not much gets past her."

"Except maybe her Cruise director." Nan frowned. "Gretchen seems two-faced; smiling and friendly in front of the senior staff, but did you see her snarl at that woman in the hallway? All she did was ask what deck the library is on, and Gretchen lit into her."

"Saw that. Told her passengers should memorize the ship's deck plans and layout before they board." Will opened the door to the promenade. "Forgets we're on vacation. I'm well aware of it, and there's time to relax in this nice lounge chair. Join me?"

Jerria teased, "You'll need all your strength before the Ping Pong tournament."

As they settled into round wicker chairs on the open deck, a skirmish broke out a few yards away. Two teens heatedly debated how to score a shuffleboard shot.

"I know, but you're in the ten-spot, and my puck landed right on top of yours, so that's ten points for me," a girl argued. A boy, probably her brother, insisted his puck was there first, so her shot didn't count. Their voices rose.

The assistant Cruise director pushed the glass door open and stepped onto the open deck. Surveying the scene, Liza giggled. "Lighten up; it's no biggie. I don't know how you even managed to land on the other puck. You both get the points, and here, I'll give you each a glow wand." She dug in her omnipresent tote bag. "You're going to the dance party tonight, right? Super."

Liza wagged a finger at the teens. "No more arguing, got it? You're here to have fun."

A woman called to Liza, asking about the Draw-A-Celebrity game scheduled for later that afternoon.

"Oh, don't miss it, it'll be fun! And I'll have prizes. I'm on my way to the Ping Pong tourney. Who's with me?"

Jerria, Will, Nan, and Charlie followed Liza up one deck to the table tennis area by the pizza grill. Four other passengers straggled in, and Liza greeted them with a grin. "Cruise ship rules, okay? First couple to get eleven points wins that round, then we'll rotate in the other teams for a playoff. You have to be ahead by two points to win the tournament. Super."

Jerria and Nan took one side, introducing themselves to Lucy and Kate. Jerria served, and Lucy easily returned it. Kate knocked the ball out of bounds. Nan hit the ball to Lucy, who smacked it over the net to Jerria, starting a six-bounce volley before

Kate reached in, sending the ball over the railing into the ocean seven decks below.

"Oops, sorry, I'm not really athletic," Kate murmured.

Liza laughed and tossed another white ball onto the table. Jerria scored three points, Lucy two and Nan racked up four in a row. Kate bounced the ball off the table twice more, then stepped back, allowing her partner to score four points on her own. With a flourish, Nan served the ball on point eleven. Lucy lunged for it, tripped over Kate's foot, and the ball shot out of bounds.

"Win!" Liza helped Lucy to her feet. "Okay, you two did great! Guys, you're up next. Super. Ken, you and Ben take this side, okay? Ken, Ben...hey, that rhymes!"

The white ball flew across the table, lobbed back and forth at high speed. Jerria and Nan cheered them on. Ben and Ken were one point ahead, then two. Charlie made that up with two swats of the paddle. Tie score; Will's turn to serve. He lobbed the ball across the net. As Ben dove for it, the ball spun to the left, landing just inside the line, giving Will the advantage. He flicked his black hair off his forehead, winked at Jerria and shot the ball over the net. Paddles poised, Ken and Ben collided. The ball squirted between them, rolling across the tiled floor. Ben groaned. Charlie and Will high-fived.

"That was close! Come on, women against the men for the final." Liza motioned Jerria and Nan to the table, whispering, "I know you love your guys. Now, beat the socks off them." Louder, she called, "Let's a have a fair fight, okay? Super. Mr Danson, your serve."

With a whoop, Will served the ball to Jerria. She swung and missed. The ball bounced toward the pool.

Jerria grumbled, "No fair! You distracted me on purpose!"

Will laughed, "All's fair in love and war."

"War, is it?" Jerria shot a grin at Nan.

Nan nodded and caught her long hair back in her shell hair comb. Will served the ball, and Nan returned it with a spin. Charlie reached, but the ball skated off the table...three times in a row.

"How on earth are you making that spin like that?" Charlie wiped his brow. "I see it coming, but when I go to hit it, it's just not there!"

Ben and Ken offered advice; typical armchair athletes. Lucy cheered for Nan and Jerria.

Kate wandered back from the grill. "I ordered pizza to celebrate the women's win."

Will whacked the ball across the net. "Haven't won yet."

Jerria swung and hit the ball. "Matter of time!"

The score was tied at nine all. One more serve, and Nan skidded the ball under Will's paddle.

"Last point. Come on, ladies! You can do it!" Liza cheered, waving her arms like a windmill. Jerria returned the shot. Will lunged, missing the ball by an inch.

"Whoo-HOO! Ladies win—I knew you would. Super! Congrats, Mrs D, Mrs C. Your grand prize is an Amsterdam Line headband for each of you. I'm in a good mood, so prizes for everyone, a pen and tablet for doodling away your days at sea. Here you go, thanks for playing...where's Miss Kate?" Liza glanced around, puzzled.

"Pizza for everyone!" Kate stepped aside to let a crew member set the steaming pizzas on a table closer to the pool. Another followed with a pitcher of root beer and a stack of plates. The players dug in.

Liza slid a slice onto her plate. "I'd better take mine to go. I have a couple of hours off, and I want to try that email again. If it doesn't send this time, I'll have to make a call from Seattle. Have fun, okay?" With a jaunty wave, Liza slipped her tote bag over her arm and crossed the pool deck.

Charlie watched her go. "She's sure a lot happier than she was in San Francisco. Must have cleared up whatever was bothering her."

"I like her. Pass a napkin, will you?" Jerria set the headband on her head. "Not really compatible with my curls, but we earned it." She was still winded, but the win was worth every sore muscle she'd feel later on.

Joel called from the railing a few yards away. "Come on, everybody, you have to see this!" The ping pong players hurried to the rail. The naturalist pointed to the sea, a few yards from the ship. "Just look at that, would you? We're in the middle of the sea lions' migration north. I can't believe I'm seeing this with my own eyes. Look for yourselves."

Jerria leaned over the teak railing to see the roiling brown blobs in the waves below. "I see dozens of them, maybe more. Joel, where are they going?"

"Did you see them near Fisherman's Wharf? They hang out there, then when they want a girlfriend, they head north. Most of them go to Astoria, Oregon. They hook up, then make their way south again." Joel didn't take his gaze off the big mammals. "I don't get the appeal, myself. They're ugly, smell bad, lazy—all they do is lay around moaning on the docks all day, occasionally fighting if another comes too close. That, and this migration, is probably the only time the males exert themselves in any meaningful way. They're socially awkward, but I guess the girl sea lions in Oregon like them. You know how it is, the new guy gets all the attention."

Finishing the pizza a few minutes later, the players went their separate ways. Nan wanted to read her Alaska guide book on their balcony, and Charlie and Will headed for the golf cage. Jerria decided to explore the ship.

Jerria came upon a group of women outside the SunSun Village lounge, surrounding a large table littered with yarn, paper patterns, and scissors. Sunlight streamed through the floor-to-ceiling windows. As she passed by, the women called to her, smiling warmly.

"Come join us! We're catching up on some needlework while we're at sea." Jerria recognized Cowboy Bob's wife, and nodded as she took the empty seat beside a woman in a red blouse. She didn't raise her head, intent on her stitches.

Before long, Jerria understood why most of the group sat clustered at the far end of the long table. Cowboy Bob's wife chattered on, speech flying as fast as her knitting needles. Jerria had a mental image of a dam with words stuffed in the cracks, pushing back any possibility of silence.

"So, everyone, tell her what you're all making," she ordered. The women obeyed, displaying crocheted and knitted projects in various stages of completion.

Cowboy Bob's wife nudged a blonde woman's pile of doll-sized quilts an inch closer to the middle of the table. Jerria examined a quilt. "Wow, this is exquisite! Such delicate stitches. Lucky little girl; any baby doll would love this." The woman's cheeks reddened, half hidden by her hair.

"I keep telling her she should sell them, make a fortune," the loud woman said, biting a yarn tab.

Jerria walked around the table, admiring each woman's work. "Oh, I like this wrap, the way you've incorporated the blue and ivory strands. I recently took up weaving, and I think I could adapt this pattern. I have a friend who's always chilly. Wouldn't this make a pretty gift for her?"

"Sure you could," the woman beamed. "It's just a rectangle; it looks much more difficult than it is. Here, you can take notes on this receipt."

"Blue and ivory are so last year. I told her to use grey and green."

Jerria ignored the unsought opinion—-Bob's wife had an opinion for everything, it seemed!–and took the pen somebody offered. She quickly sketched the design. Thanking the woman, she rose.

"If you make one, be sure to use grey and green. Grey and green; that's the way to go. Join us anytime," the talkative woman bit the end of her thread. "We'll be here every afternoon." Jerria smiled politely, reminding herself to detour on following afternoons. That woman's non-stop talking took energy she just didn't have to spare.

Making her way through the photo gallery, Jerria quickened her pace. She and Will tended to avoid ships' photographers. It was so easy these days to get a good photo with their digital camera, and at far less cost.

She smiled, remembering their trip to the Canadian Maritimes. Will had asked a man standing by the lighthouse at Peggy's Cove to take a picture of him and Jerria. The woman at his side dropped her jaw, but the man happily reached for Will's camera. They posed, and he aimed the camera...well over their heads. He was so pleased to help that Jerria didn't have the heart to chide Will for unknowingly asking the only blind man in the tiny town to act as photographer. His wife flashed a grateful smile, and a few minutes later, she doubled back and took another photograph of them herself.

The photos hung over Jerria's desk at the real estate office, both the one of her and Will arm-in-arm in front of the lighthouse, and the one of a white albatross circling the lighthouse's cupola under a clear blue sky.

Rounding the corner, she nearly ran into a woman whose blouse looked like a Bedazzler run amok. Ignoring Jerria, the woman gushed to her partner, "Don't you just love sea days? So luxurious, so peaceful, no deadlines or silly tours to take or stuff to learn about. And there's always so many tourists in cities. Too bad we'll be in Seattle in two days."

As they walked on, Jerria shook her head. Wasn't that the whole point of travel, to be somewhere other than home, to explore new places? She remembered holding Jeff's hand as they crossed Times Square when he was about five years old. He complained, "Stupid tourists!" as the crowd jostled them. She pulled him aside and reminded him that they, too, were tourists, and how lucky he was to be there at all.

Jerria stopped to snag a ginger candy from a table outside the spa. No spa treatments this cruise; last time, she'd tried a sea salt exfoliation, and her skin felt sand-blasted for days. On the other hand, a massage might feel good. Considering, she noticed a large poster by the elevator, its bold print hard to miss.

"Tonight's Barbecue Under The Stars Cancelled, due to forecasted high winds." In smaller print, she read "Sign up to win Dinner With An Officer! Drop your name and cabin number in the box by Guest Services."

Thinking back to the dinners with Captain Storkmann in Hawaii, Jerria turned on her heel, heading for the center of the ship. She filled out two tickets, for her and Will, as well as the Callister's. Penciling "4 guests" next to the names, she dropped them in the wooden box. If either couple won, they'd dine together.

She paused to watch a game of mahjongg in the atrium. The players' fingers flew; they'd obviously played before. Other passengers lounged with books, or quietly engaged in conversation. Walking past happy passengers made her shoulders relax. Will was right; stepping out of their routine was good for them.

Chapter Thirteen

Jerria clasped her earring. "Okay, I'm ready. I stopped to read the menu posted by the dining room earlier. Peking duck for me!"

Will grimaced. "Happen to notice the rest of the menu? Burgers or fried chicken, perhaps?"

"It might be fun for you to broaden your horizons." She poked his arm. "You never know, you could be missing out on your all-time new favorite food. However, I did notice prime rib and lasagna on the menu."

"Beef sounds good. Not sure I trust lasagna on a cruise ship." Will opened their suite's door, nearly bumping into Nan, her hand poised to knock on their door. Charlie stood beside her.

"I can't blame you. I'd wait until Little Italy for Italian food, myself. Are you two ready for dinner?"

They walked down three flights to the dining room. After ordering, Charlie commented on the soft music played by a trio. "Aren't those musicians the same ones playing pop music by the pool this afternoon? They're versatile!"

"I guess a small ship has crew doing double duty. I'm looking forward to the show tonight. We haven't seen the production performers yet. Will, pass the rolls, please." Jerria buttered a cheese bun and took a bite. "Mmm. I think this is the best one yet."

"Tough Trivia this afternoon," Will said. "Had no idea pineapples were the symbol of the hospitality industry."

"Maybe that explains the Hotel Manager's tattoo on his wrist," Charlie said. "Nan, how did you know Alaska has the longest US coastline?"

"And not a single sandy beach. Credit that guide book I bought at the airport. I'm enjoying the section on wildlife most, so far. I taught Marine Biology for years, but Hawaii has very different species. And the birds! I know you two take bald eagles for granted, but we don't see them in Hawaii. It's too warm for them, I guess."

"We have the best team for Trivia, no question. I don't need the prizes, but it's fun to play." Jerria buttered her roll. "How many magnets do we need?"

A tall man in officer's whites approached their table, consulting a card in his hand. "Mr and Mrs Danson, Mr and Mrs Callister, am I right?" His gold teeth flashed. "Let me introduce myself, and extend an invitation to dine with me tomorrow evening. I'm Thompson, the Guest Services officer here on the *Ocean Journey*. You four won the 'Dinner With An Officer' drawing, my favorite meal of any cruise. The Provisions officer will be joining us, along with one other couple."

Jerria smiled. "Thanks, we'd enjoy that. Who's the other couple?"

"Mr Armstrong said he's scouting out the couple married the longest on the ship. He has a thing for history. I think he's hoping for a good story. We'll meet in the SunSun lounge at six-thirty for drinks, then we'll be escorted to our table. Thank you for joining me. I look forward to it." Thompson put the folded paper in his pocket and headed for the door.

Jerria sat back, pleased. "This will be fun. I'm so glad I put our names in the box for the drawing."

Will and Charlie exchanged a grin. Will winked, "*You* did? Charlie dropped our names in the box on our way to the golf simulator."

Nan smiled, "So did I! I saw the box on my way to the cabin, and it seemed like a good idea."

"There you go; it was meant to be. I wonder who the couple married longest is?"

"I won't have it, do you understand me? I've had it up to *here* with them constantly demanding one thing or another." The Cruise director's voice rang through the open doors, oblivious to the echo-chamber effect of the dining room's foyer.

Diner's heads craned to listen. Waiters froze, midstep.

"I'm sick to death of dealing with a bunch of whiney geriatric passengers!" Gretchen's voice carried plainly. "I swear, this place is like God's own waiting room. You deal with them yourself, and leave me out of it, do you hear me?"

Gretchen strode into the dining room. All eyes on her, her jaw stiffened. "What's the matter with everybody? I'm not late, am I? You, there, go back to your dinner."

Chastened passengers resumed their meals, and conversation gradually picked up. Jerria set her napkin beside her plate and pushed back her chair. "That's it, somebody has to report her, and I—"

"Oh, Jerria, dear, are you leaving already?" Penny called to her. She and Elias approached, holding hands. "I wanted to tell you our news." Her blue eyes sparkled.

Jerria sat back down, taking a breath. "I'd love to hear it."

"You'll never guess. We were eating our dessert and the nicest officer came right to our table. He invited us to join him for dinner tomorrow! He said we are married the longest of anybody on the ship. Can you imagine?"

Elias slipped his arm around Penny. "I'm a lucky man, alright. I noticed an officer stop at your table, too. Are you the other couple Mr Armstrong mentioned?"

Jerria smiled, her anger forgotten. "Yes, we are, and I can't wait. I'm so glad we'll be together."

And before then, I'll talk to somebody about Gretchen's behavior. I can't let her ruin the cruise for Penny and Elias.

If she only knew.

Chapter Fourteen
Day Four   At Sea

The following evening, Jerria draped her dove-grey shawl over her arm. "Come on, Will, let's go. Is that the third time you've tied your necktie?"

"Won't lay straight. Don't want to get all gussied up. It's just dinner." He tugged at his collar, reminding her of their son, who also hated formal wear.

"Let me help you." Jerria tweaked the knot. "One night of dressing up won't hurt. Besides, I like being with the most handsome man on the ship." She took his arm.

The Callister's suite next door was open, and Jerria smiled, hearing Charlie's plaintive grumble, followed by Nan's scolding tone.

"What fool decided tying a silk noose around a man's neck was any way to prepare for dinner? Why can't I just wear my blue polo shirt?"

"Honestly, this isn't Hawaii. Here, put your suitcoat on. And quit all the *namunamu*." They stepped in the hallway, Charlie's face sheepish.

Jerria raised an eyebrow. "Nan, that word...what did you say?"

"*Namunamu* means complaining or griping, and our suite had plenty of that. Love your necklace, Jerria. Are we ready?"

"I like that word; it sounds like what it means. Like murmur or slush. What are those called? Onomatopoeia?"

"Hold up," Elias called as they waited for the elevator. He wore a charcoal tuxedo, the folds in his satin cummerbund crisp. "Going our way?"

"Oh, my, this is so exciting. Wait until the girls in my book club hear we dined with a real officer!" Penny fingered the pearls at her throat. "Everybody looks so nice, I must say. I don't get much chance to wear my good lace dress at home. And Elias is so happy to wear his tuxedo."

Will and Charlie exchanged a glance. *Traitor.*

Cranberry spritzers in hand, the three couples and two officers entered the formal dining room a short while later. The maître'd led them to the table in the center, under a glittering chandelier. Three waiters hurried to seat them, draping black linen napkins on their laps.

Penny's earrings trembled in excitement. "Oh, my, I feel so elegant! Thank you so much for inviting us, out of so many interesting passengers onboard."

The Provisions officer patted her hand. "Indeed, we have interesting people around us, but none as valued as you, my dear. We'll order, then please tell us about yourselves, so we can get better acquainted. I'd like to learn how you met your partners first." He suggested the filet of Kobe beef.

Solicitous waiters placed cups of soup at each setting: cream of chicken for Will, shrimp bisque for the others. Introductions began. Will told about attending a national business student competition in college. Taken in by Jerria's pert attitude and sharp intellect, he made a point of competing against her in every round. They invariably placed first and second, every time. "Drew me in like a magnet, that smile of hers. The following semester, transferred to her university in Oregon, just to be near her. Married that summer. Luckiest man alive."

"I love a happy ending." Thompson sat back so the waiters could place spring rolls on the table. "And you, Mr Callister, how did you win Mrs Callister's heart?"

"She was my boss, department head at the university in Hawaii. I fell for her my first semester teaching, after I moved from the mainland. We raised our daughters on Kauai. Now that we're retired, the division of labor is finally equalized."

Elias raised an eyebrow. "Retired? I'm not a good judge of age, but I figured you two to be much younger than that."

"Nan's full Hawaiian, and as superstitious as any of them. Both of her parents both died at age fifty, and Nan insisted we retire at forty-nine. So far, we're still here."

Nan protested, "I'm not superstitious! Just...respectful."

When the laughter died down, Thompson turned to Penny and Elias. "Now, Mr and Mrs Wilcox, you're celebrating a milestone anniversary this cruise, right? How long, and where did you meet?"

"Seventy years ago, Penny and I married in Kansas. Prettiest schoolmarm on the prairie, I always say. We met at a USO during the war. I was recovering, and not up to dancing yet, but I knew a good catch when I saw one."

"Actually, I pursued *him*," Penny smiled. "Elias was so handsome, I couldn't let him get away. Once he recovered, we danced through the years. A doctor told us it was the best therapy after what happened at Pearl Harbor."

Thompson leaned in. "You were at Pearl Harbor, Sir?"

"Yes, I was, but luckier than many. We were on Battleship Row that Sunday morning. I served on the *USS Maryland*. She took fire, but we only sustained minimal damage. The captain had us race out into the open sea when the bombs began falling. I was in the wrong place, wrong time, as they say, hit by shrapnel when a bomb fell on the main deck. Funny, how a man can be wounded, and the boys next to him are just fine."

Elias wiped his lips with his napkin. "The *Maryland* was a feisty little ship. She went on to make headlines in the South Pacific, but I missed out on that. I learned to use my legs again, once I came home, but we never could have children."

The Provisions officer stared at Elias. "Sir, you said the *Maryland*? My grandfather served on the *Maryland* at Pearl Harbor."

Elias locked his eyes on the younger man. "Is that so? What was his name?"

"Lemuel Armstrong. I named my son after him."

"Lem Armstrong? Old Lem? I can still see that skinny kid, red hair shining in the Hawaii sun. So long ago. Is he..." His voice trailed off.

The officer assured him "Old Lem" was alive and well and still regaling the family with war stories at every holiday meal. "Let me put you two in touch after the cruise, all right? Gramps would love to hear from an old friend."

"Old Lem, after all these years. Son, I'd like that very much." Elias blew his nose in a tissue, and wiped his eyes. "I can still see the bombs falling in the harbor, the screams, and those planes coming like they'd never end. Our boys–"

Penny took his hand. "Now, dear, no one wants to hear old war stories."

"I do!" All four men chorused. They made plans to get together to hear Elias' stories later on.

Jerria's heart ached, remembering walking through the National Cemetery at Arlington, reading the grave markers. Trusting young men, willing to serve their country, their futures cut short–

Elias voiced her thoughts. "So many lost."

Concern etched Thompson's face; as host, it was his job to make the evening special, not sorrowful. "May I propose a toast? To all good friends, old and new!" Glasses clinked.

"Oh, my!" Penny's hand flew to her throat. "Is that for *us*?"

Eight waiters paraded from the double galley doors to their table, plates held aloft. Pausing near their table, each tipped a tiny cup of brandy onto the

Kobe beef. Four other waiters leaned to ignite each plate with a tiny torch. Diners nearby applauded.

"Penny, it was worth every trial in the past seventy years to just to be with you tonight. I love you more than ever, my dear." Elias raised his glass to his wife.

Thompson wiped his eye. "I do love a love story."

Chapter Fifteen
Day Five   Seattle

Jerria breathed deeply, surveying the long row of bright flowers displayed on long tables. Workers rapidly arranged bouquets in white paper. "I can't decide. These lilies are so vivid, and they smell heavenly. But the irises are gorgeous. Which do you think I should buy?"

"Buy 'em both. No loss, if you enjoy them. Hurry up, Honey. Just pick one. Need to meet Nan and Charlie at the artisan honey stand in twenty minutes. Pike Place is a maze; better get a head start."

"I'll get both, I think. You choose a bouquet for Nan, will you? She'd like flowers in her cabin, too."

"Aloha! I'd love fresh flowers." Nan's voice carried across the cold Seattle market.

"Oh, there you are. Were you able to get your glasses repaired?" Jerria raised an eyebrow. "Charlie, you weren't serious about buying a salmon, were you?"

Charlie held a bag in his hand. "Yes, that Flying Fish Company drew us in. The salmon looked so good, we had some shipped home. This is just salmon jerky."

Dodging a flower cart, Nan inhaled the rich scent. "This place is amazing!" Shivering, she pulled her rain-speckled jacket tighter around her. "It'll warm up later, right, once the sun comes up?"

Will shook his head. "Sorry. Already ten-thirty. No sunshine today."

"How do people here stand this weather? It's like living in a car wash! I miss Kauai's sunshine already. While we waited for my new lens, we fed the brass pig, watched them throwing salmon, and ogled a glazed donut at least fourteen inches across. The vegetable displays look like oil paintings."

"Still vegetables, even displayed like art." Will said. "Donuts sound good."

Jerria took Nan's arm. "Let's pick out some flowers. They'll deliver them to the ship, so we won't have to carry them around. I want to go to the little shops on the lower levels. Wait'll you see the scarves and jewelry!"

As the women chose fragrant bouquets, Charlie and Will stood aside. Even this early in the day, the market was bustling with wide-eyed tourists, and vendors bent on beating yesterday's sales.

"Speaking of jewelry, you're not going to accidentally buy any diamonds this trip, are you, like you did on our last cruise?" Charlie teased.

"Hope not! Did Jerria tell you she sold the diamond necklace? Said looking at it gave her shivers; just couldn't enjoy it. Even after all we went through, that was a deal and a half. Paid the guy at the swap meet a hundred fifty dollars, and it sold at auction for just under two-hundred-twenty thousand."

"The story was all over the local news in Hawaii. I still can't believe you two uncovered an international smuggling ring! What are you doing with all that money?"

"Using part of it to remodel the house before Jerria's great aunt moves in with us. And-"

Jerria thrust a huge bouquet of purple and yellow flowers under Will's nose. "Just smell this! Looks like fairies hand-painted each petal. Come on, let's go explore the market." She handed her bouquet back to the flower vendor. "Stateroom 8502, on the *Ocean Journey*. Thanks."

Putting her wallet in her bag, Nan said, "I can't stop thinking about that donut. If we divide it in fourths, the calorie count drops by seventy-five percent. You can't beat that."

"Not sure about your math," Will grinned, "but can't pass up a giant donut."

"Just don't spoil your appetite," Jerria warned as they walked down the ramp to the lower shops. "Seattle Clam Stop is supposed to have some of the best seafood chowder in Seattle, served in sourdough bowls. I thought we'd eat a small lunch before we get back onboard later on."

"Still hate seafood," Will muttered to Charlie. "Help talk Jerria into another place for lunch, okay?"

"Give it up," Charlie advised. "Jerria sounds heartset on this place. You know you're going to face a lot of seafood in Alaska, too."

A couple of hours later, Charlie pulled Nan away from a glass case displaying antique marionettes. "Come on, enough shopping! I'm starving."

"Another doughnut?" Will asked hopefully.

Jerria took his hand. "I read a menu online. The restaurant reviews rave about the seafood, but they also have burgers. You're not going hungry."

Nan said, "Seafood chowder sounds great. It'll warm me up."

Handing their menus back to the server a few minutes later, Will buttered a sun-dried tomato roll. "Did you notice Liza? Passed her on my way to the men's room. Think it was her, anyway. Had her back turned to the wall, talking on a cell phone. Didn't hear her words, but her voice sounded distraught."

Jerria shook her head. "I didn't see her, but I heard someone crying in the ladies' room. I asked if she needed help, but she didn't answer. I hope it wasn't Liza. I like her a lot, but she does seem extra emotional."

"It must be hard on the crew, being away from their families for months on end." Nan thanked the waiter as he set steaming plates on the table. "That looks wonderful."

They tucked into lunch; three seafood chowder bread bowls, one buffalo burger, no tomatoes. Will avoided vegetables as often as he could.

The *Ocean Journey* glistened in Elliott Bay below them as a rainbow of sunshine broke through the lowering sky. "Looks like the storm is over," Nan wiped her lips. "The rainbow must be an apology for all that rain. Sailaway is going to be beautiful."

Chapter Sixteen
Day Six Victoria, British Columbia

The following afternoon, Jerria called to Will and Charlie outside the Maritime Museum. "How was it?"

"Interesting," Charlie said. "I was surprised at how many ships wrecked on the Pacific coast."

Penny beamed. "You missed a lovely tea. It was so elegant! We had tiny sandwiches, fruit, petit fours, madeleines, and scones. The waiter told me how to pronounce "scone". All my life, I thought that word rhymes with *bone*, but it sounds more like *gone*. They were served with apricot jelly and clotted cream. Very British."

Will hugged Jerria and winked at Elias. "Scones, huh? Sounds like doll food. What exactly is clotted cream?"

Elias grinned. "I assure you, you don't want to know."

Jerria glanced at her watch. "Five hours isn't enough time to really enjoy a city this size. We'd better head back toward the ship. I wonder if the marching band is still playing."

"That was some welcome, with the mayor greeting the ship and Mounties posing for photos. I read somewhere their skivvies are scarlet, like their uniforms." Nan shifted her shopping bags.

"The things we keep in our brains." Jerria's curls bounced as she walked.

Penny took Elias' hand. "Oh, look, a horse-drawn trolley! Can we catch it back to the ship, Elias?"

They crossed the street and climbed aboard. They admired the city streets as the roan horses' shoes clacked on the cobblestones. The liveryman, dressed in period costume, pointed out sights along the way. "Too bad you won't be here to see the Parliament lights go on. It's quite a sight. Have a safe trip, everybody. I hope you miss the storm."

They climbed out of the trolley at the pier entrance, thanking the driver. Penny's cheeks were red from excitement. Nan's were flushed from cold, although the bank's thermometer read fifty-nine degrees. Jerria eyed her friend, wondering how she'd handle Alaska's unstable weather.

As they set their purchases on the security conveyor belt, Will mused, "Driver said something about a storm. Hope that's the one we already went through, and not a new one."

A security agent handed his key card back. "No, Sir, I hear we're in for it tonight. Welcome back."

Three balled pairs of socks in hand, Jerria and Nan cut through the shops area onboard, on their way to the juggling class an hour later. Jerria frowned at a table displaying disposable ponchos for sale. A sign read "Prepare for the Inevitable." She avoided weather reports on vacations, but this, on top of the canceled barbecue...*Good thing Will and I don't get seasick*. She'd noticed the ship had been increasing speed. Maybe Captain McCann could outrun the storm.

A few minutes later, Jerria giggled as a wadded pair of socks hit her in the back of the head. "Not to worry, you'll get it," she assured the girl behind her. She lobbed her own sock balls high in the air, catching two, tossing them up again. The third landed on Nan's foot.

"Come on, you're doing great!" the instructor encouraged. "Some of you are so good, we should hire you for the show. That's it, don't take your eyes off the balls, er, socks. Keep working on it."

A few minutes later, he said, "Now, let's see how you do with actual balls, instead of socks. Everybody, come get three balls."

After the class, Nan went to book a massage for the next day. Jerria, carrying their six pairs of socks, headed the cabin to put them away. She passed Liza in the atrium, hosting a hula hoop contest, made even funnier by the rolling waves hitting the ship. A little girl stole the show, and Liza applauded before giving her a prize. Liza's bag held a limitless supply, from what Jerria could tell.

Further down the narrow corridor, Jerria peeked in an open door to a conference room. Glittery crystal chandeliers hung from the ceiling, partly cannibalized, tilting at odd angles. Trays of crystals lined long tables down the center of the room, sparkling under the fluorescent lights. She stopped to get a better look.

A dozen or so women and a handful of men, heads bowed, focused on projects in front of them, most with pliers in hand. Two men wired crystals to a lampshade frame. Several necklaces rested in various stages of completion. One young woman perched on a chair, prying crystals from a chandelier, lowering them into her apron's wide pocket.

Jerria caught her eye, and she nodded a greeting before resuming her task. Jerria recalled an article she'd read on a flight months ago. Chandelier prisms were all the rage, according to the article. Aficionados wired the shiny parts into jewelry, lampshades, sun catchers, even new light fixtures and stained glass windows.

Lost in thought, Jerria startled at a touch of her elbow. A twenty-something woman wearing a bright turban spoke again.

"Would you like to join us?"

"Oh, no, I don't want to intrude, but it's awfully interesting."

"Come on in. Let me show you what we're working on."

The girl's ponytail swayed as she circled the long table, introducing Jerria to her friends. Jerria admired each crafter's project. Several were fashioning delicate bracelets or necklaces of small crystals.

One ambitious woman worked on a hoop light fixture. She explained, "The trick is getting the crystals balanced just right so it won't tilt. If it's too heavy on one side, everyone will know at a glance. The jewelry makers can be more free-spirited."

"They're beautiful! " Jerria held a prism-cut crystal up to the light, making rainbows dance on the walls. "Wherever do you get them?"

The woman explained collectors sought antique crystals from vintage shops, auctions, and estate sales, as well as buying online. "And of course we trade; that's part of the fun of it."

A man with a handlebar mustache offered Jerria a chair beside him. "Sit yourself down. I found a good deal on a slew of these long cuts in Russia last month, and I'd be pleased to help you make yourself a light catcher. When the sun hits it, rainbows dance on the walls."

Jerria settled in, setting the socks on a chair beside her. "Russia? Wow. I live in Oregon, and we have long months of gloomy weather. I need to catch all the sunshine I can."

"Need to stay warm, too, I see, with six pair of socks at once," the man teased.

"Well, the captain did warn of bad weather ahead."

Chapter Seventeen

Laying out the items on the desk, she drew a deep breath. This wasn't safe; she'd rewrap the items in plastic so none of the poison would get on her hands. On the one hand, this was wrong; she knew that. Her mother would be horrified. On the other hand, after that last phone call, she had to do something, anything. On the other hand, what if this didn't work? The only toxins she'd ever dealt with were in high school chemistry class. On the other hand, she wasn't out to hurt anybody, exactly. She'd put one drop on a stray cat in port, and it just staggered for a few feet then lay down, asleep. On the other hand, if more than a few passengers became sick, the cruise line would take drastic measures, and that would buy her the time she needed. Maybe they'd even cancel a few cruises. On the other hand, if they overreacted, it could end up in dry dock. That would leave a lot of the crew unemployed for a time, but they'd understand, if they knew the situation. On the other hand, she needed a break before things turned any worse. On the other hand, she knew nothing about the liquid in the vial, beyond the skull and crossbones on the label. What if...? On the other hand, that woman...

A couple more "other hands" and she could build a fine octopus.

Dr Marsh hadn't hesitated, giving her something for her supposed headaches when she went to the Med Center this afternoon. When he turned his back to take the pills from the cabinet, she stuffed four latex gloves from the box on the wall into her pocket.

Slipping the gloves on, she held the amber liquid against the light. Her thoughts swirled, recalling the burqa-clap woman in the souk so far away. What had she said? *"You'll know when to use it, Dearie."*

Time to step up the pace.

A loud knock at her cabin door made her jump. "Yes, who is it?" Her voice shook; she swallowed.

"We have the night off. They canceled the production show because of the storm. We're going to watch a movie in the crew lounge. Want to join us?"

"Oh, um, sure. I'll meet you there." She blinked, her thundering heart pulsing under her polo shirt. She slipped the vial back in place, and slid the mugs under her bed, resolving to put them back in the Staff closet in the morning. Smoothing her hair, she pulled the door open. And breathed.

Chapter Eighteen

Heavy winds kicked up the rough sea, increasing by the hour. In her four o'clock daily update, Gretchen announced the outer decks were now closed. It wasn't safe to be on the promenade, with waves of seven meters or more crashing over the decks. "Have a good evening, and remember the casino will remain open all night."

On their way to meet Nan and Charlie for dinner, Jerria saw crew members scrambling to drain the pools before the roiling water flooded the teak decks. Seasickness bags hung every few feet along every railing and stairwell. A few peaked souls huddled in the bottom of the atrium, clutching paper bags to their faces. Even the most stable part of the ship provided slim haven from the rolling waves.

Rain streamed down the dining room windows. Quite a few tables stood empty. Their waiter asked if they'd prefer the Seasick Special, or regular menus. Jerria was intrigued. The waiter explained the Seasick Special was a steamed chicken breast served with saltine crackers and green apple slices. Jerria opted for cod with baked ziti on the side.

The assistant waiter said the storm was intensifying, and hoped the worst would hold off until after dinner service was complete. The crew had been told Captain McCann planned to skirt the storm, but it loomed huge on the weather maps. Water glasses were only filled three-quarters full. Grateful she wasn't prone to seasickness, Jerria sipped her soup.

Rain pelted the windows, and the ship creaked as it struggled through stiff winds. Between the main course and dessert, Gretchen announced tonight's production show was canceled over the loudspeaker. Winds were already gusting to forty-two knots and the barometric pressure falling fast. With waves over nine meters, dancing on high heels was out of the question.

After dinner, Jerria took Will's arm as they and the Callisters headed for the Mandarin Lounge. Karaoke was better than nothing. Passengers, trying to walk normally, swayed first to the left side, then to the right as the deck below their feet rose and fell with the waves.

They met the comedian coming out of the library. His face was as dark as the lowering clouds above. Head down, he muttered something unintelligible.

Will asked, "Did you say something, Haywood?"

"It's not fair," the comic groused. "Those wimpy dancers can't handle the weather, so *they* get the night off. What do *I* get? Another show thrown at me, with an hour's notice. I should never have signed that contract."

A woman nearby asked, "Where's your show?"

Haywood grumbled, "Mandarin Lounge, in fifteen minutes. It doesn't even a have a stage, just that dance floor. If they expect me to do a song and dance, well, I can tell you that ain't happening."

A disappointed murmur filled the corridor. "Really? We were looking forward to karaoke in the Mandarin."

The man stomped his foot like a four-year-old. "That's it, I've had it. You people don't appreciate real talent when you see it. If anybody asks, tell them old Haywood took sick, like half the passengers on this god-forsaken boat. I'm going to my cabin, and I'm not coming out for nobody."

"You know, for a funny man, he's not very funny." Jerria watched the retreating comedian. "He seems—"

"Unhinged? Come on, don't let him get under your skin." Nan gripped a railing to steady herself. "Whoa, the ship is really heaving. I think I'm going to call it a night after all. I don't even feel safe walking."

They agreed, and headed for their cabins, taking the stairs up three decks. A tall glass vase on display in the stairwell wobbled, then fell off its pedestal just after they passed. The flying glass struck a girl behind them. She yelped.

Jerria knelt beside her and wiped away the blood on the teen's arm with her green scarf. "Red and green, very Christmassy," she joked. "It's not bad, but I think you'd better get Dr Marsh to bandage it. I'll go with you, okay?"

A man's panicked voice shouted down the stairwell. "Emma? Em, where are you?"

"Dad, I'm down here!" She smiled at Jerria, tears streaking her face. "Thanks, but my dad is coming." Jerria gave her a quick hung, then rejoined Will, Charlie, and Nan.

"Getting worse." Will's brows knit. "Feels like the ship is smacking the waves broadside, not riding them. Better–"

Three clangs interrupted him. Over the loudspeaker, Gretchen's announcement sounded stern. "All passengers, all passengers, this is an urgent announcement from the bridge. By order of the captain, all passengers are requested to stay in their cabins. All guest services are now closed. If medical assistance is required, please dial 411. I repeat..."

They made their way to their cabin, grabbing the handrail. Jerria jigged her key card in the lock, bracing against the doorframe as the ship listed starboard. "Do you want to come in?" she invited Charlie and Nan. "We have a deck of cards, and a game might take our minds off the storm. Oh–!" The door flew open, and she lost her balance, stumbling across the floor. Will quickly grabbed her elbow, preventing a fall.

Nan hugged her wrap tighter around her shoulders. "I'm scared. I've never seen a ship rock like this one. How far are we from land, do you think? What if the glass doors break? What if this storm is sent by Pele? What if–"

Charlie pulled her close. "Nan, this is no time for a come-apart. I'm sure the bridge is doing all they can to keep us safe. You know the cruise line doesn't want to be on the evening news."

"Besides, why would Pele come this far north, when she lives in the warm tropical islands?" Jerria cleared papers off the table. "Come on, you can deal the cards."

Chapter Nineteen

"Will, is that the door? I can't tell, over the ship's creaking." Jerria swayed, sitting cross-legged on the bed, a few minutes after the Callisters had gone to their own cabin.

Will opened the cabin door. Penny clutched her pink housecoat around her chest. Elias, wearing blue silk pajamas, stood behind her. Both were barefoot and wide-eyed.

Penny exclaimed, "I know we're supposed to stay in our cabin, and I hope we didn't wake you, but the side of our balcony door broke off, and it's so cold in our cabin. Plus, the rain made a little river all the way to the bathroom. The carpet is all wet. I tried calling for help, but no one answered. Please, can we come in, just until someone comes?"

"Of course!" Will reached for extra blankets from the closet shelf. The floor tilted again. He helped them to the sofa, arranging an extra blanket around them. "Safer if we don't try to walk around. Here, you'll feel better with your feet on this ottoman. Take this extra pillow."

"It'll be okay, Darling," Elias assured Penny. "These newfangled ships have all the bells and whistles. They even have stabilizers, although, if they're in use, they're not much help. Why, when I crossed the Atlantic in a troop transport in the Great War, they–"

"This is no time for a story," Penny sniffed, tears brimming in her blue eyes.

"Sure, it is." Jerria pulled her robe over her striped pajamas and tucked her feet under her in the beige chair. "Telling stories at pajama parties is almost required. Let's see; the show was canceled, and I feel deprived. Tell us about the best show you've ever seen. Will, you first."

Will winked at Jerria. "Saw the *Phantom of the Opera* in Portland some time back. The music..." he grabbed a glass in midair as the ship canted to the left, "...was amazing. Costumes won awards for their detail. Best part was the female lead's voice."

Squaring his shoulders, Elias raised his voice over the creaks of the ship. "Good catch! We saw *Phantom* in Chicago, and, I agree, it was very well done. Penny, do you remember seeing *The Sound of Music* in New Orleans, the time we went with your mother?"

"Oh, yes! The actors were so talented, but the littlest girl was a scamp. Any time she thought the other actors weren't looking, she pulled faces at the audience. Delightful!" Penny leaned against the cushion.

"I love a good musical, and the older ones are the best." Jerria tucked her feet under her in her chair, ignoring a crash from the corridor. "*Guys and Dolls* is always fun. The local high school performed it last spring. We enjoyed the Osmond's show in Las Vegas, too. Have you been to Las Vegas?"

As they talked, the wind roared, the ship's heaving coming like angry breaths, with only a couple of minute's break in between waves. Eventually,

Penny's eyes fluttered and closed, and Elias settled back on the pillow, a finger to his lips. Will nodded, and Jerria turned off the desk lamp. Morning couldn't come soon enough.

Chapter Twenty

Jerria awoke abruptly. The spaces between her vertebrae, which she hardly ever thought about, contracted and expanded as the ship rolled with every wave, like an internal spinal massage. She slid out of bed, trying not to wake Will. The ship creaked and groaned. Pulling back the curtain's edge, all she saw was water sloshing against the window, and great slashes of rain caught in the balcony's light. *Is this storm ever going to end? It's like being in a washing machine!* The ship listed sharply starboard, and papers on the desk slid to the floor, along with the phone. Something fell in the bathroom.

Will sat up as the ship righted itself. "Jerria? Where are you?"

"Shh. I'm here, and I'm okay." She dug for the small flashlight she kept in the nightstand drawer. "This is the worst storm I've ever seen. See if you can stop the hangers from banging around, will you?" She swept everything on the desk and table into nearby drawers, then headed for the bathroom. She muffled a sharp yelp.

"Honey?"

"There's water on the bathroom floor, a lot of it." The ship tilted to port again, and more water spilled over the toilet's rim. "The toilet has whitecaps. All I can do is pack it with towels. I'm going to put the rest of our toiletries in the sink, so they won't fly around. Don't wake Elias or Penny."

Jerria slipped back into bed, pulling the covers over her shoulders. She woke a couple of hours later to daylight leaking around the balcony door frame. Quietly pulling back the side of the curtains, she was surprised to see the floor and glass door speckled with square salt crystals. The sun shone bright and innocent. Elias yawned and stretched, careful not to disturb his sleeping wife. Will pulled the bathroom door closed behind him, and Penny's eyes flew open.

She blinked, confused. "Oh, I remember now; the storm. Is it over?"

"Yes, it's a calm, beautiful day. I haven't heard any announcements since last night. I wonder how much damage there was. I kept hearing things crashing." Jerria came and sat beside Penny.

"Oh, my, we've intruded. Here I am, in my nightclothes!" Penny's face flushed in embarrassment. "You two have been so good to us, but we must go. Elias, dear–"

Will yawned. "Didn't plan on a sleepover at our age, but glad you felt safe coming here." He aimed the tv remote, clicking to the ship's channel. "Hmm. Thought there'd be an announcement of some sort. Usual onboard shopping spiel."

A triple clang rang from the corridor, signaling a public announcement. Gretchen's voice followed. All guest services were open, except the main dining room, room service, and bars on decks five and nine. Limited breakfast was available in the buffet. She advised avoiding the atrium and aft elevators, and said the Medical Center would open early to treat "any supposed injuries."

Jerria shot Will a knowing glance; that was ship code for "which we may try to blame on passengers, so as not to run up the incident report."

Gretchen concluded, "Trivia will be held at nine-thirty in the SunSun lounge, followed by bingo at eleven o'clock. Have a nice day sailing with us on the lovely *Ocean Journey*."

Jerria stood. "Well, she didn't sound concerned. We may as well tackle the day. Will you two be at Trivia this morning? We need you."

Elias smiled warmly. "We'll be there, soon as we dress and deal with the broken door. Thanks for everything. We're glad we could count on you. Who's at the door?"

Will opened the door, and Nan stepped in. She wore flowered yoga pants and a cream tee shirt, her long dark hair braided down her back. Clutching a soft orange shawl around herself, Nan took in her friends' appearance.

"What's this, a slumber party, and you didn't invite us? Charlie and I were wondering how you weathered the storm. I was going to Elias' and Penny's cabin next."

Jerria surveyed Nan, irritated. "How do you look so put together at daybreak? We're fine, but look at this place! I think everything that wasn't in a drawer went flying."

Nan chuckled. "Put together? I *slept* in this. If we had to make a run for the lifeboats, I didn't want to be seen in my pjs. I met the cabin steward in the hallway. Griffin said the top decks took some damage, and a lot of glassware in the bars and restaurants broke, but nothing serious. What a mess."

Sobering, she spoke to Penny. "Wow, you two, some introduction to cruising, I must say! Are you all right?"

"Oh, my, yes. That was quite an adventure! I'll be the talk of the gardening club when I tell the ladies about it." Penny's characteristic good humor had returned. "And I'm proud to say, I didn't get seasick. I've always wondered if I had that tendency, but never had the chance to test it."

"You were great, my dear. If we can weather a storm like that, we can weather anything." Elias put his arm around her.

Will said, "I'm hungry. Now, where did the Cruise director say we can find breakfast?"

Jerria laughed. "That's a sure sign the crisis has passed. How about we all get dressed, meet at the buffet in a few minutes, then head down to play Trivia? I doubt many teams will show up this morning. We'll stand a good chance of winning."

"We'd win, anyway, with the brains on our team. See you soon." Nan pulled her shawl tighter, and headed for the door with Elias.

Penny paused to hug Jerria. "Thanks so much, Jerria. I didn't want Elias to know how frightened I was."

"You're a trooper. I suspect Elias saw right through your brave act, though. He loves you."

Penny's blue eyes twinkled. "And I love him. See you in a few minutes."

Chapter Twenty-One
Day Seven   Inside Passage

Waiting for the elevator on their way to the SunSun lounge after a breakfast of muffins and fruit, Jerria peered into the atrium, roped off with Caution tape. Ceramic shards and potting soil from the tall flowerpots lay strewn across the floor. Blown glass icicles from the ceiling lighting impaled the Asian couches. Three Maintenance workers fit plywood over shattered glass doors. Crew members, armed with gloves and brooms, scurried to set the atrium to rights.

Jerria waved to John Hansson, who was overseeing the clean-up. The First Officer stepped carefully over broken glass.

"Good morning, Jerria, Will. Everyone fare the storm well?"

"You're awfully cheerful! How bad was it?"

"Cheerful now, but I admit I was in line for a seasickness shot around midnight. The Med Center had a line a hundred people long, mostly crew members! Doc Marsh was throwing needles like a dart game, as fast as his nurse could fill them." He sobered. "We came through better than I expected. The way things were heaving last night, I was afraid we'd suffer major damage, but it's all cosmetic. And no injuries, either, beyond one broken arm and a few cuts and bruises. We'll be in Ketchikan tomorrow, and it's smooth sailing from here on out."

Will shook his hand. "Let you get back to it, John. Off to play Trivia."

"That's with Liza, right? Nice girl, isn't she? Stands up for herself, too. Gretchen tried to reassign Gregg to take Liza's place at the scavenger hunt this afternoon, and Liza snapped right back. Liza's new, but working out just fine."

A few minutes later, Liza called out, "Question six. What destroyed ancient Pompeii?"

"A volcano, Vesuvius," Will whispered. Penny wrote on the scoresheet in her round handwriting.

"Next: Which letter of the English alphabet can sting, fly, and produce a common sweetener? You know this one."

Jerria whispered, "B, like a honeybee."

"True or false: A human can go thirty days without sleep, with no ill effects."

Teams fell silent, counting; several people gazed at the ceiling, looking for the answer.

Jerria poked Nan. "Come on, you're the scientific one. Do you know?"

"I was a Marine Biologist. I can tell you about bones in a dorsal fin..."

Elias leaned forward. "I think it's a trick question. A human can go many days without sleep, so long as they sleep at *night*."

Charlie grinned. "I think you're right! Write it down, please, Penny. And we'd better watch for other trick questions."

Sure enough, question twelve was, "Do peacocks lay eggs, have live births, or neither?"

A confident undercurrent of "eggs" washed through the lounge. Nearby teams confidently wrote their answers.

Nan whispered, "Ah, another one! Peacocks are male; pea*hens* lay the eggs."

"Good catch, Nan!" Jerria grinned.

"After that wild night, your minds should be wide awake. Extra prizes today for the two top teams; that staff closet behind the theatre needed cleaning out, and a lot of stuff went flying. Ready? Super. What does the British word 'rocket' translate into in American English? And did you ever wonder why Americans speak *English* instead of *American*?" Liza made a note on her question sheet. "Bonus point, since it just came to mind; who said England and America are two countries divided by a common language?"

Most players wore blank faces. Jerria said softly, "Rocket is arugula, I'm sure of that. The other..."

"...is commonly attributed to George Bernard Shaw." Penny wrote on the scoresheet. "I had my students memorize a bit of his works."

"What's an arugula?" Will asked. "Never heard of it."

"Figures," Charlie teased. "It's a leafy salad green."

"Sounded a lot more interesting than that."

Liza glanced at her paper. "Where did John Denver say was almost heaven?"

Jerria overheard a man team behind her hiss, "I know this for sure. Colorado- he loved the Rockies."

"That's not right," Jerria whispered. "I love his music. It's West Virginia."

Number nineteen: "In which country is Europe's only desert located?"

Groans filled the room. Several people complained about Liza's trick questions, but she didn't cave. "Come on, smarty-pants, you can do it. Super!"

Elias and Charlie conferred, their heads bowed. "It has to be another trick question. A desert receives less than ten inches of rain per year, and I can't think of anywhere in Europe that fits that criteria."

Penny wrote *none.*

Jerria looked around the room. Several passengers were already gathering themselves, poised to leave, sure they'd lost the game. A couple of teams looked confident. Two or three people stared out the big windows at the sun dancing on the trees. This part of the Inside Passage was so narrow, land was a stone's throw on either side of the ship. Or, as the cabbie in Boston said, a bowling ball's roll away. Only in Boston do they measure distance in bowling balls.

Liza's ponytail bounced as she paced the room. "Okay, everybody, last question! It's a religious one, so all you scholars should get it right off. Ready? Super. What is a group of alligators called?"

More blank faces, Jerria noted. *Even that pastor I met in the elevator.* She leaned into the circle. "I know this one. Our son is studying to be a vet at Cornell, and he memorized a lot of animal facts..."

"...then tormented us all with them," Will concluded. "But what do alligators have to do with religion?"

"A group of alligators is a *congregation*," Jerria whispered.

Nan high-fived her friend.

"Trade scorecards," Liza ordered, "and let's see who gets these great prizes. I have mugs for the winners and highlighters for the second-place team, all sealed in cellophane for those of you who are germaphobes. Well, except the mugs. It defeats the purpose of the handle, you know?"

In the end, Jerria's team came in first place, with the team of college students behind by one point. Liza gave each of them the promised ceramic mugs, with highlighters for the other team.

"We don't have room at home for another ship's mug," Jerria said. "Anybody want ours?"

Penny beamed. "Oh, my, yes, if you're sure you don't want them. A set of four mugs; we could invite friends over and tell them all about the cruise."

Nan pushed her mug across the low table. "Here, take ours, too; now you can invite *two* couples to your home."

Penny's blue eyes sparkled. "Oh, my, thank you! You're all so kind to us. Let's head up to the cabin and drop them off."

"First, we'd better stop at Guest Services. Griffin said our cabin might be off limits until it's repaired." Elias scooped up the mugs.

"Well, if you find yourselves homeless, you're welcome to bunk with us," Jerria joked.

"I'm sure they'll figure out something, but thank you for the nice offer."

"Oh, hello, there." A woman stopped by Jerria's chair.

Jerria recognized her from the crystals group yesterday, although her bright smile was missing. "Hi. Wild night, wasn't it?"

"It sure was. Guess I missed the forecast; I was so focused on my lampshade. I feel terrible...I was the last one out of the room we were set up in, and I should have secured things before I left." Her eyes lowered. "The chandelier fell on the box of crystals, and they shattered to dust. I destroyed eight collections, single-handedly." She blinked back tears.

Jerria rose to hug her. "Oh, now, you can't feel responsible for the storm. I'm sure the group won't blame you."

"That's what you think. They told me I should take up..." she sniffed. "...*crocheting!*"

At a frown from Jerria, Will closed his mouth. This was no time to joke about yarn being unbreakable.

She patted the woman's arm. "There, now, it's not as bad as all that. Look at the bright side. You'll have plenty of time for sightseeing in Alaska. Who knows, you might even find an old chandelier in one of the small towns."

"Sightseeing?" She stared at Jerria, uncomprehending. "Why would anyone go *sightseeing* on a cruise?" She walked away, shaking her head.

"Gee, I thought that was a main reason people traveled, to see new places." Liza tucked the score sheets in her tote bag. "Silly me. Here, take these pens with the ship's logo on them; I found cases of them in the closet. See you at the scrapbooking class later on? It's right before the towel-animal demo. Good thing I'm not teaching that; mine always look like toads. See you!"

Jerria said, "We have so many pens already. I'll leave mine here on the table. Somebody will be glad to have it. Let's go find lunch, shall we?"

With the crew working steadily, the chefs managed to serve a hot lunch in the buffet, although nothing as elaborate as before the storm. The waiter promised a proper menu for dinner. As Nan and Jerria chatted over pie, Will and Charlie left to see if the golf simulator on deck ten had been damaged. Jerria spotted Penn, and wondering aloud if their balcony door had been repaired yet. Jerria and Nan waited until Penny had filled her salad plate, then walked over to her table. Elias soon joined then with a bowl of broth in hand.

Penny squirmed in her chair, beaming. "Oh, I was hoping we'd see you soon. You'll never guess what happened! That nice First Officer said– Why, Elias, is that all you're having for lunch?"

Elias waved her concern away. "It's nothing."

"Oh, yes, you'll never guess in a million years. He said our cabin was worse than we thought. Very sad, really; once the glass cracked, the storm came right in. He said they'll have to tear out the carpeting, and the salt water ruined the furniture, too. The mattress was soaked. We were so grateful you took us in during the storm, Jerria. How ever would we have managed without you?"

Elias patted her hand. "Tell them, Penny."

"That nice officer said we can't stay in our cabin. He moved us to...oh, my, I still can't believe it!"

Jerria smiled at her excitement. "Well, if John Hansson moved you to a tiny inside cabin down by the engine room, I'll speak to him myself."

"No, no, it's a bigger balcony cabin, right in the front of the ship! The bow, he called it. There's a big balcony and we can look out and see where the ship is going. And the new steward packed all of our things, sent our clothes to the ship's laundry, and even made us a sweet little monkey out of towels." Penny smoothed her napkin on her lap. "Elias and I already decided we'll have you four come visit us when we get to Hubbard Glacier. We'll order snacks from room service and have a real party."

"Sounds wonderful," Nan laughed. "We'll enjoy our first glacier together. We'd better let you get to your lunch; just wanted to make sure you were all right."

Jerria commented as they walked through the noisy buffet, "A bow cabin – lucky!"

"I'm happy for them. Wait until Penny tells the girls in the garden club."

Chapter Twenty-Two

Walking along the open promenade, Jerria and Nan paused to watch a line of children from the Kids' Club marching past, waving paper Jolly Rogers. Egged on by three enthusiastic club counselors, their pirate song grew louder.

"They're having a great time, aren't they? With all the clean up, it's probably good for the crew to have a sea day. The Inside Passage is prettier than I expected." Nan said, as she and Jerria headed to the café for a cup of hot cocoa.

"Oh, Nan, look there, in the water! Those salmon are jumping out of the ocean, then slamming back down. Why would they do that? I wonder if they're churned up from the storm."

"I can tell you," Joel said. Jerria hadn't noticed the naturalist behind them. "The salmon are jam-packed with eggs this time of year. They instinctively know if they lay the eggs in a solid clump, some creature will come along and eat them in one mouthful. Gulp." He pointed. "See, the fish jumps up, then smacks down on the water, horizontally. The force breaks apart the eggs, so they scatter when she lays them. Better chance of survival that way. Pretty smart, don't you think?"

Jerria winced, remembering her own pregnancies, years before. Even walking hurt near the end; she couldn't imagine slamming her body from any height! Mothers sacrificed for their offspring, regardless of species. *Bet those fish never waited up for their kids to come home late at night. It's a trade off.*

Jerria and Nan took steaming mugs of hot cocoa to lounge chairs in an alcove midships on deck seven. "Perfect spot, don't you think? We can see the ocean, but we're protected from the wind." Jerria crossed her ankles. "I'm always so busy at home. Being on a cruise makes me feel lazy. I could get used to this."

Nan pulled her cardigan close. "I know what you mean; at home, I have an ongoing list of things I need to tackle, and not one of them followed me here."

"You're going to love Alaska. I'm looking forward to the little shops. I'd like to find some muskox yarn for my new loom, and a moose hand puppet for baby Rowland. Are you after anything in particular?"

"A puppet is a good idea; I'll get some for our granddaughters, too. Let's see...I'd love a native button blanket, if they're not terribly expensive, and my neighbor told me I must get an ulu. *Ulu* in Hawaiian means breadfruit, but I'm pretty sure that isn't what she meant."

"Doubt you'll find fresh breadfruit in Alaska. An ulu is a knife with a curved blade. The handle's on top, and you cut with a rocking motion. They say it's faster than a food processor once you get the hang of it. I seldom use mine, but you'll see, a lot of people buy them." Jerria chuckled. "It's funny; you can't have weapons on board, so when you get back on the ship, they'll confiscate the ulu. Security delivers them to all the cabins the last night of the cruise, functionally arming the whole ship."

She sipped her cocoa. "Oh, look, there's Cowboy Bob by the bar, dancing. I wonder why his wife never joins him. She just stands to the side with her arms crossed."

"Maybe she can't take her eyes off him, after his deployment. She doesn't look happy, though, does she? I think a cruise is a great way to celebrate his homecoming."

"Listen, did you think it was odd, the way Liza handed out prizes for the hula hoop contest by the pool? She gave three prizes each to the adults, but only a sticker to Dr Marsh's sons and the little girl. Plainly, the children were the better hula hoopers. Is that a word?"

"Sure, English is a stretchy language, and hoopers is just fine." Nan raised an eyebrow. "That girl's mother was *huhu,* furious. I think if Gretchen hadn't pulled Liza aside, she'd have heard an earful."

"And what's up with Gretchen? She's in the background of every activity I've seen Liza run. I know Liza's new, but I've never seen a Cruise director hound an assistant like that. It's as if she's waiting for her to make a mistake."

"I don't get it. It looks like Liza's doing a good job to me. She's sure generous with the prizes; almost pushy. I guess she meant it when she said she'd cleaned out the Staff closet. I don't need more photo frames, but the new passengers love all that."

Nan stretched. "It's fun, seeing Penny's enthusiasm, isn't it? She's so thrilled to be on the ship."

"I know; I'm enjoying seeing the cruise through her eyes. She and Elias are a perfect couple. You can tell they've had some challenges over the years, but they're still so much in love. I hope Will and I are that close at that age."

Nan lifted her mug in a toast. "To gooey romance!"

Later that evening, Jerria stepped out of her silk dress and pulled her flannel nightshirt over her head, her voice muffled. "That was quite a show, and I don't mean the dancers."

"Think we'll see the comedian again?" Will hung his blue shirt in the cabin's closet. "Hope he wasn't serious, shouting those threats while Security hustled him off stage."

"I've never seen anybody that angry, and in public, too. For a minute, Haywood reminded me of our kids' *Rumpelstiltskin* book, the part where he was so furious, he stomped his foot and split in two."

"Bet he's done that bit a hundred times, calling an unsuspecting audience member up on stage, making a fool out of them, asking them to turn a summersault. Plain mean-spirited."

Jerria giggled. "He didn't know the guy he chose was the aerialist from the new production team! He's the one who taught the juggling workshop Nan and I attended. Haywood looked stunned when the man did a full tumbling run across the stage."

"Livid. Gretchen called the dancers back on stage pretty fast, but still saw quite a few passengers walk out. Doubt Haywood's contract will be renewed. Might even be put off in Ketchikan tomorrow."

"It's a problem, but not our problem. I'm delighted to be in Alaska again, Will. Of all the states we've visited, I left a part of my heart in Alaska. Come on, let's go count the stars."

Chapter Twenty-Three
Day Eight   Ketchikan

Jerria sat on the balcony in the early morning chill, sipping hot cider, a fleece blanket around her shoulders. Down below, slicker-clad pier crew paced, poised to tie up the ship's lines. A forklift driver balanced a long metal gangway, waiting until the ship moved into its berth.

Gretchen's voice filled the ship; her usual morning announcement following the nerve-jarring gong. "Welcome to Ketchikan. As soon as the ship is cleared by the port authorities, we'll begin disembarking on deck four, midships. All passengers are required to be back onboard no later than eight-fifteen this evening. Temperatures are in the mid-forties, with periods of rain forecast. Rain ponchos will be for sale at the gangway..."

Jerria's mind wandered. She and Will had been to Ketchikan several times, and she looked forward to visiting the small town again today. She knew Nan would enjoy the Totem Heritage Center, with her love of stories, and Charlie mentioned he'd like to tour the Bald Eagle Rescue Center. Bald eagles often flew over Jerria's house in Oregon, but they were a rarity for the Hawaiians. Maybe the drizzle would let up as the day progressed.

The sun made an effort to break through the cloud cover, but Jerria knew any sunshine wouldn't last. Last trip, she and Will had hiked the Married Man's Trail, and she'd marveled at the thick lacy moss on every tree. Oh, and the salmon...wait until Charlie saw the creek, black with spawning salmon, making their way frantically upstream. Eager to start the day, she set her mug on the table. She slid open the door, and collided with Will, who was coming out on the balcony.

He rubbed his chest. "Ouch. Meeting Nan and Charlie in half an hour, right? Plan for the day? Want to talk out here, or in the cabin?"

"Out here; it's not that cold, although I expect Nan would disagree. I thought we'd wander the old part of town first, the shops. I'm hoping to find some caribou horn buttons and muskox wool. Then we'll ride the funicular up to the hotel to the totems, walk down the back side to the Eagle Recovery Center, and stop at the Totem Heritage Center. Last time we were here, they were carving a new one, remember?"

Will smiled as she stopped to draw breath; her enthusiasm was the main thing that drew him to her in college years ago. That, and her bouncy brown curls. "Remember you were sad because the carver invited us to a potlatch, and it was scheduled for the day after we left."

"That was an opportunity lost. Not everyone gets invited to a potlatch! After the totem center, we'll want lunch. I found a place online that offers pizza with reindeer pepperoni. We'll share one, so we won't spoil our appetites. I thought Nan and Charlie would enjoy the logger show; I know they don't do that on Kauai. It'll be a chance to rest our legs, and out of the rain, too." She continued, "For dinner, we'll go to the salmon bake south of town. It sounds touristy, but the brochure says they serve typical Alaska food and I think Nan and Charlie will love it. Don't worry, I looked at the menu and you'll be fine...although it still seems wrong, coming to Alaska and avoiding salmon!"

Will made a mental note to tell Nan and Charlie to wear their most comfortable shoes. Jerria's plan would require walking several miles, or longer if they detoured, which he knew was likely.

He was right. Before noon, they'd wandered through the little shops, had a snack of reindeer jerky, and rode the funicular up to Cape Fox Lodge. They rested in the hotel sitting room, climbed the stairs to the display loft, then headed toward the back garden to the totem circle.

Nan hesitated at the double glass doors. She skimmed a hand-printed notice, then read every word aloud. "*'Bear Warning. Bears have been sighted in this immediate area. If you see a bear, do not feed it. Move away slowly, and report to the hotel desk. Thank you.'* I...might feel better waiting right here. You go on ahead, okay?"

"Come on, you don't want to hole up inside a building." Jerria took Nan's arm. "We'll be fine. You'll like the totem poles; they each have a story. Then we'll hike down the Married Man's Trail. It's a winding boardwalk through the rain forest, really pretty, and we'll fork off to the Eagle Recovery Center. Wait'll you see how thick the moss is."

Nan hesitated. "Are you sure it's safe?" She took a breath, and pushed the door open. "Maybe if we make enough noise, the bears won't bother us."

"As I always say," Will murmured, "Either have a good experience or a good story to tell."

Jerria elbowed him.

Chapter Twenty-Four

Hours later, Jerria glanced at her watch. "It's almost time to go back to the Totem Heritage Center to catch a ride with the carver. I still can't believe he remembered us!"

Nan grinned, her face half covered by her jacket's hood. "He recognized you right away. It's an honor to be invited to a family celebration for dinner. Reminds me of Hawaii; it's common to invite extras when the *ohana* gets together." She shivered. "Except, in Hawaii, we don't wear parkas."

Jerria laughed, "If you've noticed, Nan, nobody's wearing a parka here, either, except you. Some of the kids by the school were wearing shorts and tee shirts."

"Crazy. Is it even above freezing? The sign by the bank said its fifty-three degrees, but I don't believe that. Let's go; maybe walking will warm me up."

They came around the corner as the carver finished locking the Totem Heritage Center for the day. "Right on time! I hope you're hungry."

"We sure are. Thanks for inviting us." Jerria climbed into the four by four. "I'm surprised you remember me and Will."

"Oh, yes, I remember you well. You asked many questions about the totem I was carving that year. We'll drive by it on the way to the house, so you can see it in its place." He started the engine. "We see so many tourists here, but they're all in a hurry.

You were genuinely interested, and that's rare. I'm glad you can visit tonight before your ship leaves town."

"You said it was a celebration," Charlie called over the engine's noise. "What's the occasion?"

"My niece, my sister's daughter, has been accepted to university, only the third in the family to go. We celebrate her choice to seek education. And, secretly, my sister celebrates her young man *not* being accepted. She hopes once they are apart, my niece forgets all about him."

Jerria thought back to the cabbie she and Will had met in southern France, who asked if America was safe to visit. His nineteen-year-old daughter was at a Virginia university. "She met a young man, and she thinks she has found love with him. I am her Papa, and so I must go." Families are the same in every culture.

They pulled up to a long, low house with several wings, as if it had expanded as the family grew. Several muddy cars parked at random angles on the wide gravel driveway. Seven children ran to the jeep, faces flushed from playing, swarming the car as soon as it stopped.

"Uncle Ben! Uncle Ben's here!"

A round-faced woman stepped out of the front door, wiping her hands on a ruffled apron, scolding good-naturedly. "Settle down, you little scamps; give Benson a chance to get out of the jeep. And check your manners; we have guests. Show the Eagle clan proud, now, you hear?" The children stood stock still, their dark eyes shining.

Extending her hand to Jerria, Lillian nodded. "Ah, yes, I'm happy to finally meet you."

Jerria, puzzled, introduced the others. "This is Will, my husband, and our good friends, Nan and Charlie, from Hawaii. It's so good of you to invite us."

"Happy to have you in our home. I hope you skipped your midday meal, because we have a feast tonight." She smiled at Nan, who shivered in the late afternoon air. "Come in; come in where it is warmer. Our family visited Hawaii two summers ago, with the Permanent Fund payout. Very different from Alaska, but the same spirit, I thought. I felt it in the mountains, the ocean."

She ushered them into the comfortable living room, inviting them to sit by the big window overlooking the woods. "Ben, maybe you could help with the grill. Your father and the other men are out back."

"Mind if we tag along?" Charlie asked. He and Will followed Ben outdoors.

Ben's mother put her hands on her hips. "I have a few last-minute things to tend to before the others arrive. Ben's sisters are in the kitchen. Would you mind if I leave you? I'll send a child with a cool drink...soon as one runs by."

Jerria rose, protesting. "Please, we'd be happier in the kitchen. Cooking with others is one of my favorite things to do."

Nan nodded. "Yes, please, I'd like to help, too."

Jerria immediately felt at home in the large steamy kitchen. Lillian introduced two of Ben's sisters. Before long, the women chatted as through they'd been friends for years.

"Let me try that, please," Nan asked, watching Lillian's hands fly as she chopped cabbage for cole slaw. "That's an *ulu*, right? I want to buy one for home, but I don't know how to use it." Her movements awkward at first, soon Nan filled the bowl with shredded cabbage and reached for an onion. "I'm not as fast as you, but I can see that I'd use an ulu often at home."

"You catch on quick." A sister chuckled. "Benson said you went to the logger show in town. What did you think of it?"

Jerria wiped her hands on a dishcloth. "I loved it! I know it was put on for us tourists, but those loggers had some serious skills. One carved a log into a child's chair using a chain saw in under a minute! And the way they shimmied up those tall poles was incredible."

"Did you see notice the slim man in a blue shirt with a black bandana?" Lillian opened two jars of purple jam. "He's Ben's brother, Tony. He'll be here for dinner."

The sisters laughed. "Oh, our Tony, he never misses a meal, although he's as skinny as the trees he climbs. Mama, we'd better hurry; it's almost time."

Laughing children running past the big window caught Jerria's eye. "Lillian, your grandchildren are beautiful!"

"Thanks, we like them all. It sure is easier now that we have a doctor in town; seems little ones are always getting sick or hurt, one thing or another. Did you know it was illegal to give birth in Ketchikan, sixty years it was, until a nurse practitioner came in 2012?"

Jerria startled. "How did they prevent births? I recall a couple of my babies coming without much warning."

"City council made a law. The women had to leave town the last their three months of pregnancy, go where there was a doctor at hand. It was hard on families. Families should gather when a baby's born."

As easy conversation flowed through the warm kitchen, Lillian set a huge pan of warm cornbread in front of Jerria. Cutting it, they arranged squares on a platter.

"When you left last time," Lillian said, "Benson talked about you for days. He felt a real connection with you. He said he knew you'd be back some day. It means a lot to have you here tonight."

Jerria puzzled, "I like him, too. He's a real artist. We'll keep in touch this time. I can–"

"Dinner! Get it now or go without!" Through the steamed window, Jerria saw a man striking a big cast iron triangle with a mallet. Children ran to the long wooden tables in the covered porch. Adults, more than when they arrived, moved to join the youngsters.

Lillian hustled her guests and daughters out the back door, each carrying a heaping bowl or platter of food. Men ferried metal trays of fragrant meats and fish from the grill. Jerria's mouth watered.

Once everyone was settled, Benson's father began a lengthy prayer. He welcomed the guests and family and congratulated his granddaughter on her acceptance to university. He thanked the Great Spirit for the health of his family and the pleasure of family and new friends at the table. He acknowledged the salmon and elk for giving their lives so they may eat, and offered thanks for the bounty of the garden that provided so much food for the feast. He praised the long summer days which allowed a good growing season and prayed the coming winter would be a good one, and asked that the baby lamb would heal from its cut leg when it caught in the fence on Tuesday.

When he began offering thanks for the baked beans, cole slaw, sliced tomatoes, homemade butter, and potato salad, in turn, Lillian intervened.

"Amen!" she said loudly. The squirmy children flashed grins. "Now, everybody, take what's in front of you, then pass to the left. There's plenty to go around."

"At least twice," Jerria whispered to Will, scooping roasted baby carrots onto her plate.

Grilled salmon, elk steaks, potatoes, vegetables, salads, cornbread, and baked beans circled the table. Benson filled nearby glasses with cold lemonade, then stood to refill the pitcher. Hands held more empty glasses poised at his return. "It doesn't pay to sit in the middle of the table," he lamented cheerfully, pouring the icy drink. "Hey, don't let that apple-bacon salad miss my plate."

Surveying her heaped dish, Jerria thanked Lillian for including them. "We planned to go to the salmon bake south of town so Nan and Charlie could taste some Alaskan food. This is so much better."

Laughter broke out around the table. Benson's sister said, "You have no idea how much better! They call that stuff authentic, but I worked there one summer in high school –most of us did- and those packages came right from *Chicago!* All we did was heat it up and dump it in bowls, no real cooking at all."

Lillian said proudly, "Everything on this table came from the good earth or the sea right nearby."

"Delicious. Ketchikan is a sweet town," Charlie said, between mouthfuls of elk. "Reminds me of the small towns in Hawaii. I was hoping to get a chance to kayak, while Nan and Jerria shopped, but there were more salmon than water, seemed to me. I don't know how they jumped up that fish ladder like that."

Lillian asked, "Jerria, did you enjoy the shops in town?"

"Yes, I bought a twisted silver pendant, and Nan bought a sweater and scarf, locally made. I asked about muskox wool for my loom, and the woman in the store sent me around back to her mother, who gathers the stuff. She sold me all she had. I really lucked out."

"Oh, yes, that would be Enid. She's a fine weaver."

Meanwhile, Benson's brother followed up on Charlie's comment. "Yeah, it's not a good time to kayak when the fish need the water for their journey.

Your ship goes to Anchorage, right? Kayaking by the Mendenhall glacier is easy and beautiful. You know the glaciers are alive, right?"

"Alive?" Charlie raised an eyebrow. "They're just ice."

"Yes, ice, thousands of years old, compressed so the spirits speak through them. Wait'll you hear them calving; they have a definite voice."

"The ship goes to Hubbard Glacier after Skagway, and I hear it calves often." Nan reached for another roll. "I can't stop eating; everything is so good! In Hawaii, the land has a spirit, too, but Charlie is from the mainland and doesn't always feel it. This salad dressing is delicious. Is the base buttermilk?"

"Goat's milk," Lillian said. "I wish I could give you a bottle to take home, but I know you can't bring food on the ship. Make sure you give me your email, and I'll be happy to share the recipe."

After thick slabs of homemade caramel apple pie, Benson rose. "Mama, dinner was the best." He let his belt out a notch. "I'd better be getting you four back to the port. The ship leaves in under an hour, and you don't want to have to run for it."

Jerria slipped on her jacket. "Oh, I don't know, we could do a lot worse than being stranded here. Thanks so much for your hospitality. We'll remember this evening a long time."

The family waved and called to them as Benson drove down the long driveway. Before long, they saw the *Ocean Journey,* its lights sparkling like a city apartment building. Two buses disgorged tired tourists at the curb. Benson parked by the end of the line of passengers boarding the ship.

They waved one last good bye and joined the line. Nan sighed. "I love Alaska! I'll remember this dinner forever."

As the line snaked through security toward the gangway, Jerria overheard a passenger and grinned.

"That salmon bake food was terrible. I asked for tartar, and they gave me a little bowl of raw fish. What's wrong with the good old mayo-based stuff?"

A nearby woman scolded, "That's tar*tare*, you idiot, not tartar sauce! Where are you from, anyway?"

Liza danced to canned music at the bottom of the gangway, welcoming passengers with a broad smile. "Welcome back, everybody! Had a great day? Super! Didn't you just love Ketchikan? Don't forget the hand sanitizer, okay? We don't want anybody getting sick. Did you see the eagles in the trees?"

She dug in her ever-present tote bag. "Anybody want a photo frame? First ten people who tell me what they did today can have one. And I have a mug for the first person who can tell me the name of the oldest bald eagle at the recovery center." She laughed as a barrage of stories washed over her, and eager hands reached for the prizes. "Lady Liberty, that's right! Super. Here you go. You're all going to join me for the dance-lyrics game at nine o'clock, right? Same time as the magician's show, but I guaranteed we'll have more fun."

Smiling at Will and Jerria, Liza exclaimed, "There's my Trivia champs! See you in the morning, okay? Gretchen threw a fit when I changed a few of her questions, but what she doesn't know won't hurt me, am I right? Welcome back, everybody! Super. Anybody need a highlighter? I have extras. Here you go."

Will set Jerria's shopping bag on the conveyor belt through the metal detector. With his head down, he didn't see the Cruise director barreling past the passengers until she bumped into him.

Gretchen's jaw tightened. "Honestly, people, get on the ship, already! What's the hold up?" Spotting Liza chatting at the bottom of the gangway, she shoved four passengers aside in her haste to get down the narrow ramp.

"I should have known you would be behind the logjam. Captain McCann's steaming, and here you are, passing the time of day like you're at a summer picnic. Hustle these people along, and I mean *now*." Scanning the startled passengers, she snarled. "Move your feet, will you?" and stormed back up the gangway.

Red-faced, Liza passed the line, and boarded the ship. Her smile faded, she called, "Come on everybody, pick up the pace! Come along, now."

Nan said she wanted to see if anyone had turned in her lost novel she'd left in the lounge. Jerria and Will headed toward their cabin, after making plans to meet Nan and Charlie before the show. Penny was in the elevator.

Noticing her furrowed brow, Jerria asked, "Everything all right?"

Penny replied slowly, "It's Elias. He was excited to be in Ketchikan, but by mid-morning, he said he was tired and having some double vision. We came back early, and he's been asleep in the cabin ever since. He wasn't even interested in dinner."

Jerria suggested calling Dr Marsh in the Med Center, and reminded Penny they were nearby if she needed anything. Penny nodded, then stepped out of the elevator on deck nine.

As the elevator door closed, Jerria turned to Will. "What do you suppose is wrong with Elias?"

"No idea, Honey, but remember he's over ninety. Probably just tired from the trip. Check on them in the morning. Bet a good night's sleep is all he needs."

Chapter Twenty-Five
Day Nine   At Sea

Will was wrong. In the morning, he and Jerria stopped by Elias' and Penny's suite after breakfast.

Penny came to the door, her face drawn. She whispered, "He had a bad night. Now he's sleeping so deeply, I keep checking to make sure he's breathing. I don't think he has fever, but there's a blistery rash on his hands, arm, and chest. I called the medical center. They said Dr Marsh is on his way, but I guess other people are sick, too. I'm afraid we'll have to miss Trivia with you this morning."

Jerria caught the older woman in a hug. "Oh, don't give that a thought! What can we do for you? Have you eaten anything?"

Startled, Penny shrugged. "I was going to have dinner, but I...forgot. Elias so seldom takes sick, I'm beside myself."

Will volunteered to bring her breakfast from the buffet. "Faster than room service. What do you feel like eating?"

Penny asked for a roll and some juice. Jerria offered to sit with Penny until he came back. They sat on the white sofa, facing the tall windows.

"This is nice!" Jerria admired the airy room. "I'm sorry you're having a tough trip, but this suite is beautiful."

Penny blinked back tears. "I'd love it, if only Elias was well enough to sit beside me. We've been together since...well, my friend introduced us at the

USO club during the war. He was gangly and shy and I think I loved him even then. I'm so afraid...afraid of..."

Time dragged in slow motion while Jerria encouraged Penny to talk, and tried to comfort her. "Dr Marsh knows his stuff, and I'm sure he'll be here very soon."

At last, a knock came at the door. Jerria crossed the living room in three steps, and anxiously pulled the door open. She chuckled.

"Will Danson, what is all this?"

He grinned sheepishly. "Thought Penny needed more than a bit of juice, but wasn't sure what to bring. Brought a bunch of stuff. You like breakfast, don't you, Penny?"

Jerria guided his loaded tray to the glass coffee table, shaking her head. "You have enough here for a crowd. Okay, what sounds good to start? Scrambled eggs, omelet, waffles, berries, French toast, mixed fruit, cheese pastry, or oatmeal?"

Penny exclaimed, "Oh, my, so much food! I'll set some aside for Elias, when he feels up to it. I think I could eat a little-"

A sharp knock interrupted her. Jerria opened the door to admit Dr Marsh. His hair hung in his eyes, his tie was askew, and dark circles rimmed his brown eyes.

Jerria murmured, "Have you had any sleep?"

He flashed a tired smile. "Are people still doing that? I'd better get a look at the patient; I have a list of folks to check on." As if to emphasize his comment, the radio on his hip beeped. He listened, nodding. "Yes, cabin 614, I got it. Tell them I'll be there as soon as I'm free."

Jerria put her arm around Penny. "We'd better go, but we'll check back later." She and Will slipped out, pulling the door closed behind them.

On the way to the elevator bank, Will said he'd run into Nan in the hallway earlier. "On her way back from a spinning class, she said, but was dressed in workout clothes. Didn't know she liked weaving. Anyway, told her we'd meet her and Charlie at Trivia. Head to the lounge now, okay? Stake out a good spot."

Jerria playfully poked his arm. "Oh, Will, spinning is like riding a stationary bike, only faster."

"Seems like a waste of energy to me, if it doesn't go anywhere," he said cheerfully, pressing the elevator button. "Listen."

A sharp voice rose from being the door marked No Admittance. Jerria turned stricken eyes to Will.

Gretchen.

"Look, I don't care about your personal problems. You probably caught something from a passenger. You know half of them lie on the health declaration. If you're sick, it's not my issue." Her sneer was audible. "And if you need sympathy, go talk to Liza. She's got that good-listener thing going for her. Now, quit breathing around me and get back to work."

They stepped back as the door flew open, bumping the wall behind it. A woman in a crew

uniform rushed out, holding a tissue to her face. She
didn't look up as she hurried past them.

"That woman!" Jerria fumed. "I'd like to-"

The elevator door slid open, and Will propelled
her inside. "I know, Honey, but not our concern. On
vacation, remember, and supposed to have a quiet
sea day. Think about something else."

Drawing a deep breath, Jerria nodded. Her
heart rate slowed by the time they reached the
SunSun lounge with eight minutes to spare. Teams
were already gathering for Trivia.

Charlie motioned to them across the lounge. "I
chose a good spot by the window. The sea is so calm
today. Nan's on her way; she broke a shoelace." He
looked closer at Jerria. "Hey, did you eat a storm
cloud for breakfast?"

"It's Gretchen-!" Jerria fumed. "She's
heartless. We heard her light into a crew member for
being sick. Oh, that reminds, me, Elias isn't feeling
well, so they won't be here this morning. Dr Marsh is
with them."

"Hope it's nothing serious." Charlie sat back in
his seat. "Maybe he's just tired from the trip."

"Overheard some passengers in the drink
station talking about their friends being sick, too; dizzy
or something." Will stood to let Nan slide in next to
Charlie. "Good morning."

"Aloha. I brought a plate of cookies to share;
figured no one would mind." Nan crossed her slim
ankles. "Are you talking about somebody being sick? I

was wondering why this group is so small today. Must be something going around."

"We checked on Elias and Penny earlier, and he still isn't feeling well." Jerria bit a cookie. "Maybe if he rests today, they'll be able to explore Skagway tomorrow. They're not missing much on a sea day anyway, except scenery. Oh, Nan, you should see their suite! It's all silver and glass."

Liza came in, and in the flurry of passing out papers and pencils, conversation dropped off. "Where is everybody? Sleeping in on this sunny morning? Oh, well, that makes the odds of your team winning even better. Today's theme is Fishy, Fishy. I'll show pictures of fish up here on my screen, and you write down what kind they are. An extra point for each if you know if they're salt or fresh water fish. Give me a minute to set up." Liza smiled at the group. "And get your thinking caps on, because I snagged some great prizes this morning, plus these cool pens, just for showing up. Super!"

ill sighed, resigned. "Fish? May as well go read a book. Can't stand seafood, so I'm no help at all. And without Elias's memory..."

"Stay," Charlie reached for a butter cookie. "Nan was a Marine Biologist, remember? We got this in the bag."

Liza flashed photos of fish on the screen in a grid. Nan identified most of them in a low voice. Charlie said he knew some from snorkeling in Hawaii. Jerria recognized halibut, skipjack, and a few other food fish. She loved trying new recipes. The teams murmured answers while leaders wrote on their score sheets.

Will sat silently until the last three photos. "Mackerel, and number nineteen is a variegated hake. Other is a blue fin boxfish. Saltwater, all."

Jerria's eyebrows rose. "How on earth...?"

"Cat was off her feed last month. Talked to the guy at the pet store. Remembered mackerel from the cat food cans. And a real estate client had an aquarium in his den. Guy wouldn't stop talking about his exotic fish. That's all of them, right?"

When the scores were tallied, their team scored every point correct, leaving the other teams in the dust. Liza handed out ship-logo pens, congratulating Jerria's team. "Super! I thought Elias had the brains, but look at you! Here are water bottles for each of you, and scrapbooking kits, too, cruise-themed, of course. I had some left over from my class yesterday. Gotta run." Her ponytail bounced as she left the lounge, tote bag over her arm.

The teams filtered out of the lounge. Jerria noticed a young woman eying her scrapbook kit. She extended it to her. "Here, would you like this? I'm not a scrapbooker."

"Really? For me? Oh, wow. I never win any prizes. Liza makes it fun, though, so I keep trying. Thanks a lot!"

Jerria turned to Will. "Now, let's find someone to give these water bottles to, okay? I don't want to pack them home." They passed them to a couple on their way out of the lounge. The man smiled his thanks and immediately pulled the cellophane wrapper off.

Nan suggested the naturalist's lecture on glaciology, starting in ten minutes, and they turned toward the theatre. Jerria silently wondered how Joel would present an hour-long lecture, when he was too shy to make eye contact one on one.

She worried needlessly.

Chapter Twenty-Six

The naturalist confidently tapped a pointer on the video screen on stage. Joel began, "I'm sure you've all seen the glacier on the hills around the ship. We'll be at Hubbard Glacier in a couple of days. Tidewater glaciers are the most popular things to see in Alaska, and they're not even man-made. Not many ships can get as close as Captain McCann..."

Seventy minutes later, Joel concluded with, "That's how the future of glaciers looks." As if suddenly noticing the audience, he stammered, "To me, at least." As applause filled the theatre, the naturalist fled behind the curtain.

"That was worthwhile," Nan exclaimed. "I had no idea how old the glaciers are, or how much they moved. Half a mile a year is *fast*."

"Joel did really well. I think he's more confident in his own element."

"*My* elements are hungry. How about some lunch? Like to try a burger from the outdoor grill by the pool." Will suggested. "If we stay in the glass alcove, might be warm enough to eat out on the deck."

"The sunshine is pretty, but do you think it's warm enough to eat al fresco?" Nan shivered. "Tell you what, you three go ahead, and I'll go get my jacket. Meet you on the pool deck."

They agreed, and parted; Nan headed down two decks, while the others climbed the stairs and went out onto the open deck. Several parents kept a sharp eye on their children in the pool.

"Whew, the scenery is amazing," Jerria commented. "The channel must be really deep for the ship to sail this close to land. Look at how close those little waterfalls are. Hey, can you make out that dark splotch by the big rock onshore?" She pointed over the railing.

Will squinted as the shape moved in front of the boulder. "Bear. See, there's her cub, no, two of them."

Just then, Dr Marsh's sons ran to the rail, shouting. "Mom! Mommy, come see, there's a real live teddy bear!" Their wet footprints fairly danced across the teak deck.

Jill Marsh hurried to them, carrying two pool towels. "Wrap these around yourselves, boys, it's cold. What do you see, Jeremy? Oh, yes, a black bear with her babies. Twins, just like you."

She smiled over her sons' heads. "Not exactly a cuddly stuffed animal, is it?"

Jerria chuckled. "I guess not, but it's fun seeing things through children's eyes."

"They need to let off steam, and a pool's as good a place as any. They don't even notice it's not swimming weather. I had more help last cruise, but my husband has been tied up since yesterday. I don't think he's even slept. So many people are sick."

Will frowned. "Can't be seasickness; puddles have higher waves. Thought ship's doctors only had office hours a few hours a day."

"That's what I thought, too, when he signed on, but he's on call 24/7. I talked to him a while ago. He said whatever's going around isn't something he's familiar with, so he's been in contact with the CDC. Guess they're having some big conference in Anchorage."

Jerria blanched. What could be serious enough to need the Centers for Disease Control's input?

Jeremy pulled at his mother's hand. "Come on, Mommy, let's go splash in the pool."

"Too cold for me, sweetie, but I'll come watch you two." Jill waved. "See you around."

Nan walked up, zipping her jacket. She turned up the collar, and announced, "There you are. Let's get some lunch. I hope they have hot soup."

The four friends filled plates and sat at a round table protected from the wind. Jerria idly watched three crew members scrubbing a nearby door and handrails. She bit a french fry. "Nan, Jill Marsh was saying there's some kind of illness onboard, and the doctor doesn't know what it is. I hope that's not what Elias has."

"I don't want to worry you guys, but there was an emergency team in the corridor down from our staterooms. I heard a woman collapsed." Nan sipped her corn chowder. "What could it be? I'd expect a doctor to be able to handle most ordinary issues."

"Well, we'll just keep washing our hands often and hope we don't get sick. I noticed there are more hand sanitizer dispensers around the ship." Jerria reached for a paper napkin. "What are your plans after lunch? Anyone interested in the cake decorating demo?"

Will and Charlie opted out. They wanted to join the volleyball tournament on the sports deck, as long as the ship hadn't curtailed activities yet. Jerria thought they might, since so many passengers had taken sick. Nan said she'd enjoy the cake demonstration. They ate, chatting as the scenery slipped by.

Half an hour later, Jerria shifted uneasily in her seat. Far from the expected friendly competition she'd seen on other cruises, the undercurrent in the atrium was increasingly hostile, and deteriorating fast.

The head pastry chef stood on the left end of the long table, his tall toque bent over an elegant Black Forest cake. He deftly spritzed cream swirls, evenly spaced, and set the next layer in place. Next to him stood Haywood Jacallme, his brow pinched, angrily splatting frosting between his cake's layers. Captain McCann, immaculate in her white uniform, was to his left. She was no professional baker, but she carefully spread frosting, slowly rotating the turntable, intent on her task. On the right, the Cruise director, stone-faced, stabbed a knife into a block of dark chocolate over and over. Shards scattered, unheeded.

"Next, add one-half cup of kirsch to the top layer, drizzling it slowly." The chef glanced down the line. "Gretchen, that's quite enough chopping; the block is for curls on the top, not chocolate chips. The next step... Haywood, what have you done? Your cake is *leaking*. I said a half cup, not a half bottle."

A thin trail of alcohol flowed off the raised cake stand, across the table, and onto the floor. Glaring, the comedian sneered, "Like I care. Cakes ain't in my contract." The audience roared with laughter. The comedian's face darkened, and he moved away from the table.

Captain McCann's back straightened. She said quietly, "You, there, funny man. If you don't plan on swimming to the next port, may I suggest you take your place? And not one more word, if you please."

Haywood tried to stare down the usually good-natured captain, but failed. He stepped back to his cake and grabbed his offset spatula like a dagger. The audience fell silent.

The chef held his finished cake up. "There you have it, Black Forest Cake! My staff will now serve you."

Without a backward glance, Haywood Jacallme and Gretchen left the stage.

"I've never seen a cake demo like that," Nan set down her fork a few minutes later. "Good thing they prepared samples ahead of time, because a couple of those cakes were not made with love. I think if Gretchen or the comedian had poison, they'd have sprinkled it on instead of the kirsch."

"Poison?" Jerria rolled her eyes. "They are both angry sorts, but that's going overboard."

Or, it should be," Nan laughed. "I don't know what came over them. Let's go watch the men play volleyball."

Chapter Twenty-Seven
Day Nine   Juneau

A heavy fog lay over Juneau as the *Ocean Journey* slipped through Gastineau Channel the following morning. Jerria pulled her cardigan around her shoulders, straining to see the pier below. She heard a knock at the door, but left it to Will to answer it.

He slid open the glass balcony door a minute later. "Ready for breakfast, Honey? Nan's here and Charlie's on his way." She sighed and followed him into the cabin.

"Good morning," Nan smiled. "Is the main dining room okay with you two, now that it's open again? We're in no hurry to get off, are we?"

Jerria slipped her shoes on. "Sounds good to me. We have plenty of time. We don't have to be back onboard until eight-thirty tonight."

Will opened the door to admit Charlie, who held a scrap of tissue below his lip. "Battle wound?" Will eyed his friend's chin.

"Multi-tasking gone awry. For future reference, trying to put on sneakers while shaving is a bad idea."

"So long as you're not bleeding out, let's get some breakfast." Nan led the way to the elevator, and down three decks to the main dining room. Two crew members in white jumpsuits greeted them while they wiped handrails in the corridor.

"Must be an inspection coming up," Will commented as they were seated at a window table. "Never seen so much cleaning going on."

"Or maybe they're concerned about the people who are sick. We should check on Elias soon." Jerria accepted a sheet of printed paper from the waiter. "What's this?"

The waiter apologized for the limited menu. "Captain's orders; no cold, raw, or unpackaged food until the doctor figures out what's causing the sickness onboard. He says it isn't food-borne, but Captain McCann's not taking any chances."

Jerria questioned him. What else did he know?

Glancing furtively, he confided, "We're not supposed to talk about it. I can tell you no crew or staff are sick; just passengers, and they're not from the same home towns. Doc's eliminated the galley, the pool, and the spa." He straightened. "I'm sorry the only fresh fruit this morning is unpeeled bananas and tangerines, but the chef has prepared a lovely baked stone fruit compote."

Jerria ordered, lamenting the lack of fresh pastries and breads, usually baked onboard. "I avoid croissants at home, but they're a treat when we cruise. Oh, well, I guess I didn't need the calories, anyway."

The assistant waiter set hot drinks at each plate.

Will stirred cream into his hot cocoa. "We'll get a good lunch in town. Wanted to take the Point

Roberts Tramway to the top of the mountain, but unless the fog lifts, won't be able to see anything."

Nan nodded. "I know you talked about going to Mendenhall Glacier, Jerria. What else are we doing today? I feel lazy, letting you do the planning, but you've been here before and..."

"...and we all know, if there's something worthwhile, Jerria won't let us miss it," Charlie chuckled. "We appreciate your planning, more than we can say."

Jerria smiled ruefully. "Just call me Information Booth. I can't help it. I'd be sad if we returned home and heard about something wonderful *right there*, and we didn't know about it!" She shifted in her chair, her attention drawn across the dining room where several passengers griped about the paper menus.

Those poor waiters. Hollering at the messenger won't change anything; it never worked for our kids, either. First, we'll catch a shuttle to Mendenhall Glacier. I know you men have been itching to kayak, and, Nan, if you'd like, I thought you and I could hike to the abandoned gold mine at the top of the hill."

"I'd love that!" Nan said. "I'm always up for a hike."

"Good! There's a pretty waterfall along the way, where most people turn back, but I think we'll have time to go the extra mile or so to the top. Not fast, though; I'm a grandmother, not a sprinter."

Charlie set his cup down. "Did you know Juneau is built on gold tailings from the early mine?

Hollowing out a mountain and pushing it into the bay is a strange way to build a major city."

"Especially with the history of earthquakes." Nan shrugged. "I'm refusing to think about it. Let's eat and get going, shall we? People are already getting off."

The driver of the shuttle to Mendenhall Glacier kept up a running commentary. "On the left, folks, look at that tall widow-maker. See the bald eagle at the tree's top? I've been doing this run all week, and there he sits, waiting for breakfast to come by. They do that, those eagles, pick out a favorite tree and stay there all day. National symbol, they are, but they're also scavengers and lazy. Coming up here on the right side..."

Jerria tuned him out, gazing at the passing scenery. Many of the houses had small planes in the driveway, where the family car would be parked anywhere else in America. Although Juneau is the state capital, the city is only accessible by air or water. She wondered if she could adapt to this kind of isolation.

Before long, they pulled into the parking lot across from the Mendenhall Glacier Visitors Center. Passengers piled out. On the sidewalk, Jerria shifted her daypack. "Let's split up and meet back here in time for lunch. Maybe by then the weather will have cleared."

Nan stared at the glacier, awestruck. "Those colors! The blues are deeper than the glaciers we saw on the mountains. And feel the silence? I think the fog is thinning already."

Will hugged Jerria. "Meet by the tram stop in two hours, okay? Enjoy your hike." He left with Charlie to meet their kayaking guide by the lake.

Jerria adjusted a strap on her grey daypack. How did kids get used to wearing them to school every day? "Nan, are you ready to hit the trail?"

They stopped at the low stone wall overlooking the glistening glacier, where a chunk of glacial ice rested. A uniformed ranger explained how to tell the difference between glacial ice and a normal ice cube. "If someone says it's glacier ice, look for bubbles. A normal ice cube will have one big bubble in the center because it freezes from the outside in, squeezing air to the middle. But a genuine glacier is made of many years of airy snowflakes, packed down, making lots of tiny bubbles in layers inside. Come touch this ice; it's thousands of years old."

A few tourists stood nearby, including a young family Jerria recognized from the ship. The parents herded three young children; the father had a baby in a front-pack on his chest. The girl had won the quick-sketch contest Liza held yesterday, and Jerria remembered her glee at winning a marker set.

"Kids, stay by us," the mother called. "Kate, you stop running around like that. I don't want you to fall. Curt, grab her, will you?"

Jerria snagged the little girl's coat as she ran past. "Sorry, little one, but Mommy said to stop." She returned the child to her mother. "Oh, my, did you burn your hand?"

The woman glanced at her palm, distracted. "I don't know...these little blisters popped up last night. Curt, just pick her up."

"Mom, I have bumps, too," the older girl displayed both hands. "It doesn't hurt very much, though."

The harried mother brushed aside her daughter, keeping a firm grip on her son's sleeve. "Not now, Becky! Don't start complaining. If it gets worse, we can see the ship's doctor when we get back. Hold my hand, I said!"

Jerria and Nan headed up the gravel path banking the glacial lake. Sunshine glinted on the milky water, the fog subsiding into wispy tendrils. At the water's edge a few hundred feet away, they saw a group of red kayaks slipping into the lake. Two tiny figures waved their paddles high over their heads.

"Charlie's been eager to get back in a kayak." Nan mused, "That woman's hand...I can't get those blisters off my mind. What would cause that? You don't think she's sick, do you?"

Jerria unzipped her jacket. "I remember when my kids were little, I had to use hand cream all the time. Washing my hands so often, being exposed to diaper wipes and who knows what all wasn't good for my skin. It's probably nothing."

Nan chuckled. "That might explain the mom, but no self-respecting girl that age would change diapers. Not willingly, anyway. I can't believe I'm here. This is gorgeous!"

"How do you say 'beautiful' in Hawaiian?"

"*Nani.* It's really not a big enough word for this glacier. The colors remind me of the Caribbean."

They paused to catch their breath, letting other hikers pass. Soon the trail led into a forest, and the glacier faded from view. Underbrush muffled the sounds of voices below.

"If I remember right, the waterfall is around the next bend." Jerria stuffed her scarf into her pocket. "And then it's uphill from there."

Nan caught her breath as they came to an opening in the forest. A handful of people milled around the cascading waterfall. One man pulled a crushed paper cup from his pocket. As he bent it back into shape, he exclaimed, "I've been waiting for this! Hey, everybody, did you know you can drink from any Alaska waterfall? Too cold for giardia!" He filled his cup and took a long drink. "Who wants a taste?" Hands reached for the paper cup.

Nan shuddered. "Even if the beaver-fever bacteria isn't in the water, heaven knows what germs they'll pass around on that cup. Come on, let's find the old mine."

Jerria led the way up the narrow trail, leaving the other tourists by the waterfall. After fifteen minutes of navigating steep switchbacks, they reached the abandoned mine, the end of the trail. She slumped on a fallen log, panting, rubbing her aching calves. A large rock pile blocked the abandoned mine in front of them. A rusty mine cart sagged on bent narrow-gauge tracks, long forgotten.

"Move over," Nan ordered. "You were right, this is amazing, and I'll look closer as soon as I can breathe again. I wasn't expecting the trail to be that steep."

They sat in silence for a couple of minutes. Nan shivered in the sunshine. "Can you feel that? Spirits, *uhane*, as if all the hopes and dreams of the miners are trapped in the mine. There was success here, long ago, but I feel a darkness as well."

Jerria nodded. "Imagine what the last person to walk away from that mine cart thought? The man who set the blasting caps to close off the mine; who was he? It's as if I can still hear the miners' voices, shouting to one another."

She giggled unexpectedly. "Another voice I can imagine is Will's, telling me to rein in my imagination. Come on, let's look around the bend. I want to take some more pictures before we head back down." She glanced at her watch. "Which we'd better do pretty soon, if we don't want to run for the shuttle."

The walk down was easier, and before long, they saw Mendenhall Lake glinting through the trees. Seeing no kayaks on the lake, they quickened their pace.

Will and Charlie waited on the low stone wall. They stood as the women approached. Will hugged Jerria. "Missed some excitement; saw it from the water. Ambulance came, sirens and lights, and hauled a couple of people away. Enjoy the hike, Honey?"

Jerria and Nan told about the waterfall and mine as they walked toward the shuttle drop-off point. A handful of people sat on benches, waiting.

Charlie shook his head. "I can't believe they shared a paper cup with that illness going around on the ship. Some people."

"Mom! I don't feel so good!"

Heads swiveled. The young girl they'd seen hours earlier cried out, then slid to the ground by the bench. Her father caught her arm, breaking her fall. Seconds later, her mother's knees buckled, and she silently collapsed to the stone walkway. The father stared at the thin trickle of blood from her head, as if he didn't know what to do next.

Jerria knelt, pulled a paper napkin from her jeans pocket, and pressed it on the unconscious woman's temple while Will dialed his cell phone. Charlie sprinted toward the Visitors Center, and Nan gathered the two younger children, pulling a sack of gumdrops from her jacket pocket. The man knelt between his wife and daughter, holding their hands, bouncing the baby on his chest. Helplessness sketched his face.

Long minutes later, an ambulance pulled up. The group stepped back, letting the EMTs load the unconscious pair onto gurneys. Lights flashing, its sirens shattering the stillness, the ambulance receded into the distance. The shuttle pulled in as soon as the ambulance drove off, and subdued tourists climbed aboard. Jerria wiped the fogged window, watching the bewildered father shepherd his children into a waiting taxi. As the bus turned the corner, Jerria saw a little face pressed against the taxi's window.

Chapter Twenty-Eight

"Strange goings on today," the driver called. "The *Ocean Journey* is sure keeping our paramedics hopping. A real plague ship, seems to me. Couldn't pay me to go on a cruise, no way, no how. Now, let me tell you about the best place to eat lunch, down by the pier. That crab shack is legendary! Best dill potato salad in the city, too, but you'd better not tell my mother-in-law I said that. I gotta live here, you know?" He kept a cheery banter on the way back to the pier, and the passengers' moods lifted.

Although it was early afternoon, fog still enshrouded the top of Mount Roberts. Stepping off the bus back in town, Jerria consulted her tour guide. They stood by a row of tour kiosks, debating what to do next. Will settled the matter. "Worked up an appetite on the lake. Lunch first, then gold panning, okay?"

Jerria eyed Will. He ate like their teenaged son, yet stayed slim as a rail. Life wasn't fair. "Lunch it is. Shall we try that crab shack the driver recommended?"

"No, I looked up the menu on my phone, and all they serve is crab, nothing Will would eat," Charlie said. "Anyway, I bet we can get good King crab just about anywhere in town."

A man in a plaid jacket called to them from a nearby Dogsled Tours kiosk. "Hey, if you're looking for a good local meal, my Aunt Ruth's place is the best. Two blocks up, and you won't leave hungry.

Crab and home-style stuff." His blonde dreadlocks shifted as he dug in his jeans pocket. "Here you go. The card's a little ragged, but, hey, it's Alaska. And after lunch, if you want, I can sell you a gold panning tour. Guaranteed color."

Nan wondered, "How do you guarantee we'll find gold?"

"Easy; they load the pans with dirt and salt a sprinkle of gold dust in them. That, and seven bucks, will buy you a burger in town."

They thanked him, laughing. Jerria took Will's hand as they walked.

The small restaurant was crowded, but a table soon opened up. An older woman wearing a green apron and wide smile handed them greasy menus. "Oh, did Jake send you? He's a good boy. I think he keeps his hair like that to annoy his mama." She pulled out a tablet and pencil. "How about some fresh King crab? Came in this morning. You, there, your nose is wrinkled." She winked at Will. "Not a seafood lover, is that your story? I have just the thing for you. Trust me, okay?"

They ordered King crab, and Will agreed to take his chances. As the woman bustled away, he grumbled, "Should have read the menu. Probably end up with some vegetable something or other with tofu in it."

Jerria took his hand. "Seems to me, you've been a little braver about food since you tried sweet beans shave ice in Honolulu. And there's dinner on the ship in a few hours. Would you look at the walls?

There are so many cards and photos, I can't even tell what's under there."

A man in a leather jacket at a nearby table offered, "Aunt Ruth gives a five per cent discount if you leave her something to hang up. Got a business card?"

"Good to know, thanks." Jerria smiled. "Have you heard a weather report? Is the fog supposed to clear? We're hoping to go up to Mount Roberts."

"Sorry, socked in all day, looks like, and more rain expected this afternoon." They chatted about the storm the ship had passed through. He said the winds had reached eighty-eight miles an hour a little north of Juneau. "Hurricane force, anywhere else, but here, it's just another storm."

Across the room, Gretchen nibbled a salad, her eyes on a magazine. Jerria wondered if her few hours of free time might improve her mood.

Soon their waiter carried a heaping tray to their table. Long red King crab legs overflowed the platter. Bowls of cole slaw, parsley-coated baby potatoes, and crusty rolls rounded out the family-style meal. "Back in a flash," she assured Will.

Returning to the table, she plopped down a plate in front of Will with a flourish. "That there is our famous Sled Dog, and a heap of rough cut fries. Two-thirds of a pound of homemade reindeer sausage in a big old sourdough bun. The green salad comes with it, but you don't look like a salad man to me."

She earned a grin from Will. She pulled a stack of paper napkins from her apron pocket. "Enjoy your crab, now. It's so messy, we ought to serve it in a kiddie pool, but we have plenty of napkins."

Will took an appreciative bite. "Woman after my own heart."

The others dug in, cracking crab like experts. Jerria said, "Will, you're missing out. This is delicious!"

Jerria noticed Gretchen's eyes scan the small restaurant as she paid her bill. She didn't acknowledge anyone, although Jerria recognized several patrons from the ship. After the meal, Jerria set her fork down. "I need to wash my hands. No wonder she gave us so many napkins."

As she stood, a sound like a thousand woodpeckers hammering on steel filled the building. At a glance, tourists stood out from locals, their eyes fearful.

"What on earth-?"

"Sit yourselves down now," the owner bellowed over the roar. "That's nothing but hail on the old tin roof. I know you all seen rain before, so don't get your sled dog line in a knot."

Jerria and Nan headed for ladies' room. Over the rainstorm's din, Nan raised her voice. "Might not be the best day for gold panning."

"I agree. Bad enough to be standing in a stream fed by melting snow, without getting rained on. How about touring the state capitol building? It was closed last time we were here. Alaska is a very young state, not far from frontier days, and it might be interesting."

Nan reached for a paper towel. "Good idea; I always like seeing where history happened. Let's go tell the guys."

As they approached the table, the man in the leather jacket rose and shook hands with Will and Charlie. "I think you'd enjoy that more than a lot of fancy shops, am I right?"

He nodded to Jerria and Nan and headed for the door. Will pushed his arm into his jacket sleeve. "Honey, gave us a great idea, since gold panning's out. Suggested a walk-through of the state capitol. It'll be dry."

Jerria laughed. "Great minds think alike."

The hail had turned to drizzle. "Just a few blocks, right? How do people live like this?" Nan pulled her jacket's hood up, stepping around a puddle. "At least the crowds have thinned out."

A man in a blue sweater held open the heavy wooden door to the capitol. "Would you like an official tour, or are you okay exploring on your own? On your own? Good. You're free to go anywhere you'd like, except the Lieutenant Governor's office. He's napping."

They hung their jackets on hooks in the foyer, then climbed the narrow stairs, heading for the empty House chamber. Half an hour later, they retrieved their jackets.

"Stopping here was one of our better ideas, perfect for a rainy day." Nan tucked her polka-dot scarf around her neck. "There's a raw, frontier feeling, as if those early strident voices seeped into the very woodwork."

"I didn't know the people raised money to build the capitol. Learning how Juneau came by its name was funny, too." Jerria zipped her jacket. "Imagine politicians bribing voters with beer the night before an election?"

"Not so far-fetched," Charlie said over his shoulder, heading down the stairs. "We do live in weird times. I thought the plaque about Sarah Palin was interesting. I don't know if she was vice-president material, but they sure loved her as governor. Imagine, a politician with an eighty-percent approval rating? Most days, you can't get eighty percent of any group to agree on anything, including what day of the week it is."

Grey clouds hung over the city as they emerged. Mount Roberts' top was still enshrouded. Jerria poked her head into a souvenir shop, and the others followed.

"Look at this." Charlie showed Nan a tiny vial of water with a bit of gold leaf floating in it. The vial read *Genuine Alaska Gold* in black ink. "Six dollars! Isn't this like the gold leaf you used on the mirror frame at home, Nan?"

"Probably, but it's the experience, the memory, that costs so much. Everybody knows about Alaska gold. Oh, look at this cute little stuffed puffin."

Will and Charlie wandered toward the hats in the back of the store. "I guess I can understand gold fever," Charlie said. "Take my brother-in-law. He started out playing a few hands of poker on Saturday nights. He won nine thousand dollars in one afternoon, and now it's his career. Believing the next pan will be the one holding a fortune, I can see how gold mining could turn into an obsession."

"Like shopping? Who buys all this stuff, anyway? Just about every item says *Alaska* right on it. Good marketing."

They met Nan by the cashier a few minutes later. She said Jerria had gone outside with a young woman. Nan paid for the puffin and grizzly bear sweatshirts she'd found for their granddaughters.

Jerria rushed in a minute later, and handed Will a large bag to carry. "Thanks. I mentioned I'd like to buy more muskox wool for my loom, and the clerk said her mother had some to sell. Feel how soft it is."

"Nice. What did it cost?" Will asked.

"You don't want to know. Making memories, remember?"

Charlie suggested, "Let's walk back to the ship, okay? It's not far, probably faster than waiting for the tram. Unless you're worn out from your hike."

On the half-mile walk back to the ship, Jerria told them about the woman who sold her the wool. "She said she picks tufts off bushes in springtime, when the musk oxen are shedding their winter fur. And look, she gave me a box of homemade candy. Let me rest a minute, and I'll share. My legs are killing me." Jerria passed the bag of caramels to Nan. "What's that commotion by the gangway?"

Chapter Twenty-Nine

Haywood's nasal voice carried across the pier. "Contract or no contract, they can't make me stay on a death ship. People are dropping like flies, hundreds of 'em, and that lady captain's hiding it from everybody. I'm afraid to eat or touch anything. Me? I'm outta here, catching a flight back to civilization."

A slim woman shifted a garment bag on her shoulder. "I know, can you believe it? That's why we're getting off. I heard there are no flights today, but I'll sleep on a park bench before I get back on that ship."

Strident voices rang out as Jerria and Will neared the ship. Passengers slowed their pace, while others leaned over railings on the ship above. A handful of people dragged luggage down the crew gangway, heads lowered. Jerria recognized the lead female singer, and assumed the others were entertainers as well.

From the top of the crew gangway, Gretchen shouted, "You can't walk off in the middle of your contract! You'll never work another day on any cruise ship– I'll see to that!" Several passengers stopped in their tracks. Maybe the entertainers knew more than they did.

The performers quickly loading their luggage into the backs of two vans, not looking back. Her face stormy, Gretchen watched the cabs ease down the pier. She kicked the wall and stomped into the ship.

"Perpetual tantrum, that woman," Will scowled.

"I wonder how they'll replace the production crew." Nan shifted her bag. "Maybe they'll hire locals, or hold a passenger talent show. We saw one on a cruise to Mexico, and it was surprisingly good."

Pointedly ignoring the commotion a few yards behind them, Liza and Gregg cheerfully greeted returning passengers at the bottom of the passenger gangway. "Welcome back, everybody! Who wants hot cocoa?"

Liza handed Nan a steaming paper cup. "Mrs Callister, I overheard your great idea! Super! I bet there's all sorts of talent onboard. I'll get a sign-up posted soon." She flipped her ponytail. "With your name at the top, naturally. You're from New Zealand or somewhere, right? I bet you do a mean hula."

"Hawaii. Alright, I can dance. After all, I'll never see the rest of the passengers after the cruise. If I make a fool of myself, it won't matter."

Jerria squeezed her arm. "Good attitude! I've seen you dance; you'll do great."

She craned her neck toward the front of the line, gauging how fast it was moving onto the ship. Four people carrying large grey duffle bags stood inside the doorway, showing their IDs on lanyards to the First Officer. John Hansson extended his hand to the first, but was rebuffed. She recoiled, offering a fist bump instead of a handshake. He nodded, his face solemn.

They left their things in their cabins, then met by the indoor pool, it's retractable roof closed. Will set down a dish of mini candy bars he'd snagged from the cafe. Nan sighed and wiggled her toes. "Ah, this feels like home, if I overlook the plastic plants and the big plaster elephant. It must be close to eighty-five degrees in here. I was so cold this morning, looking at the glacier, but it was wonderful. Charlie, I never asked; how was the kayaking?"

"Great! Different than Hawaii, for sure. We were able to get pretty close to the glacier's face. I've never had to maneuver around ice chunks before."

"Bergie bits. Those were *bergie bits.* Ice chunks are what slide off a snowy roof in winter." The ship's naturalist pulled up a chair. "May I join you? I led a walk this morning, and I'm frankly worn out. So many questions!"

"Sure, Joel, come join us. Listen, we've been wondering...do you know what's going on with the ship?"

"Another question!" He sighed heavily. "All I know is what I hear. The whole production crew quit, sound techs and all. Gretchen's team is scrambling to patch together some entertainment. Tonight's main show is canceled, but the piano bar singer is pretty good." He reached for a candy bar. "Cashew; my favorite. Doc Marsh is running ragged. He's an OB, for Pete's sake. He requested help, and four nurses came onboard today. His assistant said they're going nuts, trying to figure out what's making people sick. Me, I just keep washing my hands. So far, so good."

A heavy-set woman bustled to their table, dragging a little boy by the hand. "You, there, science man, tell my son here what you said about the dirty layers in the glaciers."

Joel stood reluctantly. "Duty calls." Walking toward the railing, he began, "As I said earlier, glaciers are formed by compressed snow, many hundreds of years of ice, and they move..."

Still full from their heavy lunch, the four decided to have a light dinner in the buffet as the ship sailed out of Juneau a couple of hours later. Holding her hands under the spray hand sanitizer at the entrance, Jerria raised an eyebrow. "What's going on here?"

The serving stations stood covered in plastic wrap. Crew members waited behind the platters of steaming food, serving utensils in hand. A handful of passengers took one look, and headed back to the elevators.

"Good evening." A smiling woman in a crisp uniform motioned to Jerria. "We're under red alert status, although the captain assures us there is no real risk. Tell me what you'd like, and I'll be happy to serve you."

Glancing at Will, Jerria said, "Let's see, I'd like some of that lentil soup, and the beef looks good..."

As she and the others settled into their chairs a couple of minutes later, a man nearby slammed his fist on his table. "What kind of a cruise is this? No salt and pepper shakers on the tables? If I wanted paper packets, I'd go to a fast food place. Who's in charge around here, anyway?" An officer hurried across the room, obviously hoping to quiet the passenger.

A flustered waiter set bottled water on their table, along with a basket of packaged dinner rolls. "Coffee? Tea? I can bring canned soda, if you'd like, but I'm sorry, there is no ice available."

Jerria thanked her. "It must be tough for you, dealing with crabby passengers."

"Yes, Ma'am," the waiter replied furtively, "But we're all doing the best we can."

After dinner, they decided to go listen to the piano bar singer, an Elton John impersonator, complete with glitzy costume and heels so high, Jerria marveled that he could use the piano's foot pedals at all. Within a few lines, he had every person in the packed lounge singing along.

Jerria leaned over to Nan between numbers. "Isn't it amazing, the details we keep in our minds? I haven't thought of these songs in years, yet all the lyrics come back. Think about all the numbers, passwords, and stuff we keep in our heads. It's no wonder people's names don't stick. Aunt Henrietta says memory is like a cup runneth over; things put in there years ago sink to the bottom. That's why we can remember lyrics to sing-alongs, but nobody remembers what they put their car keys."

"She sounds like a wise woman." Nan waved a bar server near. "We'd like four cans of lemon-lime sodas please, and I already know about the ice. Thanks."

Jerria headed for the ladies' room during the break. She paused before flushing. She didn't mean to listen in, but the heated voices, very low, perked her ears up.

"You crossed a line, woman. I won't have you barking at me in front of passengers like that, jerking your bag out of my hands like I was a thief. I just needed the key to the back office."

Gretchen?

"All I'm saying is, keep out of my bag. I have personal items in there, and I don't want your hands all over them. I can't risk losing my pen. Next time, ask."

Was that Liza's voice?

"I'm not interested in your stupid pen. You'd better watch yourself, I'm telling you."

Jerria heard the restroom door close. She flushed and stepped out. Washing her hands, she smiled in the mirror.

Liza straightened her collar, eyes averted. "Oh, Mrs D, I didn't know you were in here. I guess you heard that. Sorry about Gretchen; I just think I have a right to my privacy, you know?"

Jerria reached for a folded hand towel. "We're all a little on edge."

"I guess so..." Liza shook herself, then squared her shoulders, and reached for the door handle. "All the more reason to make tonight fun, right? Super!"

Jerria dried her hands slowly. What was up with Liza and her pen? She shrugged. Must be special to her, maybe an heirloom or a gift. Or it could be silly, like Will's favorite steak knife, one of a matched set of eight. Only he could tell the difference. She tucked a wayward curl over her eyebrow.

Liza moved to the piano, clapping her hands. "Your attention, please! Super. Our own Elton John's on his way back to the piano, but I wanted you all to be the first to hear about tomorrow night's entertainment. It's the *Ocean Journey's* first-ever passenger talent show, featuring you! Meet me in the theatre at four-thirty tomorrow if you'd like to audition." She scanned the crowded bar. "Not you, Mrs Callister, or you there, Cowboy Bob; you're guaranteed a place, no matter what. The rest of you, be thinking! Now, let's put our hands together for Joe the Entertainer!"

Jerria applauded with the rest. The singer had talent, no doubt, but her mind wandered. Elias and Penny hadn't come to the show, and they hadn't answered her phone calls earlier, either. She'd come to love the older couple.

I'll stop by their suite after the show, she decided. *I'll invite them to drive up into the Yukon tomorrow. Plenty of room for two more in the van, and they'll enjoy it.*

Her mind settled, she turned her attention back to the singer. *All those crystals and sequins; that collar alone must weigh a couple of pounds!*

Chapter Thirty

They waited in their seats after the final applause died down, letting the crowd disperse. Charlie asked, "What time do we need to meet tomorrow? The ship docks at 9 AM, right?"

"Yes, and we can pick up the rental can any time after nine-thirty. Sailaway is at 8 PM. We'll have plenty time to drive to Emerald Lake, and still see Skagway itself." Jerria sighed. "Wait'll you see the Yukon. The quiet is so thick, you can feel it. Would you rather see town in the morning, or drive north first?"

Nan said, "Let's drive first. That way, if we run short on time, we'll already be close to the ship."

"Good idea. Let's meet right at nine o'clock." Jerria stood and stretched. "If it's okay with you, I'd like to invite Elias and Penny along. Sitting in a van won't tire him out, and I think they'd love the drive."

"Sounds great! Charlie and I can stop by their cabin tonight. It's not too late."

"Okay, thanks. I think I'm getting a blister; the sooner I can kick off these shoes, the better."

Almost to their stateroom, Will stopped suddenly. "Uh, oh, what's going on?"

Jerria peered around his broad shoulders. Not far down the long corridor, two cabin doors had yellow Do Not Enter tape strung across them. Farther down, Jerria saw Dr Marsh and another crew member, bent over someone lying on the floor. He stood and walked toward them, his head lowered.

"Dr Marsh, can we do anything for you?" Will offered.

Startled, the doctor raised bleary eyes. "Oh, hi, there. I have to call for the fire team to carry her to the Med center. Must have set my radio down somewhere." He raked a hand through his hair. "I don't get it...over two dozen passengers have the same symptoms. I can't find a link. They collapse with no warning, and they all have a blue rash on their hands. I don't know..." Realizing he was rambling, he sighed. "Sorry. Excuse me; I need to make a call."

Jerria frowned, watching the doctor's retreating back. "Will, do you think we're safe?"

"As often as you wash your hands, Honey, no germ would dare attack you. The doc will figure it out. Let's see if there's a good movie on TV, okay?" Will squeezed Jerria's hand, then pulled out his room key.

Fifteen minutes later, Jerria jumped to open the door. Will clicked the television off as Nan and Charlie stepped in.

"Sorry to bother you, but we thought you should know." Nan pulled her shawl closer. "We went to Elias' cabin. Their suite and the one next door are blocked with that yellow Caution tape. I asked a steward in the hall about it, and he said they're under quarantine. I hesitate to call them. And did you see the same tape down our hallway?"

"Poor Penny! She must be so worried. Come sit down. We talked to Dr Marsh in the hallway. He sounded a little frantic." Jerria sat cross-legged on the bed in her green pajamas. "It's good tomorrow's another port day. He'll get some help, and we'll be away from the ship."

Charlie said, "I'm sure they'll get a handle on it. Meanwhile, we'd better get some sleep so we can enjoy tomorrow. I'm looking forward to the drive inland. I've only seen the coast of Alaska. Good night."

Jerria closed the door behind them. "Did you see Nan's eyes? I could tell she's thinking about omens and spirits." She shifted. "Can we skip the movie? I just want you to hold me close."

Chapter Thirty-One
Day Ten   Skagway

Jerria zipped her flowered sweatshirt, standing on the balcony as the *Ocean Journey* pulled into port the following morning. She'd been on the balcony nearly an hour, watching otters play in the water and the sun glinting on the short waves. It promised to be a beautiful day, once it warmed up.

Will came out onto the balcony. "Here, Honey, brought a banana and a carton of milk. Silly to skip breakfast. Tied up yet? A little ahead of schedule."

"Thanks. Look over there, to the left." She pointed down the pier to two ambulances and a van, doors agape. "They're waiting, like vultures."

As soon as the lines were secured, crew members slid the metal gangway from the ship to the pier. Uniformed EMTs walked briskly to its base, along with three people in scrubs. Jerria counted eight people on covered gurneys wheeled down the steep ramp by crew members, and two more in wheel chairs. A handful of passengers straggled behind, trailed by a line of uniformed cabin stewards toting luggage. Dr Marsh brought up the rear, and handed a stack of file folders to a woman on the pier.

"I see Penny! Oh, poor Elias!" Jerria's eyes filled with tears.

Will put his arm around her waist. "Honey, good thing. Get the care he needs."

Jerria buried her face in his shirt. "What kind of care can he get in a place this small? Does Skagway have a hospital? Ketchikan didn't even have a nurse until recently!"

After the ambulances and van drove away, they returned to their stateroom. Jerria picked up her jacket and a map, pausing to blot her mascara in the mirror. They entered the corridor just as Gretchen announced the ship had been cleared for passengers to go ashore.

Nan and Charlie met them a minute later. Nan's tan hat was cocked over one eye. "Let's go, I'm ready for adventure today. What a pretty day for exploring."

As they walked down the stairs to the gangway on deck three, Jerria told them about the ambulances. Charlie agreed with Will: the patients needed more care than a ship could offer. They'd seen three more cabin doors strung with the ominous tape.

Jill Marsh was ahead of them in the security line, grasping a twin's hand firmly in each of hers. "Boys, quit squirming! We have to wait our turn." Apologetically, she greeted the group. "They're not happy about the *Days of '49* show. I promised them colored popcorn if they behave in the theatre."

"Colored popcorn? I heard Skagway has more kinds than you've ever seen. It's worth being good for a treat like that." Charlie grinned at the boys. "Besides, you'll enjoy the show. We're going to see it later this afternoon. Did you know there's a real bad guy in it?"

Eyes wide, Jed and Jeremy stared at him. "Really?" they chorused.

"Yes, and some shooting, too. Don't give your mom a hard time, okay?"

Jill shot Charlie a grateful glance. "Thanks. Have fun today!" She slid their cards in the security slot, urging her sons down the gangway.

Nan sidestepped the photographer at the base of the gangway, a costumed goldminer holding an oversized gold pan. "Oh, the air smells wonderful here, mint mixed with pine. I can feel the history in the air."

They walked down the long pier, past tour buses, and onto the wide walkway into Skagway, chatting with other passengers. Spirits were high. Cowboy Bob and his wife were just ahead, and Jerria quickened her pace to reach them.

"Hi, there! Pretty morning, isn't it? What are your plans for today?"

Bob glanced at his wife, who kept her eyes averted. "Thought we'd take us a hike around old Dyea, if we can get a taxi ride out there."

Jerria offered to give them a lift. "Doubt you'll find many cabs in a town this small."

"Thanks, appreciate it." Cowboy Bob tipped his Stetson.

The six walked down wooden sidewalks, two blocks to the car rental place. Piling in, they headed inland, talking about the cruise so far. Cowboy Bob's wife stared out the window, silent. Jerria tried to get her to talk, remembering how assertive she was at the craft table. Maybe she only spoke when Cowboy Bob wasn't around.

Charlie eyed Bob's blue-tinted snakeskin boots. "Are you really going to hike in those fancy boots?"

"Yes, Sir, I aim to. I do nearly everything but swim in these things. My mama had them made for me. They was waiting for me when I came home. During my last tour of duty in the Middle East, I vowed I'd go back to living in my boots as fast as I could. Those government-issue boots are just not the same."

Soon they arrived at the ghost town. Cowboy Bob and his sullen wife climbed out. Lowering his voice, he confided to Will, "You gotta excuse my wife here. Since she met me in Istanbul for some R and R, then lost the baby, she's been a little bit of crazy. A quiet walk will do her some good." He assured the others, "We'll be fine, getting back to the ship. Got dinner plans for that fancy steak place onboard tonight. That's another thing about being home; I can eat whatever I please, cooked by people who know how to cook it. Thanks again for the lift."

Waving as they drove away, Will shook his head, his black hair falling over his eyes. "That is one appreciative young man. Poor woman. Acts like she's mad at the world and everybody in it."

"Maybe a calm hike will cheer her up. Let's not let her spoil the day." Jerria pulled out her map and guide.

Other than the tour buses, which they soon passed, they saw only one other vehicle. The White

Pass Railway clung to the side of the mountain like an HO scale trainset, pacing them. Before long, they arrived at the US-Canadian border crossing, where the railway stopped.

A lone border agent cheerfully greeted them from his booth, reaching for their passports.

Will joked, "Who did you make mad enough to exile you way out here?"

"How did you know?" The man's face reddened. "I admit I may have misplaced a file the boss needed on his way to the White House, but I love it here. Just look at my office!" He waved his hand, taking in the expanse of tree-covered mountains. "No deadlines, no stress, and I have the best view of any agent in America." He indicated a stone shed a few yards away. A slim porcupine strained to reach above its head, licking salt from the mortar.

The White Pass Railway broke the silence, its brakes screeching as it wrangled the siding, moving the engine on its way back to Skagway. The agent handed the passports back to Will. "Plus, I get transferred to a warmer climate once the snows fall. See those tall red poles? They mark the road during the winter. When it snows here, it *snows*. Have a good day, folks. I'll be here on your way back."

A mile down the road, they stopped at the Welcome to the Yukon sign. Three tour buses spilled passengers onto the gravel, all vying for the best photo angle. Will suggested they stop on their way back to the ship, after the scheduled tours had passed. Jerria had a detailed guidebook and map, and pointed out interesting things along the way. Stopping several times, they snapped photos of a silver mine, long since abandoned, waterfalls cascading from steep cliffs, prospector's shacks scattered higher up on the hills, old-growth cedars.

At a cry from Nan, Will pulled over. Across the two-lane road, something leaped at a small furry creature, threw its head back, gulped it down in one bite, then stared at the humans.

Nan gasped. "Poor little thing! It was eaten so fast, I bet its heart was still beating."

Will said, "At least it didn't have time to be afraid, whatever it was. That coyote is so fat and fluffy, not like the scrawny ones we see near home."

A few minutes later, Charlie called, "Stop, Will. Look, by that log. It's a grizzly!"

They watched the bear lumber into a berry patch, scooping up handfuls, oblivious to the van a few yards away. After a few minutes, it disappeared behind the bushes, and Will drove on.

Jerria consulted her guide. "Now, little ways farther, look on the mountainside on the right. There should be three Dahl sheep about three-quarters of the way up."

Charlie asked, "How on earth does the guidebook know how many sheep are in a particular place? Wait, there they are."

Will stopped the van alongside the road. "Three of them, alright."

Nan pulled out her binoculars, and burst out laughing. "Very funny! Here, take a look."

Charlie laughed, "They're fake! Plywood covered in fur, I think. I wonder how many tourists stop to see this."

"Add four more to that total." Will pulled back on the road.

A few miles farther, Will parked at a scenic overlook. Emerald Lake lay below them, its gemstone green water glistening in the sunshine. Climbing out, Nan whispered, "I can feel the silence, it's so thick. It's beautiful! I wonder what makes it that color."

Jerria read from the guidebook. "It says here it's caused by diatoms, the same kind found in the Caribbean. Wow, that's a good six thousand miles from here."

They walked down a gravel trail to the lake, admiring the gem-colored water nestled in a hollow. Jerria stretched her arms out and twirled slowly. "I love it here. Our home isn't exactly in a metropolis, but I can see why people would want to live out here."

Nan grinned. "It's gorgeous *now.* Did you see those snow markers lining the road? They had to be eighteen feet tall. Those early prospectors were tough people!"

"You have a point," Jerria conceded, "but it's wonderful today."

Charlie said, "I hate to leave, but we'd better head back. How about stopping for lunch at that bakery a few miles back down the road?"

Will agreed instantly; he was always up for a snack.

Jerria ruefully thought about her resolve to eat more sensibly today, then sighed. "Sounds great!"

A large wooden cut-out of a moose marked the bakery. "Eat Here Or We'll Both Starve" elicited grins as Will parked the van in the empty parking lot.

Nan commented, "Pretty optimistic location! Not many people pass by. Oh, look beyond the fence. Are those wild boars by the trees?"

An aproned woman swung open the screen door at the top of the steps. "Come on in! Are you hungry? I put some cinnamon buns in the oven not ten minutes ago."

"Great! Can we get some lunch while we wait?" Nan smiled.

"Sure, that's what I'm here for; saw your van coming a mile away. I can make you ham sandwiches on bread I baked this morning. My husband smoked the ham himself. We produce all of our food here, as much as we can. The good land provides. How about some nice white bean and hambone soup with your sandwich?"

Jerria's mouth watered. She settled in one of only eight wooden chairs, then asked about the boars. "Are they wild?"

"Yes, but you're not to worry about them. They come out of the woods this time of year, foraging for mushrooms. Later in the fall, they get more aggressive. Here, you rest a spell while I rustle up your lunch." The open kitchen was just a few steps away.

Jerria relaxed, taking in the teapots hanging on the wall, and displayed on open shelves. A few hung suspended from the window, making a porcelain valance of sorts.

Soon the woman brought steaming bowls of soup. "I saw you looking at my teapots. It's my mother-in-law. I guess she never got over her son selling his law practice to live up here. She says a teapot is a sign of civilization, and every time she visits from the lower forty-eight, she brings us another one. Coming out my ears, I tell you." She set a stack of calico napkins on the table. "Eat up while it's hot."

Before they'd finished the thick soup, the woman set down sandwiches, bursting with ham and spicy sliced radishes. "Four minutes left on the oven timer. You got room for a cinnamon roll, or do you want me to pack them up for the road?"

"Packed, please. I don't think we could eat them after all this, but we'll enjoy them later on." Jerria surveyed her sandwich. "I'm not sure I can even finish this much."

"Give it a good college try," the woman smiled. "I hope you like it."

They ate, relaxing in the warmth of the tiny bakery. Jerria and Nan couldn't finish the sandwiches. Will and Charlie both gobbled theirs, then ate a frosted sweet roll. Jerria wondered for the thousandth time how Will could eat so much, yet stay so slim. It wasn't fair.

Carrying a white box with four warm cinnamon rolls, Jerria thanked the baker and headed toward the van. She stopped to watch the wild boars some yards away.

Nan paused beside her. "That ham was delicious! But I've been thinking about those boars. You don't think the good land provided..."

Charlie laughed. "Don't think about it. I've seen you eat a lot worse things in Hawaii." He turned to Will. "On our first date, she ordered some kind of larvae as an appetizer, alive on a leaf. I was afraid the thing was going to crawl off my plate!"

Will grimaced. "Ew! What did you do?"

"First date, trying to make a good impression, didn't think I had much choice, so I ate it, fast as I could. I think I still felt it wiggling a week later."

Nan laughed. "It wasn't my favorite thing, either. I'd never dated a *ha'ole* before. I wanted to see how a mainlander would react. If Charlie could keep a straight face over that, he had potential."

Laughing, they climbed into the van and headed south. Jerria pointed out sights in her guide book as Will drove toward Skagway. Before long, they arrived at the Welcome to the Yukon sign, now deserted.

Jerria sighed happily. "I'm so glad we rented a car. I feel sorry for all those people crammed on buses. I'm enjoying being with three of my favorite people."

She glanced at her watch. "It's only one– twenty, more than seven hours before sail away.

Another half hour to town, then we'll have plenty of time for wandering and shopping. I read about a walking tour that looked good to me."

"The tour sounds great; we like to soak up local flavor, like you and Will." Charlie's nose wrinkled. "But shopping... Maybe Will and I can get some colored popcorn instead."

Jerria laughed. "There's a little shop at the edge of town with the best prices I've seen in Alaska. We'll be quick, I promise. And we'll go there last, so we don't have to carry stuff around, okay?"

Nan smiled, "Is that the place with the moose hand puppets? It's been on my mind since you mentioned it."

"Yes, and cute little stuffed sled dogs, too. Your granddaughters would love them. Can we get one more photo in front of the sign, with all of us in it?"

Chapter Thirty-Two

Back in Skagway, they joined a walking tour leaving the National Park office. The ranger was a born storyteller. She said the early miners were "long on hope, short on preparation." Jerria gazed at the sturdy mountains, envisioning the trek leading up to White Horse Pass, where so many had died seeking gold. She shivered, pulling her sweatshirt closed.

Jerria loved a good storyteller, and the ranger was one of the best. Within a few sentences, she had them engrossed in Soapy Smith's exploits. The last of the big-time western bad men, Soapy was a con man who took over Skagway during the winter of 1897-98. Through a combination of charm, skill, and guile, he soon controlled an underworld of more than two hundred gamblers, swindlers, and thugs.

The small group stopped in front of a small wooden building. "This was the slick, fast-talking, low-life flimflammer's office, where much of his nefarious dealings went on. His main occupation was mining the gold miners, making money off them any way he could devise, and he was a sly one."

"One thing the homesick prospectors were desperate for was communication with the folks at home. That scoundrel set up a telegraph system, charging exorbitant fees for messages sent, paid in gold up front. Of course, the telegraph operator was one of his men, and he wrote down and dutifully keyed in the precious messages. If the miners told their kinfolk they were bust, they sent them on their way. But if a miner sent word home that he'd found gold, Soapy's men would follow the prospector to his claim, and I don't mean for afternoon tea."

"Either way, the cost of sending a message home was outrageous." She pointed to an exposed wire protruding from the roofline. "And as you can see, it was no system at all, just another of Soapy's scams. The messages didn't reach back east; they barely cleared the roof."

"Poor people, to be that desperate, and with little recourse!" a woman choked out.

The ranger agreed. "Skagway and Dyea were a long way from the delicate city life most prospectors left to seek the gleam of gold, and bad actors were abundant. Soapy Smith's power seemed almost limitless until July 8, 1898, when the townspeople finally had enough. Surveyor Frank Reid lured the old charlatan into a trap, and they ended up shooting it out on one of the town's docks. We'll head there now, and I'll tell you the rest of the story. Walk this way, please."

At the end of the tour, they thanked the ranger and the group dispersed. They walked down the wooden sidewalk, stopping in front of the Arctic Brotherhood building. The front of the building was covered in driftwood, with the organization's symbol, a gold pan and nuggets, near the roofline.

Nan read from a brochure she'd picked up at the ranger station. "It says here the local chapter of the Brotherhood first met here in August 1899. 'Harley

Walker and his fellow lodge members collected over 8,800 driftwood sticks on the shores of Skagway Bay and nailed them to the front wall.' That's a lot of driftwood—none of these pieces are very big." She continued, "'The Arctic Brotherhood Hall is the most photographed building in Alaska.'"

Jerria asked, "How do they know that? I read that Deception Pass in Washington is the most photographed bridge, but who keeps track? We'd better head to the theatre. The show starts in about fifteen minutes."

They glanced in old-time storefronts on the way. Jerria paused outside the theatre to read a handbill pasted on the wall.

The Days of '98 Show has it all: live music, singing and dancing, love and rejection, comedy and melodrama, and truly brings Skagway's colorful history to life. It's been a Skagway tradition since 1925.

They bought tickets and made their way to seats in the second row of the small, dusty theatre. Actors dressed as dance hall girls scanned the audience for a male volunteer. Will cast a glance at Jerria. *Don't do it.* She winked.

Will and Jerria had a long-standing policy never to offer the other's services. A few months after they moved to Hat's Mill, Will's new friend on the town council mentioned he was desperate for help with the town's Celebrate Summer Festival. It seemed the chairwoman recently found out she was expecting twins and needed to take it easy.

Confident in his young wife's ability, Will said Jerria could pull it off, no sweat. Jerria, plenty busy with landscaping their new backyard, tearing down the ugly wallpaper in the upstairs of their Victorian house and dealing with the major kitchen remodel, plus caring for their two little children, saw it differently. Not wanting to let the town down, she stepped up, and the festival was a great success.

To get back at Will, she sweetly mentioned to the Church choir director how much Will loved to sing; all he lacked was some encouragement. The enthusiastic choir director, Mabel, hounded him mercilessly, until he was forced to attend choir practices. After a few, even Mabel agreed that the joke was on her; Will had a good heart, but his singing voice didn't match. Will and Jerria agreed never to volunteer each other again.

A woman they recognized from the ship pushed her husband onstage. A couple of the "fancy ladies" led him up the rickety wooden stairs. Near the end of the play, he reappeared on stage, looking sheepish, festooned in feather boas and lipstick while his wife's camera clicked.

Will whispered, "Blackmail material. And after making a fool of himself, and missed the whole melodrama."

After the show, they headed into the theatre's lobby, where the actors posed for photos. Most of the audience swarmed them, cameras in hand. Will steered around the dancing girls, stopping to examine a framed photo of the famous con man.

Jerria greeted the man who played Soapy Smith. "Thanks," she said. "You did great, really made the character come alive."

"Glad you enjoyed it." The actor twirled his handlebar mustache. "Thirteen years, three shows a day when the ships are in port, and I can say it never gets old."

"May I ask what you do when ships are not here? Do you live in Skagway full-time?" Jerria was a people-person, always interested in the background of anyone she met.

"I'm a high school teacher: math, science, chemistry, biology." Seeing Jerria's surprise, he smiled. "Skagway has less than a thousand year-round residents, and close to a hundred students, kindergarten through high school. It's hard to believe it's that small when a cruise ship or two are in town."

"Come on, Larry, we've seen all there is here. I want to buy that moose-poop tee shirt before they sell out. It's a hoot."

Jerria stepped aside as a woman pushed by. "But, with that few students, how do you manage to teach? You can't have much of a class discussion with so few students."

"Soapy Smith" smiled. "Ah, Alaska's not like the lower forty-eight. The schools have great funding from the oil money, and we're loaded with high-tech options. My kids video chat all day long. I may only have one chemistry student in person, but I link to others across the state. Teacher-student ratio is 1:10, so we have plenty of interaction." He snapped his suspenders, slipping back into his role as Soapy Smith. "Ma'am, so long as I'm in charge around here, I can promise you the children of this fine city get the very best of modern education." With a wink, he said, "Actually, students who transfer anywhere in the lower forty-eight often find themselves a year or more ahead of their classmates. And I brainwash them into going to college, too, as much as I can."

Another patron pulled at his arm, asking for a photo with "Soapy Smith". He bowed to Jerria. "Excuse me. Pleasure to meet you."

Stepping out into the sunshine, Nan wrapped her scarf around her neck. "Jerria, I'm glad you scouted out the melodrama. After the show and the walking tour, I feel like I really know Soapy Smith, the old *pilau ka'ne*. Are we ready to do some shopping?"

Jerria giggled. "I don't know what you said, but it sounded bad."

"No, 'bad' is *maika`i`ole*. I said he was a stinker. Come visit us in Hawaii soon; I'll teach you a whole new language."

Charlie and Will decided to stop in the fudge shop. They'd meet the women in the last shop at the end of the wooden sidewalk, where Jerria had found bargains on their last trip.

With two cruise ships in port, the normally small town was bursting at the seams. Jerria dodged a woman loaded down with shopping bags. "Either she took a head start on Christmas shopping, or the bargains are better than I recall."

Soon they entered the small store, teaming with tourists. Nan surveyed the heaped baskets, overflowing with stuffed animals, hematite jewelry, ubiquitous tee shirts, and other Alaska-themed goods. "You weren't kidding! I already see a dozen things I want, and I haven't even closed the door yet. That's a great price on sweaters."

Jerria chose a set of soft finger puppets for her grandson. Rowdy would enjoy the sled dog, moose, puffin, grizzly, and otter. She chose a sculpted salmon for her bookshelf at the real estate office, then moved to the kitchen supplies aisle.

Nan called from the next aisle, "Jerria, this is adorable! Look, it's a stuffed porcupine, like the one we saw licking the border agent's shed. The girls would love it. What do you think about the ulu? Should I get this one, or the bigger one?"

"Get one like you used in Ketchikan; you seemed comfortable with it. Or maybe both, for that price. Did you see these wooden salad tongs with the carved eagles on them? They're like the ones Lillian had, and they're only four dollars."

"May as well buy them," Will said behind her. "Spent more than that on fudge. Want me to hold some of that, Honey?" He took Jerria's hand basket, leaving her hands free.

Jerria suggested Will go pick out a couple of cambric shirts; the color would highlight his eyes, and the price couldn't be beat. Charlie followed, in search of a wide-brimmed hat. Before long, the four friends met near the front of the store. Nan had three sweaters over her arm, and a string of glossy black hematite necklaces hanging from her left wrist. She shifted her heaping shopping basket in a futile effort to keep the magnetic stones from tangling.

"Are we ready to check out?" Jerria asked, giving the shelves one last glance. At a nod, they joined the end of the line of shoppers.

s if composed by an alien symphony, cell phones ringers sounded, dozens at once. Someone dropped a glass vase, sending shards across the floor.

Jerria dug in her pocket. Will, Nan, and Charlie all reached for their mobile phones at the same time. The clerks pulled their phones from under the counter. On every aisle, customers' eyes riveted on little screens. Ship passengers read the mass text message, turning stricken faces to one another.

A woman cried, "Harry, what are we going to do?"

Chapter Thirty-Three

As if choreographed, people came to life, their voices rising, sharp with concern.

Jerria glanced at Will. "I've never seen a ship's emergency warning system by text before. What does it mean, do you think?"

He shrugged. "Just says the ship needs to sail three hours early; doesn't say why. Probably a mechanical issue, nothing to worry about."

Nan's eyes flitted across the sea of murmuring shoppers. "They look worried to me. Maybe we'd better head back right away." She set her heaped shopping basket aside.

"Now, they don't know any more than we do. Maybe the captain wants to outrun another storm. The ship leaves in ninety minutes. That's plenty of time for us to buy this stuff and finishing looking around town. Colored popcorn, remember?"

"That worked to calm Dr Marsh's kids, Charlie, but I'm not in the mood for popcorn." Lines of concern etched her face. "We'd better head back soon. If something's wrong, I don't want to be last onboard."

Jerria touched her arm. "Good idea, but we have plenty of time. Let's buy this stuff first. We can wander through the train station Visitors Center on our way back to the ship."

Nan squared her shoulders. "Okay, that's a good compromise. Go on, Jerria, the clerk is free."

After they paid for their items and headed out into the street, Jerria stopped. "Listen. The atmosphere has changed, it seems to me."

She was right; all along the boardwalks, people clustered together, their shoulders hunched, talking about the message from the *Ocean Journey*. Along the gravel path to the ship, she could make out a thin line of people snaking toward the ship.

A couple stepped around them. "Hey, lady, get a move on! Didn't you hear the ship's leaving early? I heard an earthquake is coming, and the captain wants to be out at sea when it hits."

"An earthquake? Oh, no! That'll trigger a tidal wave, and we'll all die. Come on, we need to run!" A man dropped his shopping bags, took his child's hand, and raced down the sidewalk, pushing people out of his way.

"Run, run for your lives!" Others joined the panic, shouting and running toward the pier.

Nan grasped Charlie's hand. "I know there's no way to predict an earthquake, but what if something bad *is* coming?"

Charlie squeezed her arm. "The only thing we need to worry about right now is not getting trampled. They're acting like sheep, running around crazily, without even knowing why. Let's let the crowd get out of the way, then we'll head back to the ship calmly."

Jerria had little faith in rumors, but she was glad to see Nan's attention was on Charlie. She stopped to talk to Liza, who was standing near a storefront a few feet away.

"Liza, you look lost in thought. Any idea what's going on with the ship?"

Liza startled. "Oh, sorry! I was just thinking about jelly and stuff. Did you see the eagles circling overhead?"

"Jelly? Gosh, you're like Will, thinking about random foods." Jerria shifted her bag. "Do you know why the ship is sailing early?"

Liza shrugged. "Oh, I don't know. Nothing official, that I've heard. Of course, I might have missed it. I spent my day getting hollered at by Gretchen. She's sure touchy about where stuff is set in the staff closets! I'm her assistant, and that should give me some say-so. By the time I finished, I barely had time to come onshore at all."

"Sorry, I shouldn't be complaining." She shook her head, her usual enthusiasm restored. "Goodness, Mrs Danson, it's no big deal, just a lot of hooey about some people getting sick. People get sick all over the world. Worst case scenario, the cruise line will cancel the next few sailings. That'd be super news for me. I might get transferred to another ship, away from the dragon lady."

She shifted her packages. "I'd better head back to the ship. How long can Gretchen keep up that sweet act in front of the senior staff, anyway?" Liza flashed a sudden grin over her shoulder as she walked away.

"Let it go, Honey." Will took Jerria's bags. "Let's enjoy our last bit of time in Skagway. Plenty of time to hit that bakery over there. Wonder if they have donuts. Could go for a cream-filled something."

Nan released a breath. "I guess you're right. There'll be a long line at the gangway by now. I doubt Alaska has anything like a Hawaiian *malasada*, but the bakery it is."

They crossed the street, and pushed open the glass door to the bakery. A few customers sat at small round tables. Frosted donuts filled glass display cases.

Jerria breathed in the warm, sweet air filling the steamy shop. "Mmm. Good call, Will. I'd like some hot cocoa and ...oh, it's going to be hard to decide!"

A clerk interrupted. "Which ship are you from?"

Puzzled, Jerria responded, "*The Ocean Journey*. I'd like a–"

"Whatever you want, it has to be to go. I heard the ship is leaving port to get away from some terrorist attack, and I'm not going to have a bunch of passengers stuck in my shop. I close at five o'clock, sharp, no matter what. Now, what do you want?"

Cowed, the four ordered drinks and a donut, each, then walked outside.

Will pulled out his Boston cream donut. "Strangest thing; whole town's on edge. Furthermore, this donut is stale. Travesty!"

Jerria laughed. "Mine's not good either, but I see you're still eating yours. The Visitors Center is this way, isn't it?"

They made their way to the White Pass and Yukon Railway station. With fully half of the tourists in town already on their way back to the *Ocean Journey*, the sidewalks were no longer mobbed.

"After seeing that trail over White Pass, I have to respect those gold seekers," Jerria said. "Look at this photo; it's a human traffic jam. The conditions were unbearable!"

"Jerria, wasn't one of the twigs on your family tree a gold-miner up here? Remember you and Great-Aunt Henrietta talking about that last year."

Jerria paused. "Oh, I had forgotten! Yes, she was a shirt-tail relation at best, but it's a fine story. As I recall, she and her husband came to Alaska with the rest of the forty-niners, but he died soon after they arrived. She and her sister set up a pie shop; a tent, really, in Dyea, charging prices Soapy Smith would have been proud of. The miners were hungry for any taste of home. I think they only stayed a year, before moving back south. I'll have to ask Henrietta for more details when we get home."

"Which we won't do if we miss the ship."

By the time they reached the *Ocean Journey*, only a few people lingered at the base of the gangway. Two state police cars parked near the security checkpoint, the officers deep in conversation with Captain McCann. Her face stern, she pressed her point.

"I said, they're crew members, not prisoners. I can't force them to stay onboard against their will. As far as I know, it's all four children's program leaders, and sixteen of the galley staff. You don't understand. My people are scared. I don't know how much longer I can keep it from the passengers."

Jerria knelt to tie a shoe that didn't need tying, straining to hear the officer's response. Charlie and Nan slowed their pace, Will leaning on a post.

"Captain, I'm sorry, Ma'am, but our hands are tied. My orders are to get your ship loaded up and out of port as soon as possible. You know those CDC folks are on their way. Until they say different, you're under quarantine, the whole ship." The officer held up his hand, motioning for silence while he cocked an ear to his radio. "Captain, I'm sorry, but you heard that well as I did. Your whole ship, crew and passengers alike, is on a no-fly list until we get this sorted out. Don't be getting any ideas about sneaking your people off. Skagway's a small town."

"Good call," his partner nodded firmly. "No way of telling what kind of awful contamination you're carrying. We don't want any of that here. You bossy characters from the Lower Forty-Eight; I don't trust you as far as I could throw a baby grand piano."

Captain McCann hissed, her face inches from the officer's. "What am I supposed to tell my crew? I don't want a panic. You're blowing this out of proportion. Only one death so far..."

Captain, Ma'am, please get back on your ship, and take your people with you." He raised his voice. "Everybody, move along. We need the ship out of port as soon as possible." A handful of passengers and crew hurried toward the gangway, including the doctor's family.

Jerria stood, locking eyes with Captain McCann. The officer stared back, then turned on her heel and stalked up the gangway. "Will, what should we do? Should we get on the ship, or try to stay here?"

Charlie put his arm around Nan. "I don't think we have much choice. You heard him; we can't get a flight out. I doubt there's much lodging in town."

Nan shivered. "Can we rent a car? We could drive to Whitehorse, maybe fly out of there. Or take the Al-Can into BC?"

Jerria said slowly, "There were only three rental cars in Skagway. I don't think that's an option." She gathered her shopping bags and headed for the gangway, smiling.

Liza stood at the bottom of the ramp, unshaken, misting passengers' hands with disinfectant. "Everybody had a good time in Skagway? Don't miss the talent show tonight in the theatre. It's going to be great!"

Jerria frowned. "Liza, aren't you concerned? The ship's sailing early, people are sick..."

A white unmarked station wagon drove slowly up the pier, stopping near the state patrol cars. Five people wearing scrubs stepped out, and gathered briefcases and luggage from the rear hatch. Before they moved toward the ship, each put on a green surgical face mask and plastic eye protection.

A woman nudged Jerria from behind. "Move along, will you? With all that yellow tape they're stringing up down there, we're better off getting on the ship. I don't like the look of that police officer's face. He's liable to arrest us all on a whim. The last thing we need is to be marooned here with no way out."

"Yes, come along, everybody; let's get back to our fabulous cruise on the *Ocean Journey!* The bars are open, there's live music on the pool deck, don't waste your afternoon standing here. Don't forget the auditions for tonight's talent show. Super."

Retrieving her bag from the security conveyor belt, Jerria took Will's hand. "Did you hear Liza? She doesn't seem upset at all."

"Move, everybody!" Gretchen called from the corridor. "Captain McCann wants us out of the berth in a hurry."

Jill Marsh touched her arm. "Gretchen, I can't get in touch with my husband. Honestly, is it safe to be on the ship?" Concern etched her face.

"Oh, you, too? I expected better from you, Mrs Marsh." Gretchen briskly assured her, "People are overreacting. The quarantine status just means we'll have to stay at sea, but so what; we're already going to Hubbard Glacier tomorrow. They'll figure this out before you know it."

Turning to the slow-moving line of passengers, she barked, "Move along, move it, get on the ship already. Ignore those foolish people turning back. Would you rather enjoy your cruise, or be stuck in a one-horse town?"

A man joked, "One horse? No, I saw two horses pulling a trolley through town."

"Hey, that's funny!" a young woman giggled. "Too bad the comedian didn't hear you. He needs fresh material."

Jerria knit her brow. Where was Haywood now? He wasn't involved somehow, was he?

Chapter Thirty-Four

As Jerria hung up her jacket in the cabin, the familiar gong signaled an announcement. Will propped open the cabin door so they could hear better. Gretchen's voice filled the corridor.

"We'll be leaving beautiful Skagway in a few minutes, on our way to the lovely Hubbard Glacier. Tomorrow is a relaxing sea day. Be sure to take advantage of the shops onboard. And meet with Liza for the open audition at four o'clock sharp in the theatre for tonight's talent show."

Her voice lowered. "And seriously, folks, this illness is no big deal, so don't get all bent out of shape. Only one person has died so far, an old man in his nineties, probably well past his expiration date. Have a great evening on the wonderful *Ocean Journey*."

Stricken, Jerria's eyes filled. "Oh, no...Will, the old man...you don't think...?"

Will put his arms around her. A minute later, he rose in response to pounding on their door. In tears, Nan ran to Jerria. Charlie stepped in behind her.

"It was Elias! Griffin just told me he's the one who passed away!" Sobbing, the women clung to one another.

Charlie blew his nose. "Griffin said they're calling it a cardiac event. Event...sounds like a church picnic."

Jerria reached for a tissue. "Poor Penny. What will she do, alone and so far from home?" She choked back another sob. "I...I didn't get to say goodbye..."

Gretchen stood silent under John Hansson's wrath. The First Officer had tracked her down in front of the Staff closet behind the theatre. She tried to block out his onslaught over the way she'd announced the old man's death, but she couldn't ignore his parting words.

"Captain McCann is furious. The passengers are all on edge, and you made it infinitely worse. They need a distraction. Tonight's talent show had better be the best ever, or consider yourself relieved of duty. For now, we'll call it probation."

Gretchen glared at the officer's retreating back, then slammed the closet door against the wall. "Passengers! They do love to strut their stuff, as if anyone else cares. Mr Hansson has no idea what I'm going through; he's only a new guy." She gathered eight decks of cards from the shelf, and reached deeper for another carton. "Bad enough I have to do the stupid horse race game while Liza's auditioning the show-offs; now she forgot to restock the prizes. What is she, a vending machine?" She banged the door shut, nearly breaking her key in the lock. "And what kind of fools keeps everything wrapped in plastic? I'll get her off my ship, if it's the last thing I do."

Jerria didn't feel like eating dinner. The pervasive odor of disinfectant turned her stomach. While Will went to find something quick to bring back, she sat on the balcony, wrapped in a blanket. Twilight wasn't far off. The gauzy sun hung low in the sky like a living thing, the hazy orb resentfully ordinary, unconcerned about the troubled ship cutting through the black sea below. A single tear trailed down her cheek. She admired Nan, who still intended to go through with her dance at the talent show. If not for her friend performing, she'd prefer staying in the cabin.

How could Elias be gone? His warm wit, his deep love for Penny, that amazing memory...Another tear dripped off her chin. *Murdered, that nice old man. What am I doing on another cruise ship?* She blotted her tear, hearing the cabin door open. *I want to go home.*

"Will, I'm out here."

Will came onto the balcony with Charlie. "Here, Honey, brought you a cup of chicken soup. Good for the soul."

"Hi, Jerria. Nan went ahead to the show, and I wondered if you'd mind if I hang out with you two until it's time to go."

"Of course. It's not a good time for any of us to be alone. How's Nan?"

Charlie sat in the wicker chair. "Shook up, like the rest of us. I suggested she forget the talent show, but she insisted. She said, 'Maybe it'll soothe a soul or two,' and if anyone can do it, it's Nan. Since she's been teaching hula at the rec center at home, she didn't need to practice. She made a paper flower for her hair, grabbed a couple of her sarongs and took off."

Jerria smiled faintly. "Must be nice, to get dressed with only a length of fabric and a strategic knot. Nan always looks good. Do you know what she's dancing?"

"She said it'll be a healing performance, but I'm not sure what that means. Hey, while I was getting dinner, I overheard two servers talking. They said a bunch of passengers missed the ship in Skagway. I wondered if that cowboy and his wife, hiking out by Dyea, made it back. Did they have a cell phone? How would they hear the emergency message out that far?"

"Dyea's a ghost town, what's left of it. I wondered about them getting a taxi back, too. We were smart to drive out of town early in the day."

An hour later, the theatre came alive, as if the audience hadn't a care in the world. Laughter hung in the air, as the bearded man took a bow. A passenger bellowed from the audience, "You're a lot funnier than that dumb comedian they hired!" Others shouted agreement. Wiping his brow, the young man exited, stage left. Next up was a duet singing a medley of 1950's songs, followed by a ten-year-old tumbler.

As the applause faded, Liza stepped onto the stage. "Thanks, everybody, for coming tonight. I told you we had a lot of talent on the ship! Super. Our concluding act is Nan Callister, all the way from Hawaii. Watch her hand motions; hula tells a story, just like the totem poles."

Passengers quieted. As the house lights dimmed, a single spotlight puddled on the stage.

Stepping into the pool of light, Nan raised a graceful hand. Jerria smiled at the red paper hibiscus tucked behind her left ear; leave it to Nan to improvise a flower! Seemingly unaware of anyone in the theatre, Nan exuded an exotic air even before the off-stage ukulele's notes began. Tapping her bare heels, Nan slowly swirled to the left, then back to the right. The blue flowered sarong flowed over her hips as she gently swayed to the haunting Hawaiian music spilling through the theatre. Her arms spread, hands in constant fluid motion, her body told a story of love and hope, a life fulfilled, mourning and sorrow, love beyond measure.

Jerria sat on the edge of her seat, her eyes riveted on Nan. *Amazing, how a simple dance can take in the fear we all feel, and hope. She's even portraying Elias. I wish Penny could see this.* The theatre was silent other than the soft strumming of the ukulele, the audience in rapt attention.

Nan extended her arms, encompassing the theatre, then swept down and left, as if giving her soul to the earth itself. Reaching high over her head, she pulled down the strength of the heavens, cradling it against her chest, releasing it into the audience. Jerria heard a sharp intake of breath behind her. Circling slowly, Nan outstretched her arms, dipping low into a lingering bow as the melancholy music faded.

The audience sat hushed, stunned by the beauty of Nan's dance, touched by grief and a bit of fear. Jerria heard sniffles and a few whispers. "The old man...Life goes on...We'll be all right."

Seconds later, a stagehand ran and handed a microphone to Nan. The familiar notes of "Aloha O'e" rose and swelled. Nan smiled broadly, her clear voice flowing over the audience. The lyrics flashed on the screen above the stage, and Nan motioned the audience to join in. Several passengers rose, and soon everybody was on their feet, swaying, singing, wiping tears.

Aloha ʻoe, aloha ʻoe
Farewell to thee, farewell to thee
E ke onaona noho i ka lipo
The charming one who dwells in the shaded bowers
One fond embrace,
One fond embrace,
A hoʻi aʻe au
'Ere I depart
Until we meet again
Until we meet again.

The music faded, and the audience stood in profound silence. A long moment later, someone clapped, and the theater thundered with applause and whistles. Nan bowed playfully. As Liza came from behind the curtains, Nan pulled the paper hibiscus from her hair. She reached to tuck it behind the assistant cruise director's ear, but hesitated, unsure which side was appropriate.

Liza laughed, taking the flower in her hand. "I'm not married yet, but I'll be wearing a flower behind my left ear before long. Wasn't Mrs Callister wonderful? Super. Thanks, everybody, for coming out. Don't forget the dance floor is open in the SunSun Lounge with the fabulous house band. Let's have another round of applause for our super incredible talent!"

Chapter Thirty-Five
Day Eleven   Hubbard Glacier

Warm water spilled over Jerria's aching body. She'd barely slept, fighting thoughts that raced like hamsters on a wheel. Why hadn't Cowboy Bob performed last night at the talent show, as planned? Had he and his wife missed the ship? Where was Penny now? The cruise line would assist her in getting home, along with Elias' body, but how would she manage all alone? *Coming on this cruise was a bad idea. After the episode in Hawaii, I should have known better.* She leaned against the shower wall, hot tears streaming down her wet cheeks.

Will knocked on the bathroom door. "Jerria, Gretchen made an announcement. Wasn't sure you could hear it with the shower running."

Jerria turned off the water, blotted her face, and propped the door open with her bare foot. "Thanks, I missed it. What did she say?"

"Just said Captain McCann would say something in ten minutes."

Jerria wrapped a towel around herself, disdaining the bathrobes provided by the cruise line. "We'd better turn on the TV so we can hear the captain."

While they waited, Jerria dressed in jeans and a forest green sweatshirt and swiped on mascara. Will watched her from the sofa, his eyes soft. She was every bit as beautiful as the woman he'd married almost twenty-eight years ago, and twice as spunky. She caught his eye in the mirror and smiled.

Two loud clangs rang through the ship. Jerria blotted her wet curls with a plush towel. "That gong! Nobody has an excuse for not hearing that."

She settled back against Will. Captain McCann's face appeared on the television. "Will, look at her expression. I've never seen her so solemn."

"Looks like she hasn't slept in days."

Captain McCann stood on the bridge, two senior officers flanking her. "Good afternoon, *Ocean Journey* guests. I trust you had a good day in Skagway yesterday. Thank you for making the effort to come aboard early. That move was unprecedented for me, but I felt it necessary under the circumstances." She drew a deep breath. "Which brings me to the meat of our issue. First, let me assure you everything is under control, so there's no need to panic. Let me say what I have to say, then I'll be available at nine-thirty in the theatre to answer further questions. I urge you to remain calm."

Jerria sat upright. "What is she saying?"

"Don't know, but wish she'd spit it out."

"As you may know, some of our guests have fallen ill. Dr Marsh assures me the illness does not appear to be contagious, although several cabin mates of those afflicted have exhibited symptoms as well. At this time, he is unable to identify the source. He put in a call to the Center for Disease Control in Atlanta."

Captain McCann glanced to her left. The camera panned, showing three people holding clipboards, their faces as stern as the Captain's. "Luckily, the International Council on Infectious Diseases is having a conference in Anchorage, so the CDC contingent was able to reach our ship quickly; in the neighborhood, so to speak. They'll be doing some checking to find what's causing this minor outbreak. Please let these agents do their work as you see them about the ship."

Captain McCann continued, her voice subdued. "For now, the plan is for us to spend tomorrow in Hubbard Bay, as scheduled. The CDC people say we may have to miss a port, or perhaps more, if they cannot identify the illness quickly." Captain McCann glanced at a card in her hand. "Now, I'm sure you all have a lot of questions, so let me head them off, okay? And remember I'll be available in the theatre later on if you have more. First, the illness appears to be contracted by direct contact, touching something. I'm sure you've seen our crew cleaning the ship, even more than usual. Out of an abundance of caution, I'm keeping the galley on red alert status a while longer. Next, we don't believe the people of Skagway are at any risk; as I said, it doesn't seem to be contagious. The mayor of Skagway asked us to move up sailaway purely as a precaution."

Will said, "Never been kicked out of a port before." Jerria shushed him.

The captain consulted the card again. "To date, eighty-nine passengers have exhibited symptoms.

Thirty-three have been transported to a hospital in Anchorage. Signs to watch for include sudden severe weakness, dizziness, double vision, racing heart, and a blueish rash on hands and arms. Dr Marsh says it can progress to a high fever and trouble breathing. Any passenger or crew member exhibiting symptoms is to contact the Medical Center by dialing 311 on any ship phone. Please keep washing your hands often, and watch out for one another."

Her smile didn't reach her eyes. "I assure you, we're getting on top of this. There's no need to panic. Okay, folks, that's it for now." She handed the microphone to the Cruise director.

Gretchen's voice was saccharine as she stared into the camera. "As Captain McCann said, the situation is under control. All guest services are now open, and please join our own Gregg for Gold Rush Bingo at the top of the hour, in the theatre. Liza will be holding a Guys-Against-Girls putt-putt competition in the Warrior Lounge at ten-thirty. We expect to reach the glacier at noon, approximately. That's all for now."

"Pass me my sneakers, please." Jerria slipped on socks. "What do you think, Will?"

"Didn't give us much more information, did she? Can't see staying in the cabin all day; either we've already been exposed or we're safe. Let's see what Nan and Charlie are up to."

A minute later, they knocked on the cabin next door. Charlie invited them in.

"Good morning. Did hear the announcement? What do you think?"

"I almost missed it," Charlie confided, running a comb through his hair. "That infernal gong woke me. I slept like a dead rock last night."

Nan came in from the balcony, a blanket around her shoulders. "As opposed to a live rock?" she teased. "Aloha, you two. Sounds like the captain is concerned, but they don't seem to know much more than we do."

Will suggested, "Let's get some breakfast. Worry about this later."

Jerria poked his arm. "You're always hungry. I'll come with you, but I sure don't feel like a packaged meal. If they eliminated the galley as the source of the outbreak, why can't we have real food?"

"I miss fresh fruit," Nan sighed, exchanging the blanket for a soft grey wrap over her teal sweater.

"Oh, well, let's go see what's available. We'll be in Hubbard Bay soon, and glacier-watching takes energy. I hope the fog clears by the time we reach the glacier face."

Chapter Thirty-Six

The elevator to the top deck was crowded, so they opted to wait for the next one. Liza joined them, her Staff tote bag over her arm. "Good morning, everybody! Pretty day, isn't it? I heard the glacier is very active this week, so it'll be something to see. Super. You're going to play Guys-Against-Girls, aren't you? I always led that on my other ship, and it's a blast. You'll have time before morning Trivia."

"I don't think we'll be there," Jerria said. "Today's a day for scenery, so we plan to be by windows or outdoors this morning. Nan's never seen an active glacier. Plus, our Trivia team dissolved. You heard about Elias Wilcox, right?"

Liza's smiled dimmed briefly. "Oh, yeah, him. Well, here, take some prizes anyway. You've done so well, I bet you'd have won again. Do you want flashlights or these plastic passport covers?"

They declined, but Liza insisted they take them. As soon as she left the elevator, Jerria set hers on the handrail. "Somebody will be happy to have that. I don't need another flashlight."

After a breakfast of packaged pastries, canned peaches, and hot cereal, they headed for the game room. Its floor-to-ceiling bowed windows provided a good vantage point while keeping the winds at bay, and they had the room to themselves. Will reached for a Scrabble set, but for a few minutes, they were content to watch the scenery glide by. Dall sheep and mountain goats clung on the steep rock walls.

"This very minute, major cities are bustling with millions of people," Nan commented. "It's hard to believe this is the same planet. There's so much nothingness."

Jerria nodded. "I know, Alaska isn't called the Last Frontier for nothing. It's also called Seward's Folly, but it looks like a fine purchase to me."

"I read he paid four cents an acre," Charlie put in. "Cheaper than dust."

"And a whole lot prettier. Have you ever seen so many waterfalls in one place?"

Charlie dumped the Scrabble tiles onto the table. "Waterfall...how many points would that be?"

Each drew tiles, and concentrated on the game. Evenly matched, the points were close until Charlie's last turn.

"*Maximize*. I was afraid I'd be stuck with those tiles." He counted twice. "Seventy-five points."

Will clapped him on the shoulder, and Jerria congratulated him.

Nan smiled, "You beat us, by far! Maximize is even a real word. Sometimes when we play at home," she confided, "I suspect he's throwing in horticulture words to trip me up. Good for you, Charlie!"

They swept the game pieces into the box, and turned their chairs to face the windows. The *Ocean Journey* watched as the ship slowly made its way into the bay, the craggy cliffs on both sides drawing closer. Small chunks of ice bobbed in the water below. Will suggested they go up to the top deck. "Be near the face soon. Don't want to miss the full experience here behind glass."

Nan glanced at the rain-streaked windows. She asked them to wait; she'd be back soon. Before long, she returned, looking decidedly rounder.

Charlie raised his eyebrows. "Did you put on weight?"

"No," she retorted, "I put on wardrobe. I'm willing to brave the weather, with enough layers." She wrapped a thick scarf around her neck, tucking it into her parka's collar. "Ready?"

Chapter Thirty-Seven

By the time they'd climbed the four flights to the upper deck, the sleet had turned to thin rain. They staked out a spot under an overhang. Ahead lay the Hubbard Glacier's face, and dozens of passengers gathered to be the first to see it. More stood in the observation lounge, protected from the elements.

The *Ocean Journey* slowed, gliding through the inky water, tall cliffs rising on port and starboard as the bay narrowed. Its engines only a low hum, the silence of the bay pressed in on the ship. Crew members offered plaid wool blankets. Nan gratefully wrapped two around herself, while Jerria and Charlie took one each. Will zipped his waterproof jacket.

Jerria surveyed nearby passengers arrayed in Alaska-emblemed ponchos, jackets, sweatshirts, even suspenders, and chuckled. "They'll look silly wearing that stuff at home, but at least they're warm."

She heard a scuffle and a thump across the deck. Heads swiveled. A man lay on the deck, his nose bleeding, unmoving.

"We were just standing here, and he fell over!" a woman cried. "He's not going to die, is he? Help, somebody!" Two passengers and a crew member ran to his side.

A medical team quickly removed the fallen man, and passengers turned their attention back to the scenery. As the ship gradually eased up the fjord, ice from the distant glacier bobbed in the water below, thicker than earlier, bumping against the hull of the ship. Someone joked about the *Titanic*. No one laughed.

Joel stood a few feet away, binoculars in hand. "We may not make it all the way to the glacier's face. Captain McCann's very cautious of the ice, but we're going as far as we can go safely. Hubbard Glacier is about seventy-six miles long. Did you all see the colors of the bergies? You can see how much ice is underwater compared to above the surface. It's the same with the glacier itself. Nearly two hundred eighty feet of ice is under the water and..."

Three moose and a calf nibbled bushes on the shore, silently watching the ship glide past, unconcerned. A while later, three white-jacketed crew members circled through the passengers with trays of steaming mugs. "Hot soup, anyone? Beef barley soup here."

Most passengers accepted the mugs, cradling them in their hands, soaking in the warmth. A woman shied away, insisting, "How can you trust food, when so many people are sick? I'm not eating another thing until I'm back in civilization!"

A nearby passenger snorted. "Some people need an excuse to lose some weight. Take any incentive you can get, lady. You look like a walrus in that coat."

"How dare you! I paid good money for this new coat, I'll have you know. I certainly don't need to lose weight, you big oaf!"

"Hey, no skin off my nose, if you're one of those people who can't see what's in the mirror. You aren't even smart enough to know boiling soup kills germs."

"Well, I *never!*" She took a swing at him, sputtering. The man ducked. Swiftly, her partner grabbed her arm.

"Come on, let's go on the other side, away from him. We don't need to be around stupid people. Obviously, he doesn't know a thing about fashion."

Her face flushed, the woman stalked across the deck to the far railing.

Joel raised his voice, his eyes flickering back and forth. "Look, there's an otter on that bergie, holding its favorite rock. Every day, they choose a rock and carry it with them. It comes in handy for opening clams and other snacks. Keep an eye out for seals, too. They look like floating logs at first, until you make out their faces."

Jerria shook her head. "Tension's rising. I hope they get a handle on this soon."

Captain McCann's voice came over the loudspeaker, muffled by the surrounding cliffs. "Good news, on two fronts. First, you'll be glad to know the CDC folks agree we can revoke the red alert status in the galley. That means our talented chefs will be serving a full menu, starting with dinner this evening." She chuckled. "I expected that; I can hear your cheer even up here in the bridge. Second, due to our schedule change, we're in no rush to leave Hubbard Glacier today, as long as we're out of the harbor by dusk. So relax, take in the beauty, and enjoy the day, folks."

A man nearby sighed. "All we have is time."

"Time, and a decent dinner tonight," Will grinned. "In danger of losing weight myself."

As the ship gently rounded the bend, Hubbard Glacier's face came into view just as the sun broke through the clouds. Even from a distance, its vivid colors rising three hundred fifty feet above the water caused a collective gasp. Captain McCann eased the ship closer.

"I didn't know glaciers have a voice. No wonder the early people believe they're alive. With all that creaking and groaning, I can feel its spirit." Nan stared. "That huge piece to the left is definitely leaning. Do you think it'll calve while we're watching?"

"Sometimes they hang like that for a long time, so there's no way of knowing," Jerria replied. "There it goes...oh!" An iceberg the size of a ranch house sheared off, crashing into the sea. A wave crested with ice splashed over floating floes. Two sea lions tipped into the water. Passengers clapped.

"I saw a documentary, where people actually surf on the waves made by glaciers calving. I love to surf, but that's plain foolhardy." Charlie pointed to the water. "Look, there goes a lifeboat."

One of the small boats from the *Ocean Journey* skimmed across the bay, dwarfed by the massive glacier. Two orange-overalled crew members dodged iceberg bits, guiding the boat closer to the glacier face. Another ice shelf calved free, sliding into the sea, triggering a tall wave that raced swiftly toward the lifeboat. Jerria's heart skipped a beat, watching anxiously with others lining the rail. The crewmembers frantically turned the boat's bow into the oncoming wave, riding the crest like a roller coaster. Passengers breathed a collective sigh of relief.

Danger passed –for now- Jerria watched a man in the boat lean over the side. Using ice clamps, he and his partner wrestled a chunk of ice into the lifeboat, waved, then maneuvered the little boat back toward the ship. On the port side, a davit lowered into the water. The boat rose, crew, ice, and all, to the Promenade deck. A few minutes later, they came onto the upper deck, pushing a cart with the ice chunk they'd retrieved on it.

Joel pulled the cart to the open deck. "There you are. I was afraid that wave would swamp you guys. This piece is a beauty. Come closer, everybody. The older, denser ice is the deeper blue and... Oh, no, you don't!"

Joel stepped in front of the glacial ice, his arms spread protectively. He glared at the two white-aproned crew members bearing ice carving tools. "No. Way. This ice was probably fluffy snow about the time of the Crusades. You two are *not* turning it into a race car or dragon!"

Taking one look at Joel's face, the ice carvers retreated into the ship.

Nan shivered as the afternoon progressed. "That breeze feels like somebody left the freezer door open. But I'm enjoying this so much! Oh, I think it's going to calve again."

After the berg broke free, the four friends retreated to the lounge, where they could watch the scenery behind glass. The ship gradually backed out of the narrow fjord, toward open sea. A waiter offered mugs of hot chocolate.

Nan cradled her hot cocoa mug in her icy fingers. "You were right; I'm never going to forget this!"

"It's been a gorgeous day," Jerria agreed. "I keep thinking about Elias and Penny. They would have loved to see the glacier. I wonder how Penny is getting on."

Nan loosened her wooly scarf. "All she can do is go on living until she feels alive again. I thought the illness had run its course, but then that man collapsed on deck earlier..."

"Oh, no, you don't," Will's eyes twinkled. "Can't go worrying. Come on, time for a game of shuffleboard before dinner. Men against the women, and losers buy dinner in the dining room."

Jerria stood. "You're on! But dinner? That's already paid for. How about you and Charlie bring me and Nan hot fudge sundaes before bed, since we're going to win?"

"Maybe skip the ice cream and just bring me a bowl of hot fudge. I don't think I'll ever be warm again." Nan sighed. "The ship doesn't have an *indoor* shuffleboard court, does it?"

As they waited for the aft elevator, Jerria overheard a woman comforting a girl in the nearby stairwell.

"Don't cry. I agree, it's not right, and I know you played your best, but it's just a game."

"But, Mom, we *won!* Liza gave the second place team cool water bottles, and gave us *stickers!* She said we weren't old enough for water bottles, but it's not like they had beer or something in them. It's not *fair!*"

As the elevator door closed, the girl's last words carried plainly. "I'm never going on another stupid cruise in my whole life, and you can't make me."

Jerria sighed, remembering her own daughters' drama over the years. At that age, everything was a crisis. Still, it did seem odd that Liza awarded prizes unfairly. Perhaps the girl misread the scores.

Chapter Thirty-Eight

Forty-five minutes later, Jerria high-fived Nan over their victory, best three out of five games, brushing aside the men's excuses. Hearing their laughter, John Hansson paused as he walked the promenade deck. He joined the good-natured teasing.

"Really, Will? You expect anyone to believe the ship's motion threw off your shot? We're only going about four knots. And you, Charlie, distracted by a wave? Yeah, right—you lost, fair and square. Congratulations to the ladies."

"You seem to be in a better mood," Jerria eyed their old friend.

"Keeping up the act as best I know how. We're supposed to be in Valdez tomorrow, and there's already been some complaining about missing the port. Keeping passengers distracted from the quarantine is a challenge, and I think it'll be worse if we have to stay at sea much longer." John shook his head. "We have enough supplies and food for a few more days. We're scheduled to resupply in Anchorage. Captain had a memo saying the storm delayed the shipment. Maybe we'll arrive at the same time."

He brightened. "We're making some progress, though. Only six new cases today. The CDC and Dr Marsh have narrowed the poison to a rare plant toxin. They say it's called rowsh, from the hemlock family. The CDC folks were pretty excited to identify it. Apparently, it's only found in the Middle East. We're trying to figure out who's been there recently, who could have had access to it. It'd be a lot easier if this itinerary required the ship to keep control of everybody's passports, as they do in more exotic ports."

Jerria leaned forward. "I can't believe someone's deliberately poisoning people. Do they know how it's spreading, John?"

"Yes, it's by direct skin contact, and it doesn't take much, I understand. The trouble is, anybody could have put a couple drops of the poison anywhere. They've run tests all over the ship, and nothing showed up. They're pretty sure it's been placed deliberately. We're trying to figure out the connection; what have all the sickened passengers touched that others haven't? Why are some cabin mates affected, but not others? Four of the victims are in pretty bad shape, including one of the doctor's sons. Doc says we may need to set up an airlift if they get any worse."
He glanced at his watch. "Break's over. I'd better head back to the bridge."

Jerria shivered. "Deliberate...Elias was murdered."

As the sun dropped behind the mountains, Nan pulled her jacket closer. "I look like a marshmallow with so many layers on, yet I'm still cold. Let's go get ready for dinner. Jerria, we need to save room for our sundaes later." They walked ahead of Will and Charlie, who still grumbled about their loss.

Their waiter presented leather-bound menus with a flourish. "Everybody's happy tonight. Cooks happy, chefs happy, diners happy. How about I bring you one of each appetizer while you decide on your dinner?"

"Yes, please," Jerria smiled, her good intentions forgotten.

She surveyed the dining room. Although a fresh-cooked meal was a draw, many chairs stood empty, out of illness or fear, she surmised. She turned her attention to the menu. So many choices!

This far north, the sun set late in the evening. After dinner, the friends sat on the pool deck, protected from the chill wind by the retractable ceiling, watching the sunset through the glass wall.

Jerria relaxed in her chair as the light in the sky faded. "Have you ever seen such colors? Looks like God pulled out the big box of crayons. And Joel said the Northern Lights will be visible later on. What shall we do this evening?"

With no evening show scheduled, passengers seemed at loose ends. Several paced the outer deck, while others read books in public spaces. The movie had been relocated to the theatre, since the onboard cinema only sat thirty. Jerria had seen the show at the tiny theater at home, and didn't care to watch it again.

She suggested they go sit in on the karaoke hour. "Although no one's going to sing as well as you,

Nan. You had the whole audience caught up in emotion last night."

"Thanks. I think the passengers were hungry for an outlet, with all the tension on this cruise. I figured leading a song was better than heading up a witch hunt."

On the way to the Mandarin Lounge, Charlie said, "The officers are doing a good job of keeping the cause on the down-low. John only told us because he knows us well. I'd guess most passengers have no idea somebody is deliberately poisoning people."

"Good thing! Nan's right; that would trigger a witch hunt for sure." Jerria reached for the hand sanitizer as they entered the lounge. "Look at us; this is a habit now, without even thinking about it."

Will rubbed his hands together. "Won't protect anybody from poison, but regular germs may as well die, too."

They took seats in the back of the lounge. On the dance floor, a woman crooned into a microphone, her voice as ragged as the notebook holding the lyrics. A sprinkling of passengers sat facing the front, while others waited their turns, fidgeting. One yawned, then walked away.

Somebody muttered, "Is she ever going to stop wailing? She sounds like my cat when he's about to cough up a hairball."

In the middle of the third song, Jerria hissed, "She shows no sign of stopping, and I can't take much more of this." She suggested a game of Hearts.

"Good idea. Have a small errand to run, then we'll meet you in our cabin." Will winked at Charlie.

Jerria watched Will's retreating back. "After all these years, I love that man more than ever. What do you suppose they're up to now?"

Nan chuckled. "You forgot they owe us a prize, didn't you?"

"The sundaes? Yes, I did forget." They walked down the deserted hallway. Jerria shook her head. "I can't help thinking about what John said. I find myself looking at the other passengers differently, wondering who of them could deliberately kill Elias, and make others so sick. Are they still on the ship, or did they get off in one of the ports?"

"I know. What would make anyone poison people on a cruise ship? There are so many places to commit a crime without paying cruise fare first. Do you think the poison is targeted at a specific person, or is it random? Too many questions."

Jerria pressed the elevator button with her knuckle. "Look at me; I'm afraid to touch anything. Maybe it's like that guy on the news last month, the one who burned down three houses in his neighborhood to make his insurance claim look believable. John said the poison could be as little as a drop or two; it could be anywhere. And why choose something that exotic? They had to know somebody would figure it out eventually. I've heard some criminals actually *want* to be caught, like a sick game." She pulled out her key card.

Jerria opened the door and sprawled on the bed, scooting a towel lobster out of the way. "Griffin makes cute towel animals. Why can't we just enjoy our cruise? I hate feeling on edge all the time. I wish we could figure out who's behind this."

"Let's see if we can narrow it down." Nan reached for a pad of paper and pen on the desk. "Honestly, how do you keep your cabin this tidy? It's as clean as the minute you walked in on Day One. Ours has clutter everywhere."

"It's only neat on the surface. Don't look in the drawers. We need to think about this logically. Every criminal has to have means, opportunity, and motive, right? What could a bad guy have to gain by poisoning people?"

Chapter Thirty-Nine

By the time Will and Charlie entered the cabin carrying two sundaes apiece, Hearts had been forgotten. The women were deep in thought, scrawling on papers. They barely acknowledged their husbands.

Will protested. "What's going on? Never ignored a hot fudge sundae before."

"Oh, sorry, thanks, it looks good. Help us out here, will you?" Jerria reached for her sundae. As they ate ice cream, Jerria filled the men in. "We know the CDC people are hunting for the poison itself. Dr Marsh is tied up caring for the sick passengers. The officers are trying to keep passengers calm, knowing it'll be a madhouse if anyone finds out it's not just a routine virus or something." She licked her spoon. "Mmm, homemade fudge sauce. But the rest of the staff..."

Nan interrupted, "They're all busy. We were trying to narrow it down, maybe figure out who's being targeted, or who had access to the poison. Besides, Elias was our friend, so we have a stake in this. We've met a lot of people on this ship, being involved in the games and classes. I've been going to the gym every morning, and the exercise classes have been full, but the numbers of people playing ship games are smaller every day."

Jerria kicked her shoes off. "Why is that? Usually the games are a big draw."

"Thinking about categories of people?" Will asked. "What about the children onboard? Hate to think of them being targeted."

"Well, I hate to think of *anybody* being the intended target." Charlie scooped whipped cream. "Far as I can tell, the kids' group looks the same to me. And the teen club sure puts out a lot of noise. Good idea, to put that by the pool. What if it's not specific people being targeted? It could be random. Should we focus on a *place,* instead?"

"What about the dining room?" Jerria asked. "Every passenger goes there a few times every day. Would that be a good venue to poison people?"

"Maybe," Nan interjected, "but how? The only thing every guest touches is the hand sanitizer spray dispenser. You don't think..."

"No; more people would be sick if the poison was there. John said the toxin is unstable, not something a person could store a long time. Let's think about who might have been in the Middle East recently."

"Met a couple in the photography class who talked about working in Yemen last year. Said they were going back in a few weeks. Don't know how long the toxin lasts." Will reached for a paper napkin. "Charlie, remember the archaeologist at the golf simulator? Did he say where he worked?"

"Interesting line of work, but I'm pretty sure he said his latest dig was in New Zealand." Charlie's brows knit. "I remember Haywood, the un-funny comic, saying he wanted to kill his wife with something exotic. I wonder if he had access to a Middle Eastern poison. Is there any way to find out where crew members have traveled?"

"Good question. We can ask John next time we see him. Where is that woman from, the one we met at the cooking class, with all the silk headscarves? She wraps them differently than *hajib*, though." Nan set her spoon down.

"No, she's not Middle Eastern. She said she had surgery recently, and wanted to hide the scars." Jerria wiped her lips. "I talked with a woman from Saudi Arabia in the library. She said she taught at a rug-weaving school. We talked about fibers and yarns. I'd hate to blame a fellow weaver. Besides, she was so pleasant, I'd never suspect her of hurting anybody."

"If we're going by personalities, I nominate the Cruise director. We've been on close to seventy cruises, and I've never met anyone as sour as Gretchen. But what would she have to gain?" Charlie reached for a pen. "Come to think of it, I haven't heard her make any announcements since yesterday morning. Maybe she's sick, too."

"If it's a crew member, may never figure it out." Will sipped his water. "Captain McCann said at the cocktail party they come from sixty-something nations. And Griffin said about twenty percent are new this cruise. Lost cause, if it's one of them."

Charlie shook his head. "I doubt it'd be a crew member; they really value these ship jobs. A waiter told me on another cruise, he can earn more in one contract than he'd earn in five years at home. I don't see them throwing that away."

Jerria shook her head, her curls bouncing. "Besides, where's the motive? Somebody must have a *reason*. What about that man I told you about, the one who brought crystals from Russia?" Jerria tapped her fingers on the table. "Is Russia close enough to get rowsh?"

Nan sat back. "We're going in circles here. I need to clear my head."

Jerria remembered Joel said it might be clear enough to see the Northern Lights tonight. They put on warm jackets, then trooped up to deck ten. Captain McCann had announced the upper deck would be unlit once the sun set, in hopes of making the Northern Lights more visible.

Jerria pushed open the outer deck door. In the moonless light, she made out a handful of figures. Somebody near the railing said in a muted voice, "You're just in time. The Lights are beautiful."

Eerie green and yellow lights writhed across the pale night sky like a living entity. Colors swayed, cascading, tumbling across the starry heavens. Jerria envisioned a soft blanket, shaken by unseen hands.

Joel's voice was soft in the chilly night air. "We're lucky tonight. The spectacle is unpredictable, and swift, as you can see. Look closely, and you might make out more colors; purples, reds, even blues. It's caused by ionized gas particles hitting the earth's atmosphere, making this curtain of light. Amazing, isn't it?"

Jerria released breath she hadn't realized she'd been holding, her soul relaxing, pushing swirling thoughts of the criminal onboard aside.

Waves of bright hues danced overhead, filling the night sky. *Reminds me of waves on a beach. Here the ship itself is hurting, but Nature goes on, unconcerned.* Will held her hand in the darkness, and she leaned on his shoulder.

Chapter Forty
Day Thirteen   At Sea

"Come quick, Honey!" Will called from the balcony. "Couple of gray whales, right over there."

Jerria woke, startled. Wrapping a blanket around her shoulders, she stumbled onto the balcony, rubbing her eyes. The night's jumbled dreams fled as she focused where Will was pointing. Against the grey early morning horizon, she made out plumes of mist rising, a sure sign of whales spouting. Gulls circled, eager for a breakfast of fleeing fish churned up by the giant mammals. Jerria drew in a chilly breath, spellbound.

A gray whale leaped, spy-hopping not forty feet in front of them. As it dove deep, its fluke splashed the sea, scattering gulls on the surface. A wave of sour fish odor washed over them. Jerria stood spellbound, her bare feet on the cold metal floor forgotten. It surfaced, and she watched the whale glide away until it vanished on the horizon.

Will beamed, as delighted as if he had placed the creature there himself. "Good morning, Honey. Fine start to a day, right? Felt bad, but knew you'd enjoy the whales."

"Thanks for waking me. I think I can still smell its fishy breath." Jerria sank onto a deck chair, damp from the overnight dew. "Morning. I was looking forward to flying over the glaciers by helicopter in Valdez today. Instead, another day at sea. Yesterday felt so long. I wonder if the activities staff will add more things to do, to keep passengers' minds off missing the tours they had booked today." She pulled the blanket tighter around her shoulders. "Valdez is less than seventy miles from Anchorage. How long do you think we'll have to stay at sea, not allowed to land?"

"Reminds me of the Caribbean, where the ports are so close together, can often see the next one from the port. Don't know; guess the CDC will be pretty strict about lifting the quarantine. Last thing they want is for potentially contaminated passengers to get on planes and spread the poison across the globe. On the ship, everybody's contained."

"You're right, but I'm still disappointed about missing Valdez. And I don't like thinking about a killer onboard with us." Jerria stood. "I'd better get dressed. I can hear Aunt Henrietta going on about catching a cold. She'd be upset if she knew I was outdoors in my pajamas, too. Let's keep busy today, so the time will pass faster."

After a hot breakfast, Jerria and Will took the stairs to the lounge in time for morning Trivia. Charlie and Nan were already waiting.

"Did you see the whales this morning?" Nan asked. "I was on the jogging track, and suddenly somebody hollered, 'Whale!' and about thirty people ran over, hanging over the railing. It's okay; I wasn't in the mood to run anyway. It's easier to get motivated at home, where it's warm."

Will laughed. "Often thought the quickest way to clear out a cruise ship buffet line would be to yell 'Whale!' No matter how many we see, people still make a mad dash to see new ones."

"Wonder where everybody is this morning? Sleeping in, maybe, since it's another sea day? It's not the same, without Elias and Penny." Charlie surveyed the sparse assembly. Liza stood by the tall windows, staring into space.

Shaking herself, Liza turned from the window and called cheerfully, "How's everybody today? Good? Super! Come get your papers, and we'll get started in a couple of minutes."

Nan retrieved a score sheet from the piano and took her seat. "Maybe more people are sick...but the gym was crowded. It doesn't make sense that game-players would be sickened more than, say, people who work out or lounge by the pool all day."

Jerria glanced at a nearby team. Hearing them discussing changing their team's name for luck, she said softly, "I can't shake the feeling that I already know who...what we talked about last night. I keep going over conversations in my mind. Did somebody say something I can't quite put my finger on? Did I see something that didn't sink in?"

"Ready? Question number one: What U.S. state shares the longest border with a foreign country?" Liza tapped her pencil on the piano.

"Texas? No, it's Alaska," Will whispered. Nan nodded as she wrote the answer.

"What is the largest member of the deer family?" Liza giggled, "Let me give you a hint. There's a big bronze statue of one in downtown Anchorage."

A woman nearby snorted. "How would we know that? The ship hasn't been to Anchorage yet. We didn't even get to Valdez. I paid good money to see the ports, and I had an Alaska Pipeline tour today..."

Liza swiftly quashed the murmurs spreading through the room. "Okay, everybody, it'll be okay. Just write your answers. Today's a great day. Did you hear I added a flower-arranging class at eleven-thirty? Super."

"Liza, I forgot the question." A man held up his hand. "Read it again."

Liza waggled a playful finger at him. "Now, listen up, the largest deer, remember?"

"Moose, right?" Jerria leaned in so other teams wouldn't overhear. "So far, the questions are Alaska-themed."

"Next question: Name the two main clans in Alaskan native culture."

Jerria heard Lillian's voice in her mind. *"Show the Eagle clan proud, you hear?"* The other clan was Raven; she was sure of it.

"Let's move along, okay? Super. What's Alaska's state flower? Remember, now."

Will whispered, "Gave us a hint. Forget-me-nots, those little blue things."

"Did you all see the Northern Lights last night? Pretty amazing, and the sky was so clear. And whales this morning; really, an extra sea day is wonderful. No more grumbling, got it?" Liza moved in front of the window. "Ready for the next one? Super. What's the scientific term for the Northern Lights?

Teams bowed their heads, quietly debating the answer. Nan whispered, "It's Aurora Bor-"

Gretchen's sharp voice pierced the air. "Liza! You missed the staff meeting this morning. What's your excuse this time?"

Liza's head jerked as if she'd been slapped. "I...I was running late and...You said not to be late again, and I had to set up the projector for—"

"You foolish girl! That's stupid five different ways. I said, if you can be consistently ten minutes late, why can't you be consistently on time?"

"I'm sorry. Anyway, I figured you were sick and..."As if suddenly aware of the passengers' eyes on her, Liza straightened. "Gretchen, I'm in the middle of Trivia here. Can we talk later?"

"Why did you think I was sick?" Gretchen smirked, "Oh, you can bet we'll talk later, while you're packing your bags. I'll teach you to miss one of my staff meetings!"

Liza straightened her shirt as the Cruise director stalked out of the lounge. "The Wicked Witch is gone. Back to the game, okay?" Her smile shaky, Liza read the next question. "How many named glaciers are there in Alaska?"

Trying not to think about Gretchen's outburst, Jerria's mind wandered. Since Skagway, Trivia games had been sparsely attended. Some passengers were bored or frustrated, she suspected, and Penny and Elias were gone. How many regular players missed the early departure from Skagway, like Cowboy Bob and his wife? Cowboy Bob came clearly to mind, his five-inch silver belt buckle, several different Stetsons, at least four pair of boots, sharply creased jeans. *Who irons denim?* Such a nice young man, but his wife sure seemed unfriendly. You'd think she'd be happy to have him back from the Middle East–

Jerria's stomach turned. "Cowboy!"

Nan stared at her. "Cowboy? *That's* the name of the town where the Heli-Ski Search and Rescue team is based?"

Jerria lowered her voice, conscious of the other teams around her. "I just remembered something. Didn't Cowboy Bob serve in Iraq or somewhere like that? Could he be the one who–"

Liza clapped her hands. "Okay, everybody, trade papers with another team for scoring."

Mechanically, Nan scrawled "Haines" and leaned back to trade scoresheets with the team behind her. "Jerria, what are you saying?"

Nearby, a woman locked eyes with Jerria, her face flushed. Had she overheard?

"I'll tell you later."

When the scores were totaled, Jerria's team came in first... again. A man wearing a plaid shirt slammed his fist on the table in front of him. "Again? I don't care who wins, so long as it's not *them*."

Will chuckled, "Look, man, take the prizes, we don't want them. Just here to play a game."

Liza intervened. "Here, I have enough prizes for all of you. Take them, I insist. Super. It's all about my pen."

Several passengers rushed forward, hands eagerly outstretched for the plastic-wrapped trinkets.

Nan sat back. "What does a picture frame have to do with a pen?"

Jerria responded, "I don't know. I can't decide who's more aggressive, Liza trying to give stuff away or those people grabbing it."

Chapter Forty-One

Jerria's novel dropped into her lap. As calm as the glass-enclosed pool area was this time of day, she just couldn't concentrate, and she'd been trying for a good half hour. She kept thinking about the helicopter that landed on the upper deck earlier, an airlift. Someone by the snack bar said the blanketed form on the gurney was very small. A child...what if it was one of Mr Marsh's twins?

She'd run into the First Officer in the atrium earlier, and confided her suspicions about Cowboy Bob, or more likely, his wife. John said cabin stewards were tasked with packing the belongings of passengers who'd missed the early sailaway in Skagway, and they hadn't reported anything amiss. She mentioned what the comedian had said about killing his wife with something exotic in San Francisco. He said he'd pass her concern to Captain McCann.

"Captain McCann is reluctant to search cabins of staff or crew; we have to work with them, you know! But if we don't figure it out soon..."

The ship moved lazily through open water, hardly making a wake, as cut off from the rest of the world as surely as if it had been on another planet. The morning's wan sunshine had gradually faded over the thin dark line on the horizon, overtaken by grey clouds. Thick snowflakes drifted from a sympathetic heaven on the beleaguered ship.

Nan settled into the lounge beside Jerria. "Hi. Did you see it's snowing? I remember the first time I saw snow, on the Big Island. I thought it was white feathers from the *ne' ne!* I guess I was about three years old. How's the book?"

"That'd be a lot of goose feathers." Jerria set the book aside. "I can't even tell you what I'm reading. Foggy-brain, that's what it is. My mind feels like I'm looking through the wrong end of a spyglass. I can't get my thoughts into focus. It doesn't feel like a normal sea day, does it?"

"No, the ship itself seems sick, kind of listless." Nan put her feet up. "I went to the gym, but there's a sign on the door. Classes are canceled today, something about instructors not being available. Seems to me, if the ship wants to avoid a mutiny, they should add more things to do, not less."

"Did you see that poster in the atrium? There's a Mystery Dinner this evening in the specialty restaurant. It said the production crew will act out a mystery while blending in with diners, like a dinner within a play."

"Oh, Charlie and I attended one of those on another ship. It was a lot of fun. We haven't even seen the production crew; we wouldn't know them from the other passengers."

"It's limited to thirty people. If we're interested, we'd better sign up soon."

"Okay, let's do it. People are so on edge, they'll be looking for any diversion." Nan stood. "Am I the only one to think it's funny, to attend a pretend mystery inside of a real one?"

Chapter Forty-Two

Jerria smoothed her lipstick in the mirror and smiled at her reflection. Her blue dress set off her blown-glass necklace nicely. "Will, can you help me with my zipper? Thanks. Are you ready?"

Will thrust his arms into his suitcoat sleeves. "Another dress-up night. Think you booked this mystery dinner on purpose. Hate wearing a suit on vacation. You look beautiful, Honey."

"Thanks. Don't complain; dinner will be fun, and it'll take our minds off the real mystery under our noses. I'll get the door–it's probably Nan and Charlie."

Nan stepped in, adjusting her green wrap over her shoulders. "Ready? Love your dress!"

"Thanks; there's a new boutique at home. Where's Charlie?"

"He's coming. He teases me about taking a long time to get dressed, but may I once again point out *he's* not ready yet?"

"Read the invitation?" Will waved the card. "Says here the theme is a celebratory dinner to congratulate the owners of the Pickleworth Pie Company on their success. A note says we're the lucky stockholders, but to be on the lookout for nefarious opportunists."

Charlie tapped at the open door. "Let's go. I hope you don't mean me; I'm slow at tying my necktie, but I'm hardly ever nefarious."

At the entrance to the restaurant, they showed their invitations and walked in. Black and white helium balloons covered the ceiling. Five linen covered tables, set for eight, ringed the room, leaving the center open. The *Ocean Journey's* trio played soft jazz filled the room in the corner. Gregg greeted them, and a white-coated waiter escorted them to one of the tables. Jerria suppressed a thought about Gregg; her legs hadn't recovered from the yoga class.

Jerria settled into her seat. "They really transformed the place! Reminds me of those award shows, with the podium and low centerpieces. I hope there won't be any long speeches."

Nan picked up her place card and turned it over. "Blank. Good; I'm not one of the auxiliary characters. How about the rest of you?"

Each card was blank, leaving them free to enjoy the evening. Other diners streamed in, filling the tables. Jerria smiled at John Hansson across the room. She recognized some of the other passengers, but not all. Liza sat at the table next to theirs. She wore a checked A-line dress instead of her usual staff polo shirt, and dove into conversation with the woman seated beside her.

A couple with sharp British accents soon joined their table; Jerria couldn't tell if the accents were real or put on for the evening. She introduced herself, Will, and the Callisters, but was met by vacant stares.

"And what are your names?" she awkwardly prompted.

They exchanged a glance, and said in unison, "We really couldn't say."

A middle-aged woman and her teen-aged son were the last to be seated at their table.

"This is dumb." The boy pulled at his collar. "I hate this stiff shirt. I don't see why I had to leave my game in the cabin. I could've turned the volume down."

His mother flushed. "I told you–"

Jerria made an effort not to roll her eyes. She had no tolerance for spoiled teens. "Hi, I'm Jerria, and I'm sure we'll need your help figuring out the whodunnit."

He blinked through thick glasses. "The... what did you say?"

Nan explained, "It's like a play on stage, except we don't know who the actors are. During dinner, a crime will happen, and it's our job to figure it out. They'll probably throw in some random clues to complicate things, so pay attention."

A waiter closed the restaurant door, and Jerria squirmed in her seat. *A crime's about to occur.*

Chapter Forty-Three

Gregg clapped his hands and the passengers quieted. "Welcome, everybody. Tonight's going to be fun. During your lovely buffet dinner, a story will play out. It's your job to eat, mingle, ask questions, and look for clues. At the end, we'll reveal all. For now, let me introduce the main characters, Mr and Mrs Pickleworth, of the Pickleworth Pie Company."

Jerria grinned as a man and woman stood and walked to the podium; she'd have identified them as actors anywhere. The heavyset man wearing a tuxedo waved his hands expansively. "I, of course, am Phineas Featherby Pickleworth the third, of Pickleworth Pie fame. We are here to celebrate our latest venture on the famous television program, *Make Me A Million*. Once the hosts tasted our delightful lime-coconut cream pies with gingersnap crust, well, they were sold. Pickleworth Pie Company stocks have soared since the program aired, and I can most assuredly assure you..."

The mousy woman by his side, every bit his opposite in a drab grey silk, tugged at his sleeve. Somebody giggled.

Mr Pickleworth brushed her aside, then finally acknowledged her insistent pulling at his arm. "Whatever is it, Dear? Can't you see I'm in the middle of most important business? Can't you wait? What did you say? Speak up!"

Fingering her strand of pearls, Mrs Pickleworth stood on tiptoe and whispered something in her husband's ear.

"What's that you say? Dinner? They're hungry? Why, of course...why don't you tell them yourself?"

Mrs Pickleworth stepped to the podium and whispered into the microphone. "Dinner is served, unless you have something better to do, in which case, I surely understand, and I apologize for intruding and I..."

Gregg, at the side of the room, interrupted. "Thank you, Mr and Mrs Pickleworth. We'll hear more from you both later on. For now, our guests are invited to come select appetizers from either of the lovely action stations. And please take time to mingle." He clapped his hands. Jerria squirmed, irritated. Did he have to keep doing that?

Will stood and pushed back his chair. "Action stations? What ever happened to calling them buffet lines?"

Jerria smoothed her dress. "A rose by any other name...The antipasto platter looks delicious. I didn't realize I was hungry until just now."

They filled small plates with hot and cold hors d'oeuvres. Waiters circled the room, passing champagne and limeade in fluted goblets.

Liza bumped into Will, juggling her plate. "Whoops! Sorry; tight quarters. Isn't this just super? I'm so glad I was invited. Do you think there'll be a murder tonight, Mr Danson?"

The corners of Will's mouth turned up. "Well, it *is* a mystery, so something has to happen. Keep thinking about those balloons on the ceiling; one could pop and we'd think it was a gunshot."

"So long as it's not poison; there's been enough of that already. I wonder who it'll be. That young man at your table looks pretty risky to me. Enjoy your dinner, Mr Danson. Super."

Jerria watched Liza move away. "Will, that was odd, don't you think, for her to bring up poison?"

Will shrugged. "Just on edge."

Jerria stood with her back to the wall, watching the other guests move from group to group, introducing themselves. She bit a prosciutto-wrapped fig. "So, what do you think so far? It's confusing, not knowing who the actors are. Have you identified anybody yet? Mr and Mrs Pickleworth are obvious, but who are the others?"

"I'm wondering about the Brits at our table," Nan said. "They certainly are closed-mouthed. It could be cultural, but really, on a cruise ship, introductions are expected."

"That couple over there, with the matching vests and gold chains, seems out of the 60s." Will tipped his head their way. "Hard to tell if it's a costume. Supposed to mingle; going to find out."

The First Officer strolled across the room, nodding at Will as their paths crossed. Dark circles under his eyes overshadowed his usual warm smile. "Hi, all. Did you try the garlic shrimp?"

"Hello, John. I'm surprised you're able to get away. Looks like you could use a nap."

He adjusted his tie. "Yes, I sure could, but Captain McCann says we need to keep up appearances, and that includes showing my face at onboard events."

Nan lowered her voice. "Any progress? How long do you expect the quarantine to last?"

"We haven't figured it out yet, but only three more took sick today, so that's something. Most passengers accepted today as an ordinary sea day, like any other missed port. Not sure how long that'll last. If we don't make our disembarkation date in Anchorage on Thursday, things will be more dicey. Once they start missing flights home and the oncoming passengers for the next cruise realize the ship isn't there for them...Well, we're doing all we an."

A middle-aged woman in a sequined cocktail dress all but dragged a bearded man to their group. "See, Tom, look closer at him." She pointed at John Hansson's crisp white uniform. "He can't be a real officer. Nobody wears dress whites anymore, and look at the cheesy gold stripes on his sleeves; he's definitely one of the actors. Wait and see." Without so much as making eye contact, she pointed across the restaurant. "And over there, her in the flowered dress. Nobody would wear anything that garish in public; it's a costume, I tell you."

"Good thing I wore a toned-down outfit, or who knows what she'd say." Jerria giggled at John's discomfort. "Don't worry, John; *I* believe you're real."

Gregg clapped his hands. "Everybody, please take your seats for the salad course. Once you're settled, I'll introduce more characters."

The passengers' conversations died down as they moved to their seats where green salads and breadsticks waited.

Gregg introduced several other characters in the story: the nervous secretary, a shifty employee, Mr Pickleworth's attorney, a nosy neighbor, Mrs Pickleworth's friend from college. Jerria smiled at the stereotypes, right down to the lazy brother wearing cuffed jeans and white socks with Birkenstocks. Each took a minute to explain how the Pickleworth Pie Company's new good fortune would change their lives.

The woman wearing white capris and a loud yellow blouse elbowed her way to the podium. "I'm Jody Louise, and I've been dear, precious, lovely Mrs Pickleworm's closest, very best friend since our days at Miss Lelly's Finishing School For Girls." Her over-the-top syrupy-sweet voice elicited chuckles from the diners. "What's that you say? Pickle warp? Pickle what? Pickle*worth*? Not Pickleworm?" She flung her feather boa over her shoulder. "Well, really, what's in a name? The important thing is, now that she has all that money, a girl needs a dear, dependable friend she can count on, and that's me."

Mr Pickleworth's shiftless brother wrestled the microphone from Jody Louise's hand. "If there's any money to be had, it's *mine.* Let's get that clear right up front." He tugged at his mis-buttoned shirt. "I put up with that pompous airbag of a brother of mine my whole life, and I deserve a payout. I'm telling you–"

The family attorney shouted, "According to my records–"
The secretary waved a stenographer's notebook, and other voices chimed in.

Gregg clapped his hands and spoke over the din. "I see the main course is ready. We'll give the others a chance to speak once you've filled your plates. Feel free to talk to the actors while you get your dinner."

Jerria rose with the others, and headed toward the steaming buffet tables. "Duck, beef, pasta, and salmon. They really went all out." She speared a duck breast and spooned scalloped potatoes onto her plate. "Will, you might like the creamed peas. They're pretty well disguised."

"No, thanks, too green. Roast beef looks great."

They filled their plates and returned to the table. The British couple had their heads together, oblivious to anyone else.

"This salmon is so good." Charlie buttered a roll. "I've got my eye on the secretary. She's a little too smooth, very much in character. She's even wearing sensible shoes."

"Since when do you notice shoes?" Nan chuckled. "I wonder what will happen. Sometimes a Mystery Dinner includes a murder, a shooting or stabbing. The last one Charlie and I attended had the main character fall off a balcony to his death, which was pretty funny, since it took place in a one-story restaurant like this one. I think he fell all of two feet onto a mattress. The fun part was figuring out who killed him."

Jerria scanned the room. Nothing seemed out of the ordinary.

The woman beside Nan wiped her son's chin with her napkin. He protested, "Geeze, Mom! I'm not a baby!"

Jerria remembered her own kids at that age, and how she'd impressed good behavior on them. "Shape up, or I'll embarrass you in public" was a good-natured threat to her teens if they stepped out of line. She never thought seriously about what such a follow-through would involve; perhaps chaperoning a school dance in her fluffy slippers? In any case, all four of them grew into respectable adults, and–

The lights flickered twice, and darkness fell. A scream rang out.

Chapter Forty-Four

In the thick darkness, someone screamed again, a plate crashed, something bumped the table. Jerria's breath caught, her heart pounding. She reached for Will's hand. A second later, the lights flashed twice then stayed on. A silence filled the room, as thick as the beef gravy.

Heads swiveled from the scene to a woman screaming over and over, her hand to her throat. Jerria leaned into Will's chest. "Okay, enough, we heard you, the lights are back on. That's the friend, right?"

Will nodded. "Overacting, but sure has everybody's attention."

Jody Louise waved her arms, shouting, "It's Mr Pickle-wiffle! Pickle-weasel!" She lowered her voice. "Look, whatever his name is, he's dead on the floor by my foot."

Diners stood to get a look at the actor. Mr Pickleworth lay still with a long plastic butcher knife protruding from a red cellophane blood stain on his tuxedo shirt, his hands neatly clasped on his stomach.

Gregg clapped his hands again. "There you go, everyone, the murder. Go ahead and eat your dinner while Mr Pickleworth recovers, and I'll send the detective in soon."

Charlie speared a broccoli stalk. "Recovers? How's he going to recover from being stabbed to death?"

Jerria giggled. "Maybe it didn't penetrate his starched cummerbund." She reached for the bread basket. "Will complains about his every time."

The teen turned reproachful eyes on her. "That's dark, man. And they say *my* generation is cold."

"They're acting, remember?" Nan explained. "They dragged him off, but I'm sure he's standing up and eating his dinner in the kitchen by now. Now, help us figure out who had the most to gain, the motive, for killing poor Mr Pickleworth."

Over dinner, conversation swirled as passengers speculated on who murdered Mr Pickleworth. She nudged the British woman at her side. "Come on, play along. Who do you think killed the old guy?"

Eyes intent on her salmon, she murmured, "I really couldn't say."

Jerria sighed, exasperated. "Well, the rest of you, who do you think had the most to gain?"

Charlie sat back to let the waiters remove the dinner plates. "I think the nosy neighbor knows more than she's letting on, but I can't see her motive. She wouldn't be in the will. You know, I wonder if it's one of the ship staff, playing a part not yet revealed. Could it be John? And that man in the blue jacket over there; isn't he the drummer from the band?"

Gregg moved to the podium. "Everybody, may I introduce Detective Jasper?" A chuckle rippled across the restaurant as the "detective" stepped from behind a curtain.

Wearing a Sherlock Holmes-style deer slayer cap and tweed jacket, the Elton John impersonator waved his pipe and took a bow. "At your service. Let's get down to business, shall we? By a show of hands, who thinks Mr Pickleworth was stabbed?" Holding his hand up to deflect the chorus of boos, he continued. "Okay, okay, we agree he's dead. Let's see who has the best motive. Mrs Pickleworth, come to the front, if you please."

After a quick interview of some of the actors, Gregg interrupted the detective. "Dessert, everyone. We'll solve this crime as soon as everyone returns to their seats."

Jerria chose warm peach cobbler and a slice of lime coconut cream pie labeled "Pickleworth Pie Company." *Nice touch.*

A woman stopped her on her way back to their table. "You're the woman who weaves, right? I'm Amy; we met at the craft group on day three. I didn't get a chance to ask about your new loom. You said it was easy; do you remember the brand?"

"Oh, yes, I remember you. It's an Abernathy grasshopper-style number three-oh-eight, birch wood with a double shuttlecock on the warp and woof frame section. I wanted one with the free-sliding harp slide to prevent tangles." Jerria smiled at the woman's blank face. "Sorry; I remember all that because I researched so much to get one I'd be happy with. Let me write it down for you. Will, do you have a pen and paper?"

Will dug in his suitcoat pocket and came up with a receipt. "Write on this, but no pen." No one else at the table had a writing tool, either. If the British couple had one, they couldn't say.

Diners milled around the dessert display. Jerria set her pie on the table. "Wait a moment; the assistant Cruise director is here. I know she carries a box of golf pencils in her bag."

Jerria made her way across the restaurant, scanning the crowd. "John, have you seen Liza?" He shook his head.

Oh, well, I know she keeps her pencils on top of her bag; I'll just borrow one. She won't mind. Jerria nodded at the diners at Liza's table. One said the assistant Cruise director had stepped out to use the restroom. Jerria knelt and pulled Liza's Staff tote bag from under the chair. She extracted a short pencil from the box on top.

A shriek came from the doorway. Before Jerria could stand, Liza ran across the room and grabbed her hair, screaming. As they toppled, Jerria instinctively ducked. Her foot hit the table leg, sending plates crashing to the floor. The tote bag's contents scattered. Liza grabbed Jerria's hair, pulling at her dress with her free hand.

"My bag! My bag! That's my ticket back to my pen! You have no right–"

John and Will leaped into the fray. John caught Liza around the waist, pulling her off Jerria. Will helped her to her feet. Diners stared, confused. Liza burst into tears.

A man grumbled, "This is stupid. Who ever heard of a mystery dinner with two crimes? And now my dinner's ruined."

His wife took his arm. "I agree, they're not doing it right. Let's go, Henry."

Shaken, Jerria leaned on Will. Two Security officers rushed in. John let go of Liza, and the two men pulled her into the hallway, pinning her arms behind her. She wailed, "My bag...it was all for pen..."

Jerria stood, wincing; her back hurt. "I don't know what happened. I just borrowed a pencil; she has plenty. I didn't..." Will guided her to her seat, holding her hands.

Seeing all eyes on Jerria, Gregg clapped his hands to restore order. "Now that the little...er...diversion is over, let's put our heads together and get back to Mr Pickleworth's murder. Detective Jasper, would you please tell us your theory?"

John knelt and gathered the items flung from Liza's tote bag. As the detective took the microphone, John gasped. "Oh, *no*. It can't be!" He held a slim vial of amber liquid up to the light.

Jerria's stomach lurched at the clear skull and crossbones label on the vial.

Nan choked, "*La' au ma' ke!* Poison!"

Confused diners' eyes swiveled from one scene to the other. Anxious murmurs filled the room. *Three* crimes? How much of this was acting?

The detective flapped his arms, angry. "Hey, man, it's my scene, not yours. And Mr What's-his-name was stabbed, not poisoned. Remember, the red cellophane? The big plastic knife?"

John barked into his radio.

Jerria reached her limit. She put her head down on the table, tears flowing freely. "How could it be Liza? She's so happy all the time. Why..." Nan patted her shoulder.

The British couple silently stood and walked out.

The teen at their table exclaimed, "Oh, I get it now! Those stiff-up-your-lip people must be the ones who stabbed the fat guy when it was dark! But why is *she* crying? And who was the lady they hauled out? What is the officer holding?" His mother shushed him.

Detective Jasper thrust his microphone into Gregg's hand. "You can forget about me ever doing another mystery dinner. I wanted to watch the movie. You dress me up like a cartoon character and put me in a madhouse. I didn't even get to say my lines." He stormed out, bumping into Captain McCann.

"Houselights, if you please." Captain McCann took charge. "As you can see, there's been a disturbance. I'm sorry to say, dinner is over. Thank you all for coming. Gregg, if you would please, escort them out."

Standing, a passenger shouted, "I paid good money for this. I demand a refund!"

The captain turned impatient eyes on the man. "Okay, okay, I'll refund your money, and Gregg will see to free drinks as well. Please, everybody, clear the room. Just *go*."

Mollified, the man led the way. "Free drinks on the captain! Everybody follow me!"

Soon only the officers, Will and Jerria, Nan and Charlie remained. Jerria sat back, wiping her eyes on her linen napkin.

Captain McCann spoke sharply. "Okay, tell me what happened here."

"I borrowed a pencil from Liza's bag," Jerria sniffed.

"And this fell out." John Hansson held up the amber liquid.

Captain McCann sat down heavily. "One of my own staff? What motive could Liza possibly have to try to kill passengers?"

Chapter Forty-Five
Day Fourteen

Jerria slumped in the deck chair, rubbing her neck. Not even dawn, and already her head throbbed. No sense staying in bed; her tossing and turning only served to disturb Will.

Why did I ever think coming on a cruise was a good idea? Nan was right; there were omens all around, and I missed them. I should have stayed home, overseeing the construction project. It's just that the ocean calls me...Next time, I'll hang up on it.

One more day to get through; even though the officers knew the culprit, they thought it best to take another sea day. How long could they quash the swirling rumors?

John said Captain McCann decided it'd be better for the passengers to hear what happened once they were safely on land. There was still time for a mutiny, after all, if they knew their lives had been in danger all this time. John Hansson promised Jerria an update sometime this morning. He didn't owe them anything, but they were friends.

Dawn's first glimmer of light lightened the eastern sky. In the milky darkness, Jerria made out several dolphins splashing alongside the ship. *As omens go, that's a good one.* She quietly slid the suite's glass door open. She could still get a couple of hours' sleep before Will woke up...unless her icy feet on the back of his knees disturbed him.

Jerria reclined in a lounge chair midafternoon, fifteen minutes before the movie was to start. The snow flurries of yesterday were a memory. Overnight, a warm front moved in, and Gregg announced the comedy would be shown outdoors on the big screen above the pool. In Alaska, "warm" was relative.

They agreed a funny movie was just what they needed. Jerria went early to stake out good seats for Will, Nan, and Charlie. She'd taken four plaid wool blankets from the shelves by the snack bar, then picked up another for Nan. If the temperature dropped, they could wrap up. For now, she was comfortable with her windbreaker undone. Little white clouds skittered across a clear sky.

What a cruise! She closed her eyes in the weak sunshine, going over what John had told them earlier. Only vaguely aware of other passengers settling in around her, her eyes flew open, startled, when she heard a sharp, "Tsk, tsk."

An elderly woman draped a second, then a third, blanket over Jerria, tucking them in snugly. Without a word, she folded another and coiled it around her face like a hood. Satisfied, she stood back, hands on hips, eyes crinkling. "I don't want you to get cold, dearie. I'm somebody's mother, you know." Before Jerria could speak, she was across the deck, heading for the blanket shelves on blue sneakers.

Will came up behind Jerria, blue eyes twinkling. Wordlessly, he pulled out his camera and took three quick shots. Jerria sighed; without fail, *those* were the kind he sent to the kids.

"Hey, you two, this is a fine spot," Charlie approached, hot pizza in hand. Nan followed with plates and a big bowl of popcorn. A bartender brought up the rear with a pitcher of soda.

"What is this, a party?" Jerria unraveled herself and swung her feet to the deck floor.

Nan zipped her jacket. "Absolutely! At home, I always smuggle snacks into a movie, usually wasabi peas or roasted seaweed, but today calls for pizza. You feeling all right, Jerria? You don't usually bundle up, and it's not even cold out here. You're not getting sick, are you?"

Before she could speak, Will passed his camera to Nan. One glance, and she burst out laughing. "You do attract unusual people, don't you? I love that about you."

"Well, it's been an unusual cruise." Jerria slid a slice of pizza onto a plate. "I can't stop thinking—"

"I know, too much thinking, too much *mana'o*." Nan patted Jerria's hand. "I can't believe it, either. But we'll talk later; the movie's about to begin."

The movie played on the big screen, people around her laughed, but Jerria couldn't keep her mind on the plot. Thoughts spun through her mind like bright chips in a kaleidoscope. What would become of Liza? How could anyone that pleasant be out to hurt people, and why? How was little Jeremy? Where was Penny now? She hadn't even said goodbye.

At last, the closing credits rolled across the big screen. Passengers stirred, gathering themselves together, headed off to the next activity. The Activities staff had no games or dance classes scheduled today, but Gregg had added a couple of workout sessions and Joel hastily pulled together a slide show on Alaskan mammals. The ship's ice carvers promised a demonstration by the pool before dinner.

Jerria sat up, fluffing her unruly curls. "I think I'm still sore from that yoga class Gregg tortured us with days ago, so I'm skipping his aerobics class. I wonder what the officers are doing today."

"I'm sure they're swamped. The paperwork alone must be killer. So to speak." Charlie suggested a mini golf game on the top deck.

Nan tucked her scarf into her jacket. "Good idea; you men can bring us another dessert when you lose." They laughed and walked up the curved teak staircase.

A little over an hour later, Jerria sipped her milkshake on the promenade deck. The golf game had been interrupted by about a dozen passengers trampling Hole Nine. Someone hollered "Whale!" and the volleyball players left their game, heedless of the golf balls in their path. It never gets old. Jerria had been six strokes down before the stampede; milkshakes for all.

John Hansson had joined them for a few minutes before his shift on the bridge began at the top of the hour. Jerria shuddered, replaying his words in her mind as he walked up the curved teak staircase.

He'd filled them in a little more, a perk of his long friendship with Nan and Charlie in Hawaii. She almost wished he hadn't; sometimes, ignorance was easier on the stomach. How could Liza...

Nan interrupted her thoughts. "Liza seemed so sweet; if anyone was out to get us, I was sure it'd be Gretchen."

John had said the Cruise director, while innocent, felt responsible, and had put in for a leave of absence as soon as the ship reached Anchorage. Liza, meanwhile, was in the ship's brig, under guard.

"She'll be charged with two counts of manslaughter, at least, for Elias Wilcox and the woman from Ohio. That could change; still have a dozen people in critical condition in hospital. I don't know how many cases of attempted murder on top of that. If they count the people she poisoned, it's serious enough, but if a judge decides every passenger onboard was at risk of being a victim...well, she'll never see the light of day."

John said Liza had opened up to Captain McCann. In San Francisco, she'd had a phone call from a friend saying her former boyfriend was "flirting up a storm" and told Liza that Penn Campbell had fallen for Angela, the lead performer on his ship. That must have been when Will and Charlie saw her crying in the park.

John explained Liza hoped if a few passengers took sick for an unknown reason, the next few cruises might be canceled, and she'd have a chance to transfer back to his ship, where she'd originally been scheduled to work. Not sure how she thought that'd get her back to *Ocean Spirit*, but she obviously wasn't thinking clearly. She'd put poison on the game prizes. That explained why the more active, involved passengers were sickened, but not the ones who read or hung out by the pool.

"How did she get the toxin? Dr Marsh said it's unstable." Nan wondered.

John said Liza transferred in just before this sailing, along with quite a few other new staff and crew. After the previous assistant cruise director slapped a passenger, "we scrambled for anyone across the fleet who could take her place. Liza was on a ship in Oman, Jordan, when Headquarters flew her in. She must have picked up the poison there." He sighed. "Liza's in a bad way now. She's out of her head, raving about destiny, sequined jelly, and a camel market. Doc's probably going to sedate her if she keeps shouting. We don't want her to do herself an injury." Standing, John smoothed the crease in his trousers. "I'd better get up to the bridge."

"Putting poison on the game prizes explains a lot," Nan mused as he walked away. "No wonder they were always wrapped in plastic. And I guess that's why she pushed prizes on adults and didn't give any to the children. There must have been some poison on those mugs we won and gave to Elias."

"We won a lot...could have been any of them. That doesn't explain how the doctor's son got some, though, unless he took a prize while Liza wasn't looking." Thinking of her own kids at that age, Jerria said, "Very possible."

"It still doesn't make sense to me. How would poisoning passengers get her transferred?" Charlie snapped his fingers. "But, wait, I get it. All those times she talked about her pens...I think she meant her *boyfriend*. John said his name was Penn, right?"

They sat in silence, lost in their own thoughts. Jerria's heart went out to Liza. She was about the same age as her own daughters, after all, and love did make people do crazy things.

Jerria chose two crab toasts and a cracker with smoked salmon from a tray offered by a smiling waiter. His crisp uniform shone bright white under the twinkling lights on the top deck that evening. A couple hundred passengers turned out for the farewell party. The *Ocean Journey* would dock in Seward tomorrow; they'd booked a transfer to the Captain Cook Hotel in downtown Anchorage.

Jerria stood with her back against the teak railing, balancing her snacks and drink. In front of her, the party was in full swing, with live music and people dancing. They had no idea how close they'd come to death. Beyond the bright lights of the ship, the moonless night hung heavy, foreboding.

In some measure, Liza got her way; the next two cruises were canceled. John said they were bringing in high-heat sterilizers like they use in hospitals. What if Liza had put poison somewhere besides on the prizes? If the media learned of the incident, passengers would cancel upcoming cruises, and Amsterdam Cruise Line stocks would take a nosedive. If Liza wasn't already facing serious charges, they'd probably find a way to hit her with that, too.

Nan offered Jerria a small bag of spiced cashews. "Cashews aren't very Alaskan, but they're good. I just heard they're getting a new comedian, next time the ship sails. You can't go wrong with a name like Annie Palmer."

"Sounds familiar. Won that tv competition, right?" Will said. "Dance with me, Honey?"

Jerria moved into Will's arms, her head on his chest. In a world where even sweet people could poison strangers, she clung to Will's steadiness. Sanctuary.

Chapter Forty-Six
Disembarkation Day Seward/Anchorage

On the motor coach to Anchorage, Jerria dug her cell phone out of her tote bag and turned it on. Now that the dust had settled, it was time to check in on the family. The kids were so caught up in with their own lives; most likely, they hadn't given their parents' cruise a thought. Rissa would be busy with the baby (Rowland was teething), Amy tied up with her wedding plans, Sierra and Matthew doing field work for the state Biology department, Jeff in the middle of final exams, but she'd send them a text and let them know she and their dad were staying a few extra days in Anchorage.

She frowned when the screen lit up, text messages cascading over one another, filling the screen, scrolling down. "Will, would you look at this? I have over thirty text messages from the girls!"

Will turned away from the window. "Not like them. Everybody all right?"

Jerria skimmed the texts. "I think so...yes... uh, oh, they're concerned about us. They say the ship's quarantine is all over the national news. I was hoping they wouldn't hear about it. Oh, Amy used all capital letters; I'd better call her first when we get to the hotel. Here's one from Jeff. Odd; usually, when he has exams, he forgets we're alive. What on earth–?"

"What does it say?"

I'm not sure. His texts look like Morse code to me. It's from four days ago. Here, can you make it out?"

In Jeff's usual terse style, it said simply :

R U ok? Hen got mad. Aced exams. Took Ur car 2 Ogden. Road trip! What a hoot.

Jerria stared at the screen. "I need a magic decoder ring to read this. 'Are you okay?'– I get that, but the rest...What do you think?"

Will ran his hand through his hair. "A mad hen? Thought his focus this semester was large animals, not birds. Never heard a hen hoot. Don't get it."

"He took my car? He's supposed to be at Cornell another week, not on some wild road trip! Jeff's more responsible than this. Does this say he finished his exams?" Jerria gulped. "Oh, no. *What a hoot*...Will, that's something Great-Aunt Henrietta says all the time! How could Jeff know that?"

"Must be together. Henrietta's staying in Utah, right?" Will put his arm around Jerria. "Must have called Jeff somehow...maybe Rissa gave her his number."

Jerria's curls bounced. "This is crazy! Is that what Jeff means by 'road trip'? What about his finals?"

"Jeff's not going to throw a semester away. Arranged to take his exams early? Declared a family emergency or something."

"I need to call him! Do you really think he flew home from New York and drove to Utah to bring Henrietta to our place? I'm not sure he even remembers her."

"Good eleven-hour drive, plenty of time to get reacquainted." Will grinned. "Honey, can't you just see them? A ninety-four-year-old and a nineteen-year-old in a car for that long? Jeff's a good kid, but can't imagine them even agreeing on what music to listen to."

Jerria giggled, her eyes sparkling. "What a hoot...I hope that means they're enjoying one another. Forget the radio. Jeff loves a story as much as I do, and Henrietta's full of them. And if he talks about his veterinary program, she'd be interested. A woman who ran over a thousand head of cattle knows something about large animal husbandry. He'll learn more from her than a whole semester of college."

Walking into the Captain Cook's lobby half an hour later, Jerria sighed. "Ah, this is beautiful. I'm thinking cruising isn't for me. What would you think about a nice camping trip next time?"

Will's deep laugh vibrated through the lobby. "Not time to give up. Talked about another trans-Atlantic, and haven't been to Panama Canal in years."

"I guess you're right. It's just that this trip hasn't been very restful."

"Back to reality in a few days. Henrietta's already at our place, Jeff's home, help Amy plan wedding, play with the baby, maybe that contract for the house on Pine will be waiting..."

Jerria grimaced, then laughed. "You have a point. Reality is overrated. How does Australia sound?"

If you enjoyed Murder On Deck, please take a minute to leave a glowing review! I read every single review, and the 5 star ones absolutely make my day. Week! Five star reviews are a really big deal, like leaving a $100 tip for your cabin steward. It will take you under three minutes to write a one-line 5 star review, and you can do it anonymously if you wish.

Other Books by Deb Graham

Peril In Paradise a cruise novel

Tips From The Cruise Addict's Wife

More Tips From The Cruise Addict's Wife

Mediterranean Cruise With The Cruise Addict's Wife

How To Write Your Story

How To Complain...and get what you deserve

Hungry Kids Campfire Cookbook

Kid Food On A Stick

Quick and Clever Kids' Crafts

Awesome Science Experiments for Kids

Savory Mug Cooking

Uncommon Household Tips

Made in the USA
Monee, IL
06 May 2022

95917764R00184